# THE
# LOST

# THE LOST

## ANNO INITIUM 2

### DINKO SKOPLJAK

Podium

*For my daughters*



Translation from German edited by Sarah Rimmington

Cover design by Marcus Dorau

ISBN: 978-1-0394-2046-5

Published in 2023 by Podium Publishing, ULC
www.podiumaudio.com

# THE
# LOST

# CHAPTER 1

# FARM

Over the nagging of her senile father-in-law, Miriam smiled at her children. She didn't mind that they didn't smile back at her. *My God*, she told herself for the hundredth time that month, *they are leaving childhood behind faster than is good for them*. But they were alive and well—while the fabric of society was crumbling around them.

They ate in the late summer evening light at the centuries-old table, which was darkened by use. Golden rays filtered through low windows into the ancient dining room of the farmhouse. Miriam brushed a curl from her face. Surreptitiously, she watched her daughter, who, as usual, was ignoring what was happening around her and spooning the last morsels of the nutrient-rich meal—spelt burgers with steamed carrots and zucchini—into her mouth.

Lena didn't like it when her mother stared at her. She was reaching the end of puberty and she was homesick. But most of all, she missed her friends. Miriam knew that. She was sorry her girl had to be stuck in that house. Instead of going out and whiling away the day with friends, doing everything that teenagers normally did, she was spending all of her time, day in and day out, with her family. And a long way from civilization—or what was left of it.

During the day, Lena worked with Joanne, preparing enough food to get them through the coming winter. They cooked fruits and vegetables, freezing them and making juices. There was rarely a part of the day when she was detached from the music player and her headphones. She never complained about how she was now forced to live.

Still, Miriam felt her daughter's unspoken frustration, the kind only parents can empathize with. With a lump in her throat, she watched the thirteen-year-old get up and disappear into the kitchen.

Miriam's attention switched to Lucas, Lena's brother, who was four years younger and grinning mischievously at his grandfather's demented rant. Her mood brightened a bit. She loved the little swirl that made his short, shaggy hair stick out right at the top of his forehead. Lucas exchanged an annoyed look with his father, who in turn was troubled by the danger posed by his old man. Only yesterday, Miriam had had to help calm the doddering old man, who was roaring into the otherwise silent night, and bring him back to bed.

Afterward she had lain awake for hours, discussing things with her husband. It was only a matter of time before until his bellowing lured the infected to the farmstead. After much to-ing and fro-ing, they agreed they would give her father-in-law a mild sedative before bedtime so they would have less to worry about at night, at least. During the day, there was always someone to look after him while the rest of the community guarded and mended the barriers around the farm or struggled to bring in food and any survivors from the surrounding area, though it was becoming increasingly difficult to find anything or anyone more than six months after the outbreak. Everything they could reach on foot had already been looted, and the people who had once lived there had disappeared.

While Miriam was thinking about how to organize the rest of the day, her husband got up from the table and turned to her. "Is it all right if I stretch my legs a bit?" The worry lines between his eyebrows had deepened. She knew it was wearing him down not to be able to give his father the care the old man needed. Whenever his discontent got the better of him, he did the rounds of the palisades, inspecting them. Now it was that time again.

She looked at him and nodded. "Sure. Luke can help me with that," she replied, glancing at his plate and cutlery. "Are you going to take Tobi?" Hearing his name, the black-and-tan pinscher looked up from his spot in the corner. He wagged his tail happily, as he always did when he sensed a walk was on offer.

"Of course," her husband replied, whistling for his four-legged friend. "We'll be back before sundown." He stepped over to her and leaned forward.

Miriam reached out to him for a fleeting kiss. But this time it was an unusually long one. At first, when he kept ahold of her after a few seconds, she hesitated. The last time they had touched was several days ago and so she savored every moment. She melted in the maelstrom of his warmth. Miriam only noticed that he had detached himself from her once he had already stepped out of the door.

George Morel's heavy boots thumped over the worn stone tiles. As he walked, he pulled on a light jacket that smelled of dog. They were storing and drying the clothes below the steep stairs where Tobi rested during the day. The idea was that Tobi's smell would mask the smell of humans and prevent the infected from picking it up. Sometimes George even let the dog sleep on his jacket. The playful pinscher, who had lived on the farm for six years, occasionally slept in one of the children's beds, curled up under the covers behind their knees. George spotted him in the yard, waiting impatiently by the Renault. His legs stiff and his tail agitating, he peered over his shoulder, anxious for George to open the door. He was immensely fond of riding in the car and had probably assumed a joyride was in store.

"Not today, buddy; we're going to walk this time," George called with a grin, striding off in the opposite direction. Tobi trotted after him, somewhat disappointed.

At the massive gate made from boards and beams, he nodded to the guard who was eyeing him from the platform above. The tall, camouflage-clad woman returned the salute only after three seconds. She came down the stairs and unlocked the gate.

"Thanks," George said. "I'll do the rounds and check everything out."

The guard looked at him questioningly. "But we already did that today," she countered, "and everything was fine. I can personally confirm that."

"Yeah, I know. Actually, I only want to stretch my legs," he said conspiratorially. She gave him a suspicious look but stepped silently out of the way and pulled open the gate.

In his camouflage gear, George blended into the forest. In front of him, Tobi had fled over the clumsy threshold through the barest of cracks, into the open. Behind him, he heard the entrance being barricaded again. As usual, he took the path to the right. He immediately turned his attention to the fence, knowing that the pinscher would follow him anyway.

The palisade had been built over months and had grown considerably since their arrival. George pulled and shook branches and trunks to check them for stability. Now he could scarcely remember what the forest had looked like before. In the beginning, they had woven fallen trees and felled logs together between standing trees, creating a giant hedge. It had taken weeks to fence in the whole yard. They had finished just before they were discovered by a smallish band of wandering corpses. It had been relatively easy for the farm community to fend off this initial attack, despite their lack of combat experience. They had used large numbers of homemade weapons made out of hoes, plowshares, and other agricultural tools. Well-aimed thrusts through the fence had been enough to eliminate the undead.

But after the second attack, six weeks ago, one of the infected had made it across the buffer zone and caused some casualties. The next day, they had the idea of directing additional stakes outward at a slant, their tips pointing downward.

Since then, there had been one other raid, with no fatalities for the community. The new stakes impaled three of the undead, preventing them from climbing any farther. This made it easy to kill them. They had burned the corpses far away from the farm.

Having finished his first round and finding nothing to criticize, George spontaneously decided to make an additional check of the alarm mechanism. They had created a large circle around the farm and divided it into a dozen sections like precisely cut pieces of pie. Thin nylon strings stretched at chest height between the trees, creating the circumference as well as the pie pieces. If these were set lower, as they had been at first, the alarm would be tripped by stray animals. Since the outbreak, however, most of these had now fled to higher ground in the foothills of the Alps, so the risk was relatively low. In the middle of the farmyard, where the ends of the cords met, were fixed several wooden boards with writing on them to indicate the region of the forest they were connected to. When one moved, you could immediately tell from which direction visitors were coming.

George knew the inspection would take an hour at most—assuming he didn't find anything in need of repair. So he had plenty of time, and he'd be back before the last of the light faded. Having reached the trees marked with a ring of red paint, he focused on the string. He ran his hand along the transparent thread, watching for any faults. He followed the line, and in a short while he stepped out of the forest onto the asphalt path that led to the farm.

Checking the alarm system had become second nature to him. Instinctively, he let his mind wander. He calculated in his head that it had been almost seven months since they had escaped from Paris and reached the safety of the farm. Seven long months, and yet his memory of it was as clear as if he had stormed into the apartment to get Miriam and the children only yesterday.

"Why don't you answer your damn cell?" he had snarled at her, his roar scaring her beyond measure.

"I was in the car when you called. I just forgot to call you back," she had retorted. Miriam was indignant at his outburst and had scarcely been able to compose herself.

George ignored her furious tone. During the drive home, his panic had gotten the better of him. "If you can see that I'm trying to reach you, you should fucking answer," he blustered. "Are the kids here yet?"

She shook her head. "Should be here any minute."

"Oh, crap," he cursed, pacing nervously. "We have to get out of here! I can't tell you all the details right now, but we have to get out of Paris immediately!"

"What d'you mean, get out of Paris?" was all she could come up with.

He sighed, pinching the top of his nose between his thumb and forefinger. Hoping she would pick up on his tone, he tried to speak more calmly this time. "There really isn't time to explain! You pack our things and I'll pack the kids'!"

"George, what are you talking about?"

"JUST PACK THE FUCKING BAGS, WILL YOU!"

He had never spoken to her like that before. Not to say they never argued. But this time he saw her catch her breath. He had crossed a line.

All the blood had drained from her face. "Don't speak to me like that, George Morel! You tell me what the hell is going on!"

"Look, it has to do with the incidents over the past couple of weeks," he replied placatingly, not meeting her eye. He searched for the right words. "Something bad is heading our way. We only have days, maybe even hours, to get to safety."

*　*　*

"George, what are you talking about?" It wasn't that she didn't believe him. On the contrary. She knew he juggled sensitive information daily, so an invisible trickle of fear crept down her spine. And yet she had no idea what was going on with him.

"That's all there is to it, Miri!"

She suddenly hated him using his pet name for her in this situation. He continued, a little more subdued, "We need to pack. Call your mother. Tell her we're coming to her tonight. With my father. And tell her to stock up as many supplies as she can."

Then he left her on her own in the kitchen. Shocked, she quickly went over what he had said. She reached for her phone, which was on the table, and dialed a number. It rang. With her other ear, she heard the printer start up in the study. While she was thinking that she had talked to her mother on the phone just yesterday, the older women picked up. "Hello, dear, couldn't you wait to talk your old maman again?"

Maman was well over sixty but didn't look old at all. She lived at the foot of the Alps, where she ran a modern agricultural business. Pictures danced across Miriam's mind's eye: Joanne in earth-covered work clothes, her gray hair tied in a messy chignon. In the evenings, once all the work was done, she liked to wear bright, flowing robes and let her long hair ripple down over her shoulders.

It was probably the farm that was the source of Joanne's vitality, thought Miriam as she heard the cheerful voice. A longing for the place she was born flared up in her.

"Hello, Maman," she said—and faltered. What was there to tell? How was she supposed to explain the situation to her mother when she herself knew nothing about it? There was no doubt George was in a hurry, but he was also being irrational, and that wasn't like him.

Miriam decided to get straight to the point. "I have something important to tell you, so please listen carefully to what I say. We're coming over to you this evening." Maman was silent, apparently waiting for her to continue. "Something's going on here. Something even George is afraid of. And I mean really scared. The kids will be back from school any minute, and he means for us to set out right away." She remembered her father-in-law, who lived in a retirement home. "Oh yeah, we'll be bringing Erick with us. And George said to gather as much food and water as you can."

"All right," Maman replied pensively. "I'll get everything ready here. And"—she paused for a moment—"does all this have to do with what's been happening over the last few days?"

"George says yes. And it's far worse than the media reports." Miriam felt her uncertainty mutate into fear.

"Please drive carefully. And call me now and again so I know what you're up to!" *So I know you're all right.*

"Of course, Maman. Thank you." But Maman had rung off. Miriam imagined Joanne leaving the house directly and heading for the supermarket. She might be a bit headstrong and stubborn, but she certainly wasn't naïve.

In the study, George waited impatiently for the printer to spit out the email. Before the last sheet had been fully ejected, he pulled at it roughly, leaving a torn corner stuck in the printer. He folded the pages and tucked them into his back pocket. He hurried from room to room, the soles of his shoes slamming against the matte herringbone parquet, packing suitcases. He took some games, too. Who knew how long they would have to hole up for? Lengthy hikes would probably not be on the agenda this year, and they'd need something to keep the kids busy.

George set down the luggage and went into the bathroom where he unceremoniously emptied the laundry bag into the bathtub and stuffed all the toiletries into it.

Miriam was waiting by the front door. Heavily laden, he made his way toward her down the long hallway. She had put on her jacket and did not meet his eye. He swallowed sheepishly, put the bag down, and took her gently in his arms. She stiffened, looking past his shoulder.

"Miri . . . I'm sorry." The apology sounded trite, even to him. "I shouldn't have spoken to you like that."

"No, you shouldn't," she replied curtly. But she didn't seem inclined to argue.

George squeezed her tighter. "Please trust me this time, without us having to talk it all through. And when the kids get here, we have to present a united front and get them to leave right away. Please!" He put all his powers of persuasion into his voice. "Can you do it?"

Miriam rolled her eyes in annoyance. But before she could reply, they heard two pairs of shoes thumping up the stairs. He let go of her and opened the door before the doorbell rang.

George breathed a sigh of relief. He saw how surprised the children were and said, "Hello, you two! You have three minutes to get your things from your rooms to take to Grandma's house. Quickly! And only as much as you can fit in your backpacks! I've already packed most of what we need." He tapped the Samsonite suitcase.

"We're going to Grandma's? Today?" Lena blurted out. Lucas was wide-eyed.

"Do as your father says! Now! We'll explain everything in the car! Off you go!" Miriam rarely raised her voice with the children. But when she did, they knew it was better to pay attention immediately. Normally they would have cheered loudly at the prospect of a trip to Grandma's, but they could clearly sense the tense mood and suppressed the impulse.

George hurried out of the apartment with the suitcases. He wanted to leave right away, but Lucas had to go to the bathroom urgently. He was itching to get going, and it was a long time before the boy returned.

"Do you need to, as well?" he asked Lena, more grumpily than he intended. She shook her head and gave him a disparaging look, the manner of which only adolescents were capable. "Okay, everybody into the car, then!" he ordered.

Only when they were sitting in the vehicle with their seat belts fastened did George awkwardly pull out the documents. He handed them to his wife with his smartphone. "Kids, we're going to pick up Grandpa Erick now, and then we'll be on our way."

"What about school?" asked Lena.

"Maman and I will let the school know you won't be coming in for the next few days. We'll think of something—maybe you could have caught a cold . . ."

Relieved, he heard Miriam answer for him: "Honey, you watched the news with us yesterday—those strange cases of illness on the south side of town." George watched in the rearview mirror as both children nodded. "Well," she continued, "the disease is spreading fast. We want to wait until it's all been cleared up and sorted out before we come back. There's not much point putting ourselves at risk when we could be taking a little vacation at Grandma's."

That was a damn smart move on her part, George reflected. The kids were less accustomed to questioning what she said than what he said.

As he raced to the retirement home, he wondered if this was the way the world was, or if he had failed to communicate with his children as a father.

"You can't just take your father away on a whim! In his condition, he needs specialized help."

As politely as possible, George dismissed the objections of the surprised nurse, and hurriedly pushed the wheelchair in which Erick Morel was sitting toward the elevator. He felt more than saw Miriam walking beside him, carrying the bag containing her father-in-law's belongings.

"I'm calling security now!" the nurse yelled after him threateningly. The silver door slid sideways into the wall. The three of them went inside. George instructed the elevator to go to the lowest level of the complex, where the children were waiting in the car. For the umpteenth time that day, he felt overwhelming impatience, this time due to the slowness of the elevator. Then it stopped. Behind him, the door opened. He stepped backward, pulling the wheelchair with him, into the sparsely lit basement parking garage.

He stopped abruptly, looking around anxiously. He saw the car only a few meters behind him. Inside, the children's faces glowed ghostly in the pale fluorescent light. Across the roofs of the parked cars, he could make out no movement.

They were alone. Even though he could hear nothing but the clicking and popping of pipes and cooling engine hoods that were the usual sounds in underground garages, his alarm bells were ringing.

Miriam seemed irritated by his behavior. "What's wrong; why aren't you moving?" she asked. Her voice sounded strangely removed from him.

He heard himself reply, "I don't know. Something's not right here . . . Hurry up, let's . . . get my father into the car."

He wheeled the old man to the left side of the van, opened the door, and told Lucas to take a seat in the back row.

"Oh man, why can't Lena sit in the back?" Lucas grumbled.

"Because her legs are longer than yours," George replied sternly. The boy squeezed his slender body over the armrest and dropped into his assigned seat. Snorting with anger, he pulled on the seat belt and reluctantly buckled himself in.

"Miri, will you please pull the wheelchair away as soon as I lift Dad up?" She nodded. Then he helped his father, who seemed as though he had only just woken up, to his feet. Erick opened his eyes in amazement and spoke in a trembling, brittle voice.

"What . . . what's going on? What are you doing with me?"

"Hi, Dad. It's me, George."

Erick looked around as if surprised to be spoken to. "George," he said, confused. "What are you doing, my boy?" His father had actually recognized him. This sort of thing happened sometimes, though less and less frequently.

George replied calmly, repressing a flood of tears, "We're just going on a trip, Dad. It's all right. Look, the kids are there, too. Kids, say hello to Grandpa."

"Hi, Grandpa!" called Lena and Lucas. They waved at their grandfather, who gave a crooked smile, as though he were wondering whether his reaction was appropriate.

George gave way to his impatience, pushing Erick inside quickly. "Lena, can you fasten Grandpa's seat belt?"

"Sure, Dad," she replied, starting to comply with his request. George shut the door gently.

"What do we do with the wheelchair?" asked Miriam.

"We'll leave that one here. There's no room left in the car."

Then he stepped closer to her and gently put his hands on her hips. "Miri, about earlier—I'm really sorry."

She surprised him by pressing an abrupt kiss to his lips. Her words were like a balm to his stressed brain: "There's nothing to apologize for. I read the report on the way here—you did absolutely the right thing. I'm sorry I didn't trust you right away. I shouldn't have put you in that position." He almost laughed out loud as she changed her tone. "You're lucky the roles weren't reversed. I would have given you hell if you'd reacted the way I did."

Relieved and ashamed all at once, he looked at the tips of his shoes. Miriam kissed him again. "Hey, it's all good now. But let's please go— quickly. I have a really bad feeling about this."

"Yes," George replied, frowning. "Me, too." For a second, he had been able to ignore the warning sirens in his head. "The hairs on the back of my neck have been on end ever since we got out of the elevator." But he was reluctant to let her go now that they had regained their usual intimacy. She broke away from him, going around the vehicle. George bent down to pick up his father's bag.

Before Miriam pulled open the door, she asked him across the roof, "Do you smell that?"

She had scarcely finished speaking when George heard footsteps behind him. A horrible stench of excrement and decay hit his nose. He turned around immediately. A figure was running toward him, only five meters away. Ever since he had left the elevator, his muscles had been tensed, ready for fight or flight. His senses had noted the impending danger, but he had been too preoccupied with his father to take the appropriate action.

The shadow was approaching at a frightening speed. George's survival instinct took over. With a twisting motion, his upper body transferred momentum from his hips to his right hand, which held the bag. The centrifugal force caused it to lift, moving faster. The bag caught the attacker on the side of the head. There was a dull thud as his face hit the hood of the adjacent vehicle.

Three more figures were speeding toward him just as fast. He dropped the bag and yanked open the driver's door. Miriam, meanwhile, had gotten in as fast as she could. He heard her seat belt click into place a split second before his door slammed shut—and a grotesque, white-eyed face smashed against it. The car shook. The children yelled. Miriam gave a shout of surprise and hammered at the lock button with her fist. All the doors gave a click. George started the engine. Another figure jumped at the vehicle head-on, while the one at the side screamed in rage and smashed its forehead against the glass.

The window suddenly became a spider's web of thousands of tiny cracks.

"JUST DRIVE! NOW!" roared Lena.

Lucas's shrill screams rang in his ears.

"Beat it!" shouted Erick, tapping the window shakily.

George shifted into first gear and set off, his tires squealing for the second time that day. The silhouette to his left took another swing, but only hit the B pillar, albeit with full force. More attackers encircled the car. Mercilessly, he ran over two of them and raced through the garage. In the rearview mirror, he could see the figures rushing after the vehicle. Then they stopped abruptly, changed direction, and disappeared into the twilight of the underground parking lot. With the exit in his sights, George hit the gas so as not to lose momentum on the incline. They shot out into the dusk. The underside of the car crashed against the asphalt.

"Dad, what were those people?" Behind him, Lena was breathing frighteningly fast. She paused slightly after every word. Lucas on the other hand was sitting with his eyes wide open. He looked around continuously, his slender hands clutching the handle above his right shoulder. Erick was staring out the window in confusion. Miriam shivered and brushed one or two curls out of her eyes.

Without taking his eyes off the road, George, breathing heavily, tried to answer—though he wasn't sure he was right. "Remember what we talked about when we left?" At the same time, he kept an eye out for danger—and ways to avoid it if necessary.

Lena tried to remember. "Um, about this weird disease?"

"Exactly—about this weird disease. Roughly speaking, it causes people suffering from it to lose their minds and attack other people. I think the people in the garage had been infected."

"Attack?" Lena said, her tone demonstrating conclusively that she didn't think he was taking her seriously. "I kind of got the feeling they wanted to kill us."

"Well, it comes down to the same thing. But the important thing, kids, is that you mustn't let anyone bite you, scratch you, or spit on you—and you must never come into contact with the blood of the infected! If you can see that someone's been infected, run away as fast as you can. No matter who it is. AND I MEAN IT! Even if it's Mom or Dad or anyone else in the family. Do you understand that? You have to run away so you don't catch it!"

They both nodded, presumably as frightened by his tone as by the experience they had just been through.

"But isn't there anything that can help?" asked Lena.

Miriam looked at her.

George sighed. "I don't really know, love. I'm afraid nothing like that's available right now." The situation was so serious they could almost feel it physically, settling like a lead weight on the family.

George steered the vehicle at a snail's pace through the evening rush hour. His concentration did not waver. The sky had lost its luminosity. Instead, it was the streets around them that began to shine, as stores switched on their signs and cars their lights. It had begun to drizzle.

"Miri, see if there's anything on the news, please," he asked quietly.

"Why didn't I think of that before?" she whispered. "I'm in so much shock I can't think straight."

"Tell me about it," he said breathily. She rejected a few stations, and then the interior of the vehicle was filled with a female voice. It wasn't studio quality. George realized she was reporting live.

"*. . . people with the disease were sighted to the south of Paris for the first time. As the police told us, the situation is now under control. The infected have been taken to an undisclosed hospital, to be quarantined. However, eyewitnesses report that the police had to use huge force—people are talking about live ammunition—to resolve the situation. Several police officers are also said to have been injured in the confrontation. We don't have any more details at the moment. An extensive area around the scene has been cordoned off, and a forensic investigation is underway. The area is swarming with heavily armed police. They have . . .*"

The reporter stopped speaking. Short, popping sounds could be heard in the background, closely followed by a steady rattling.

The sounds were unmistakable. The speaker hesitated before continuing. Some of the words were almost inaudible, as if she kept turning away from the microphone and then back to it again: "*I can hear—I don't know if you can too—shots! They've started shooting again. I can clearly make out bursts of machine-gun fire. Now I'm also seeing people running, even some of the police officers are taking to their heels. Oh . . . my God, people are rushing at the police officers. They . . . What's that . . . ? Many of them have extensive wounds on their bodies; they're running toward the police barricades. It looks like they don't much care about being shot. Where are so many of them coming from, all of a sudden?*"

Another pause, which was dominated by background noise. Then the announcer spoke for the last time, cursing. "*Oh, putain!*" The words were followed by a muffled sound as the microphone hit the floor. Just as George heard angry, jerky screeching that seemed to be getting closer and closer, Miriam turned off the radio.

"Drive, for God's sake, drive—just get us out of here!" she told him, unbuckling her seat belt.

He watched in amazement as she wriggled past him and took a seat between Lena and Erick. He observed in the rearview mirror how she reached back to her distraught son and spoke in soothing tones to both children.

Lena was crying and typing on her smartphone. George assumed she was sending warnings to her friends. Miriam took out her cell and hopefully did the same. It was lucky they had the leaked documents and could photograph them as proof, he thought.

George glanced around, saw no sign of police anywhere, and switched to the opposite lane. He almost ran over a figure in a trench coat who had walked between the stationary cars to the other side of the road. An angry choir of horns sounded behind him. Undeterred, he accelerated. Before anyone could approach him, he turned left onto the next best side street. He knew his way around this part of town.

Until he reached the freeway access road, he didn't think it was necessary to observe the traffic rules.

They reached the farm late in the evening. The children were tired and withdrawn. They'd been so anxious during the trip that they hadn't slept a wink. Once in their grandmother's arms, they finally relaxed. Lucas had bravely held it together the whole time, but now began to cry. Lena put her arms around him and kissed his forehead. Strangely detached, George watched the scene and realized that Miriam was similarly emotionless about what was happening. *We're in shock*, he thought. *And with today's bloody events, who could blame us?* He couldn't give in to exhaustion just yet, though. There was a lot more to do.

Before pulling open the rear door of the car, he examined the cracked driver's side window closely. Capillary action had drawn a dark liquid deep into the cracks. George made a mental note to clean the vehicle tomorrow and disinfect the stained areas. Then he turned to Erick. With Miriam's help, he maneuvered him into the house. Together they took the confused man to the room Joanne had prepared for him.

Through the thin wooden walls of the old farmhouse, George heard the children heading into their rooms. Lena and Lucas went to bed right away. They obviously didn't feel like eating dinner. He was glad Miriam didn't insist on it today.

Late into the night, the two of them sat at the table with his mother-in-law, discussing what to do. He watched Joanne's expression darken as she finished reading the report. Once again, he was surprised at how matter-of-factly she took the sinister news.

"I went shopping today, right after we talked on the phone. Just like you asked," she said, turning to Miriam. "And I've already stored it all in the pantry."

She listed the food she had purchased. Together they then checked what they had and what they still needed. To ensure they got what was missing, they wrote shopping lists for the coming days. Finally, George was too tired to join in the conversation. His bed was calling, and he was only too willing to answer.

The next day he started building the palisade. George was no craftsman, but he was not entirely without talent. He would have to get used to hard, practical work quickly, because he assumed normality would not be returning any time soon. *If it ever does.* In any case, he had knowledge of the impending catastrophe and a razor-sharp mind, which would help him make the right decisions quickly.

In the forest that surrounded the farm, the children were helping him gather fallen trees and branches. George privately reproached himself for putting them in danger the previous day. On the other hand, it had made them realize how real a danger the disease was to them. So there was none of the annoying discussion that usually flared up when he or Miriam tried to suggest their cooperation was needed. Today they understood what was at stake and worked hard to help build the palisade.

The dead material from the undergrowth was easy to interweave into the living trees and bushes. The nearest hardware store, where he might have found industrially manufactured fencing, was sixty kilometers away in any case. So they would have to make do with natural building materials. Some of the healthy trunks were the width of his arm, others were broader than his shoulders. They selected the sturdiest of them for his project. George was under no illusions about the ability of a gate barely two meters to withstand an onslaught by the kind of vile creatures they had seen yesterday. For now, however, it was all he could do. One option would have been to escape by air, but then they would have had to leave Erick and Joanne behind. Erick was too sick, and Joanne wouldn't want to fly on principle. Besides, George wasn't sure they would succeed in containing the disease. It was more likely that it would gain a global foothold. So even if they left the country, sooner or later they'd be in the same position as they were now.

He and the children had built a palisade ten meters wide by the time Miriam returned. They had also tested their work for weak points. Where branches and vines gave way, they strengthened the fence. Gradually, they began to enjoy the work.

The children hooted with delight every time they hurled themselves against the gate—and it held. George was not happy about the volume of their shouts, considering it increased the risk of being heard, but that day he deliberately said nothing. He wanted Lena and Lucas to enjoy themselves for as long as they could. By evening, the fence measured twenty by two meters. Miriam's and Joanne's eyes widened as they looked at the work. He was immensely proud.

In the weeks that followed, more company arrived. People from the surrounding villages had fled higher and higher into the mountains in the vain hope of escaping the plague. These included people skilled in crafts and agriculture, who had had to abandon low-lying farms and fields. Since there wouldn't be any seasonal labor this year in any case, it was easy to accommodate the refugees in the summer accommodation. It was not long before they had made the barracks habitable for the winter months. George remembered with pleasure how well the work had progressed as more refugees found their way to them. The construction of the palisade progressed quickly, and the fence grew taller. They got the fields tilled after all and planted herbs and vegetables in the greenhouses. Over the decades, Joanne had developed a system that almost guaranteed there would be seeds and roots at the end of the season to provide a harvest the following year. Sustainable agriculture also enabled them to produce vast quantities of top-quality food that they didn't even have to sell. From the surrounding villages and settlements, they brought in food, toiletries, tools, and clothing—even weapons when they could find them. And once they had set up the alarm system, life became a little safer—it had kept out three contingents of uninvited guests . . .

Damn it, where had the string gone? George looked around in confusion. It was nowhere to be seen. He couldn't remember when he had lost contact. Tobi was pacing restlessly in front of him.

Where in heaven's name were they? In the twilight, he wasn't sure he had ever been in that part of the forest before.

Since they had arrived at the farm, his focus had never slipped. He had always been able to concentrate fully on everything he did—contrasting his earlier habit of letting his thoughts wander when performing boring, routine tasks. Now he couldn't remember anything from the last hour.

Was this another absurd and useless superpower? The hairs on the back of his neck rose abruptly. He held his breath so that he could listen more closely to the sounds around him. The forest was rustling far louder than he was comfortable with in the descending darkness. Tobi whimpered. George bent down and stroked his ears. He moved his other hand to his hip, freeing the ax he always carried from its holster.

"Shh." He tried to calm the pinscher, who was squirming more and more violently. The rustling intensified. A good stone's throw away, he made out a figure. It was moving toward the farm, dragging its feet through the foliage, shoulders drooping. George caught sight of the rear guard. His stomach clenched. Countless creatures were shuffling through the thicket. Even if they didn't get to the farm itself, they would come damn close. Under no circumstances could he let that happen.

If he tried to fight their superior numbers, he was bound to lose. There was only one strategy that made sense. He thought for just a moment and then straightened up, shouting at the top of his lungs, "Hey, you looking for me? Over here, weirdos; come and get me if you dare!" His voice sounded far more confident than he felt. The advancing zombies stopped and looked around. "Over here! Hey, OVER HERE!" He waved his ax high above his head. Everything fell silent for a moment as they located him. "Tobi, get out of here!" Instantly, the dog leapt away. George lost no time in running after him. Rotten branches broke under his feet. He could hear hungry, angry sounds at his back. The leaves rustled like deafening white noise. Branches whipped him in the face. Arms raised, he tried to protect himself against injuries. Tobi was pelting through the undergrowth far ahead of him. George had trouble even halfway keeping up with him. He forced himself to focus his awareness on the imaginary path in front of him, to give himself no room for fear. But the sounds coming from behind made him tremble.

Then he emerged from the forest onto a broad road. The land sloped steeply away on the other side. The pinscher was turning crazily in the middle of the road, probably because he couldn't decide which way to run. George immediately recognized where they were. He had often driven this way with the family on vacation. To the left, the road descended deep into the valley. To the right it went up to the pass, where there was a fantastic view of the foothills of the French Alps. He leaned both hands on his thighs and breathed heavily. For heaven's sake, had they really run this far? They were a good eight or nine kilometers from the farm.

He looked back, seeing almost nothing in the darkness of the forest. But that made the sounds of his pursuers all the more clear. Tobi scuttled across the asphalt, charging up the hill.

George looked after him and saw a car that had been left on the higher bend, likely with an empty tank or a broken-down engine or something. The dog stopped at the abandoned vehicle, stood on his hind paws, and scratched at the door like a mad thing. George ran after him, hoping the car would be unlocked. When he reached the vehicle, he jiggled the door handle. The door opened without offering any resistance.

Relief flooded through him. He jumped in, a fraction of a second after Tobi had disappeared inside. The pinscher's back fur was on end. Panic-stricken, he bounced back and forth as if the seats were red-hot.

George locked the doors, grabbed the dog, and pressed him to his chest. Tobi tried to break free, panting continuously through his jowls.

A scream rang out, and the two occupants froze.

On one hand, George's view of the road was obscured. Someone had stuck scraps of paper to the inside of the windows. He couldn't see what was happening outside. On the other hand, this was a good thing, because it meant he couldn't be seen. He put a gentle hand on the dog's muzzle and stroked it. Tobi relaxed in his arms. The immediate risk that he might bark was averted. He was managing not to whine, either. George could not help feeling that the animal knew exactly what was at stake.

He could hear many feet shuffling by the car, barely an arm's length away. Grunts and screeches pressed in on them almost unmuffled, making the pinscher flinch every time he heard them. Every now and then the vehicle shook as someone caught the side mirror.

The daylight drained away, but the menacing sounds outside the vehicle continued. George hardly dared move. The ax was still in his fist. Except for the stroking motions of the fingers of his other hand, he sat motionless. Tobi had now curled up in his lap but was still wide awake.

George tried in vain not to think of the pain his family would feel if he did not return. Fear seemed to fire his darkest imaginings and the most horrifying scenario formed in his mind: He would transform—and stagger back to the farm to attack Miri and the children.

Did the undead's human memories mean anything to them? Would he—if he became one of them—know where the farm was? Would Miriam be capable of killing him for a second time, before he could harm her or the children? If the infected discovered him now, he would rather throw himself into the abyss on the other side of the road.

His body ached from sitting still. He estimated that another hour had passed. Gradually, the noise subsided. The shuffling of feet increasingly died away. George waited until he was sure he could only hear the usual sounds of the forest. Then he carefully opened the door. It was now pitch dark outside. The interior lights did not come on. The vehicle's battery was dead. Nevertheless, it would be worth taking back with him, he thought—he might be able to connect it to the farm's solar power system, if he survived the night . . .

It was almost as dark outside the car as it had been inside. Stiff-legged, he got out. He had been suppressing the urgent need to relieve himself for a long time.

Tobi yawned and stretched, making a high-pitched sound. The sky was cloudless and the light from the stars was dim, so he could only guess at the pale path beneath. A few meters ahead of him, the dog scurried across the road, his claws clicking like soft Morse code on the asphalt. George ran about a hundred yards from the car and swiftly did his business. He didn't want the smell of urine anywhere near the vehicle they were going to spend the night in. It made little sense to trudge through the forest in the middle of the night without a halfway reliable means of finding their way. Tobi would have been a great help, of course, but what use was that if George couldn't see him in the darkness?

They made themselves as comfortable as they could in the car. George reclined the front seats and stretched out.

Tobi climbed onto his stomach and trampled out an imaginary nest before curling up and burying the tip of his cold nose in George's armpit. George stroked the short fur on his back, feeling the vertebrae strung together like marbles underneath. It was a warm summer's night, and they would not freeze. But what would happen when the temperatures dropped? They had enough firewood on the farm to last the upcoming cold season; they had made sure of that in recent months. But could the wandering corpses survive sub-zero temperatures? Or would they freeze to death? George was hoping for the latter. That would put an end to the horror, he thought. Humanity would just have to survive this one winter.


"Is Dad back?"

"No!" Her tone was harsher than she had intended, but Miriam attributed that to the turmoil going on inside her. Lucas was too sleepy to be hurt by it. He sat down on her lap, resting his head on her shoulder.

The room was lit by candles, making the shadows flicker. At the table opposite, Lena and Joanne were playing cards. Both of them looked tense.

Miriam struggled to keep her fear in check. She brooded over what might have happened to George.

The wall clock had long since struck midnight, and he had not returned from his inspection round. After the sun had set, she had set off to raise the alarm, but the guard had beaten her to it. In the farmyard, she came upon a group of people who had just been divided into search parties. Elle, who oversaw the evening watch at the gate, was giving them urgent instructions. "Clara, Mathis, and Sylvie, you take the west side! Hugo, Louanne, and Yanis, the east side! No more than fifty meters from the fence! Call out at normal conversational volume—no louder! Miriam, Maxime, and I will take the road. Does anyone have a gun for Miri? Thank you, Theo. Only switch on your flashlights for short periods! We'll all meet back here in twenty minutes at the latest! Is that clear?" Her tone left no room for argument. The gate was unlocked, and the search parties streamed out into the darkness.

Miriam walked down the middle of the road, with Elle and Maxime on her left and right sides. "George!" she called as loudly as she dared. Each step took her deeper into the forest, and her fear increased. Every noise sounded like the undead making ready to attack. She tried in vain to steady her trembling hands, hoping her voice would not break.

On either side, she could hear the other two, taking it in turns to call George's name. Their flashlights flared sporadically. Where the nylon wire crossed the driveway, they found his footprints in the foliage.

"He went this way," Maxime speculated. He held his flashlight close to the ground and shone it in the direction George had taken.

"Okay, change of plans," Elle said after pausing briefly to reflect. "Maxime, you go back and let them know at the farm. Miriam and I will follow the trail as far as we can. It may well take us longer than twenty minutes, so wait for us at the gate!"

Maxime nodded and ran off.

The two women hurried ahead, following George's route along the alarm system. Dry leaves and branches crackled underfoot with every step. After about three minutes, Elle stopped. Throwing caution to the wind, she kept her flashlight on, waving it in a wide arc in front of her.

"I can't make heads nor tails of it," she mused aloud, illuminating the path they had come along. "I can only see his tracks, not any others. Up to this point he stuck closely to the thread. But here, where the thread bends, he just went straight on. I wonder what made him do that."

Miriam thought but couldn't come up with anything. "I can't explain it. It doesn't seem like him at all."

Elle nodded. "There's nothing to suggest he ran off. The trail looks normal. Now what? It wouldn't be wise to follow him farther. I suggest we head back and start again tomorrow morning. Maybe he'll be back by then anyway."

They turned around and walked back through the night to the farm. Miriam was relieved Elle couldn't see her tears in the dark.

Too upset to join the others in the farmyard, she went straight into the house. Apart from waiting, there was not much she could do. So she tried to calm her—and her children's—raw nerves.

"No," she said again, more gently this time, "but I'm sure he'll be back soon." She got up and carried Lucas back to his room.

"Will you stay with me?" he asked, half asleep.

"Of course," she assured him, and lay down next to him in the bed. She tried to remember the lullabies she hadn't sung in years and was amazed how much she could remember despite the current circumstances. Grateful that the singing was keeping her from thinking, she quietly sang one song after another.

She had only intended to stay with him until he went back to sleep, but when she was woken by a loud call, she was surprised to find that the sun had long since moved high in the sky. Lucas had used her upper arm as a pillow, and it had gone numb. Without waking the boy, she pulled it out. The voice called out again, and Miriam realized it was Lena. She was abruptly wide awake. She rushed down the stairs and out of the house.

"Lena, where are you?" she cried. "LENA?"

"Here, by the gate!" Her daughter sounded almost hysterical. "Quick!" Miriam broke into a run.

Other voices mingled with Lena's.

She hurried around the corner. Any women and men who had weapons had stationed themselves at the gate and were watching what was happening in the forest. A number of people were crowded around Lena, trying to hold her down. Suddenly, she broke away and sprinted into the forest.

Miriam ran faster than she had done in all her life.

George woke up slowly, struggling to shake off a dream. He had dreamed he could hardly breathe. He felt a weight on his chest and saw a black shadow hovering over him. There was just enough light for him to make out the silhouette of the pinscher.

"Hi, Tobi," he whispered, relaxing a little. Something wet brushed his lips. Amused, he turned his head to the side and lifted the dog onto the seat next to him. "Lovely—a French kiss! Did you sleep well?" he asked his four-legged friend, stretching as best he could in the cramped car. Tobi mimicked the movement and yawned. "Lucky you! I got no sleep at all. Feels like I spent the night drinking. Well, what d'you say—shall we head back?"

The pinscher panted as if affirming his suggestion. George focused on the sounds around them. He couldn't hear anything unusual or threatening. Numerous birds were announcing their eagerness to find a mate.

George looked around the vehicle. Since the apocalypse had broken out, he had become accustomed to keeping an eye out for useful items wherever he went.

He folded down the rear seat and rummaged in the trunk. The first aid kit was empty. He fished out a black bag from under one of the seats. It was surprisingly heavy for its handy size: It contained two thin computers encased in aluminum, complete with charging cables, which he put back after weighing them up for a moment. There was little point in lugging them around. If they were password-protected—which he was sure they were—they would be of no use to him. Out of the blue, he wished he could get Julienne to crack the codes for him. He wondered what had happened to her. He would probably never know.

In the glove compartment, he discovered a notebook filled with writing. He leafed through it carefully. To begin with, the writing was neat and elegant, slightly slanted to the right.

The paragraphs were long, almost long-winded. But the more recent entries became shorter and more scrawled. On the final pages, George could barely make out individual letters. Many sentences consisted of only three or four words. The huge change in the writing suggested the writer had undergone a transformation. On the first page, George identified a name and wondered what "Eva" might have written in her journal. He didn't know any German—but Lena did. She learned the language at school and was doing well at it. George felt a twinge when he thought of his family. He decided to give the notebook to his daughter—but he would use the last two blank sheets for his morning toilet.

He peered out through a torn corner of the paper covering the window. It wasn't the best angle, but there was no one directly in front of the door. Very carefully, he enlarged the tear until he had a clear view of his surroundings. The coast seemed to be clear. He opened the door slowly, ready to close it again immediately at the slightest sign of danger.

Before he could react, Tobi squeezed through the crack to freedom. George held his breath. Nothing happened. He waited a few seconds before following him, ax in hand.

They walked to where they had left the forest the night before. The foliage, which had been trodden down by many feet, would show them the way back. The width of the trail testified to the sheer number of pursuers who would have caught them had they not encountered the broken-down vehicle. *My God, so many people*, thought George, shocked.

He put the diary in his inside jacket pocket and made use of the pages he had torn out.

Just under an hour later, with the sun high in the sky, he found himself on the path leading to the farm. Tobi had hurried ahead as soon as he recognized the area. The road, which was only wide enough for a single vehicle, ended at the gate through which he had stepped out into the forest yesterday.

Delighted, he jogged toward it. From a distance, he waved to the guard, who admitted the joyfully barking pinscher. The gate was torn open—Lena rushed toward him.


A summer breeze wafted through the open window, carrying the scent of pine trees. Lena had dozed until the afternoon, making up for her lack of sleep the previous night. She stretched and opened her eyes. Her wristwatch showed four p.m. The diary lay on the pillow next to her.

Papa had given her the notebook he had found during his nighttime excursion. She had intended to read it right away but had been overtaken by fatigue. Relieved that her father had returned unharmed, she had finally been able to relax. Now she picked up the notebook. She was immensely pleased to be reading German again and opened it to the first page. The very same moment, excited shouts rang out from the farmyard. She sighed, put it back on the pillow, and went over to the window.

A group had gathered at the gate. They had quickly taken up their weapons and positioned themselves at the fence. A distant humming sound was getting louder. From the platform above them, the guard pointed down the path that led into the forest.

A few seconds later, Lena spotted a vehicle approaching at a sedate pace. She narrowed her eyes. An old white Citroën came to a stop twenty meters from the gate. The driver opened the door and struggled out while the engine chugged and labored. The man was stout and wore a filthy sweater that might have once been blue. His skull was nearly bald except for a matted crown of hair. His pants had umpteen patches, and his rubber boots had also seen better days.

Alfons, the pig farmer. Lena knew him vaguely from her grandmother's stories. The farmer was not a nice person, she remembered. Joanne had often had dealings with him and the farmers' association he belonged to—and had not enjoyed it. Alfons and the association saw Joanne's radical way of working and her animal protection activities as a threat, and not a year had gone by without them filing spurious lawsuits in an attempt to make her life difficult.

A larger and younger version of Alfons now got out the passenger side. *That'll be the son*, Lena thought to herself. He, too, was wearing tattered clothes and boots covered in mud.

The sentry called to them from the platform. "Who are you? And what are you doing here?"

Lena pricked up her ears.

The man introduced himself. "My farm is a little way down the road," he called over the sound of the engine. "This is my son, Thomas."

Joanne appeared in the yard. She was wearing light-colored garments and had a purple scarf around her shoulders. She briefly took in the scene and then walked calmly toward the gate. The guard saw her coming and waited for instructions. Joanne climbed the ladder to the observation deck.

"Hello, Alfons," she called down. "What brings you here? And turn off the engine, please. The noise will just attract the transformed. Besides, there's no reason for us to be yelling at each other." He obeyed and silence fell. "What can I do for you, pig farmer?"

He lowered his eyes awkwardly, but his posture betrayed the anger he felt at her condescending tone. It was several seconds before he spoke. "We're running out of supplies, Joanne. In two days, we won't have anything left to feed the cattle. And if I slaughter the hogs now, I'll have to throw away over half of them. There's no one to take the meat off my hands."

Lena counted two heartbeats before her grandmother replied, "You shouldn't have sold your cold stores, Alfons."

"How could I have known what was coming, Joanne? Who would ever have thought this would happen?" he lamented.

"We often discussed the future of agriculture, pig farmer," said Lena's grandmother. "But for you and your kind, change was out of the question."

"My family has been raising pigs for three hundred years." He was almost bellowing. "It's all we know, Joanne."

"And now it will be your downfall," she said calmly. Lena gulped at her grandmother's tone.

"Are you going to send us away again, Joanne? Thomas has a three-year-old son and a wife at home. Are you going to leave us to starve?"

No one dared breathe. Joanne stood there for half a minute without moving. Across the distance, she looked directly into Alfons's eyes.

Only when he looked away did she turn and speak quietly to the guards at the gate below. A debate broke out. Some shook their heads firmly. Then, after some back and forth, they gave in. Four people went over to the camp that had been set up in the barn. The others continued to guard the gate.

"Drive closer, pig farmer," Joanne instructed Alfons.

Father and son looked at each other. Silently, they got in. The engine turned over half a dozen times before it started. Alfons drove toward the gate. Just before he reached it, he turned the vehicle around. At that moment the guards returned. They were carrying green plastic crates filled to the brim with fruits and vegetables, cereals, flour, and preserving jars. Lena had prepared much of it herself.

She heard Joanne say calmly to her people, "Take it to his car, please."

And then a little louder to Alfons, "That should tide you over for the next three weeks. But you should think about moving here. Winter is coming. The undead are roaming the area. And we always need helping hands."

Through the open gate, Lena saw Alfons's incredulous expression. His son and a guard had just lifted the last crate into the car. "And what am I supposed to do with my pigs? Let them starve?"

"No, just release them. As you said yourself, you have no more use for them. And not even zombies are interested in animal flesh."

"They won't survive even three months in the wild, Joanne. They'll make it to winter at the latest . . ."

"If they stay with you, they won't last two weeks, pig farmer." Her voice had taken on an unpleasant harshness. "I didn't know it was so important to you that they lived to a ripe old age."

Angry and ashamed, Alfons lowered his gaze and twisted his hands together.

"Think it over," Joanne said in a more conciliatory tone. "We have enough work, and you are hardworking people. You're welcome anytime."

Alfons and his son nodded and got in. Lena watched as her grandmother climbed down carefully and disappeared into the house. Meanwhile, the guard barricaded the gate again. Barely a minute later, the classic car's roar had faded into the distance.

For a while she wondered what Alfons and his family would decide. Would they release the animals and come to the farm after all? The tension between him and her grandmother made that seem very unlikely.

Lena left the window, went back to bed, and finally began to read Eva's diary.

# CHAPTER 2

# NORTH SEA

The sea was churning up under the wild north wind. I looked at her furtively under the mainsail. Standing erect at the main mast, her back stiff and pressed firmly against the ten-meter metal post, Franca was staring toward the mainland. Her combat boots were planted on the grooves of the deck. In her posture I could see disappointment and resignation. Anger at not being able to control those emotions. Or was it just my imagination? Were those my own feelings?

Hanna and Verena were watching from the stern. It was their parents who had contacted us through Dr. Koller and asked for help.

Sixteen-year-old Hanna had not uttered a sound for a very long time. The injuries and the psychological stress she had been subjected to had taken their toll. She had also lost her hearing during the attack on the villa. Despite what she had suffered, she played a part in the community, but she was given to introspection. Most of the time she hid her face under a scarf that she wrapped around her head as if she were living in a desert. Surprisingly, her weapons of choice during combat training were firearms. Like Franca, she wore her dark brown hair in a braid that fell down her back beneath her headdress. I wondered if she was secretly emulating her.

Her sister, who was three years older, had cared for her devotedly from time to time. Verena was the interface we used to communicate with Hanna. Like everyone else, the nineteen-year-old had been trained to use firearms in the basement of the villa. Ever since, she had carried a Glock at her hip. The long blond strands of her hair fell loosely over her shoulders and framed her narrow face, which was tanned from having spent many days at sea.

Marcus sat astride the windlass. His top priority was to get home. Alone, if necessary, he once said resolutely. We had consulted the rough map of Europe and calculated that it was five hundred kilometers from Berlin to his hometown.

The three young people were a close-knit team. In Hotel 23, they had spent weeks fighting for survival together, and this had forged a lasting bond. Which had been further strengthened by being confined on the yacht.

Autumn was just around the corner. Temperatures had been low for days, and the sky was gray. We wore just about all the clothing we had. "Unusually cool for the time of year," Patrick, who stood next to me, said again. His hands turned the wheel smoothly. We headed toward the north pier at the entrance to the Port of Amsterdam.

Only a week before, a medium-strength hurricane had crossed our path. It had not had a huge impact on us since we were able to ride out its fury in the shelter of St. Anne's harbor. We had sailed in in good time and moored at two buoys. The pier protected us from the raging waves that were thundering just two hundred yards away to the northwest. Nevertheless, our tense and uncertain faces were splattered with salt spray. No one had expressed the need to go on to the island and pay a visit to St. Anne. The Mallorca experience was still in our bones. Some of us went as far as the long Alderney pier in the dinghy to stretch our legs. At night we saw one or two lights in Newtown. But neither we nor the islanders were eager to make each other's acquaintance. We had plentiful supplies. Drinking water was streaming out of the sky. We stayed there for four days.

As soon as the hurricane had passed, we hoisted the sails, and they took us northeast. The sea continued to churn, and the swells were huge. However, the worst of the storm was over. The water rushed by beneath us.

That day, Waltraud and Jens called a meeting. Eva sat at the wheel, and we gathered there. Waltraud started speaking several times, but barely managed to utter a sound. She was obviously having a hard time putting her thoughts into words. Then she looked each of us in the eye one by one and announced, "Guys, I know how shitty this sounds, but Jens and I are getting out."

Stunned, we looked at Jens, me hoping he would contradict her. His careful movements reminded us that he had been wounded—and that we had lost a friend in the process. Jens's wounds had now healed. Looking back at us, he nodded resolutely. "I have no idea if my parents are still alive, and the uncertainty is really getting to me. All I know is that they were recently in Amsterdam. That's the only place I'm likely to find them. They would never give up the house." He took a deep breath. "Waltraud and I will travel with you as far as IJmuiden Beach—but that's where we part ways."

That was it! Just like that! A done deal. I stared at him in amazement and puffed out my lips in disbelief.

Only then did he lower his eyes.

"I understand," Franca said in a strained voice. "Normally I would have suggested we go with you, but we have to get the kids home." She jerked her thumb toward the bow, where the three of them sat watching us. "And I don't think we can get to Berlin overland. So we'll stick to the Hamburg route as planned. I can't afford another failure."

I remembered that Franca had flown to Spain on a mission to bring a young man back to Italy. She had not succeeded—her protégé had become one of the undead during the rescue operation.

"Under any other circumstances . . ." Waltraud put in apologetically, but Franca went on. Her chin was trembling.

"In the past few weeks, I've thought constantly about what happens next. I already knew our little community couldn't last forever. This . . . conversation was something I was expecting, even if I didn't know who would make the first move." Her voice softened and rose half an octave. "But it's not just about the girls for me. All my life I've been an outsider. I had great parents, but I was parted from them at an early age. The few friendships I had—if I had any—were mostly with colleagues. And I never had much success with partners. What I mean to say is that if I ever had anything like a family—it was you guys." She tried in vain to hold back her tears. Between sobs, she laughed and wiped her cheeks. "I don't want you to change your minds; no way. I just want you to know what this time with you has meant to me. Oh, and if you're wondering how I suddenly got so emotional," she said, sniffing again, "it's a therapy thing they tortured me with in rehab. Opening up. Trusting. Telling the people you care about how you feel about them. Before the pressure inside destroys you."

The mood was already uncomfortable, and we smiled awkwardly. We pretended to accept each other. To understand each other. To be free comrades who had marched alongside each other for a while and were now going their separate ways. I wasn't buying any of the bullshit. Without the community, our asses would soon be on the line.

"This sucks! You'll barely survive two days out there on your own." No one gave any heed to my objection.

Franca continued, "Tomorrow we'll divide the weapons and food fairly. You don't need the yacht, so we'll keep it." Waltraud and Jens nodded.

Then Eva detonated the next charge. "We . . . no, not we—I," she corrected herself. "I've convinced Patrick"—Patrick signed speech marks with his fingers behind her back as she continued—"that we should sail to Iceland."

"Guys! You're not serious, are you?" I couldn't believe it. "If you break up our community, you condemn us all to death!"

"Let it go, Backup," Franca placated me wearily. "There's no point in getting worked up."

But what about me, I wanted to shout. Where did I belong? Where was I supposed to sail?

As if she was reading my mind, she said, "You and I will take the children to Germany. After that, we'll see." Waltraud, Jens, Eva, and Patrick were silent.

Franca retreated into her badass cocoon again.

In the days that followed, I proclaimed my displeasure openly, but inside I was bleeding. To distract myself, I made plans about how we could get to Berlin. Whenever the hopelessness increased, I studied the map. From Hamburg, we planned to sail up the Elbe. But now, just outside Amsterdam, where our community would disperse, there was nothing to conceal the reality of the situation.

"Unusually cool for the time of year," Patrick said. I made no reply and continued to busy myself with the ropes. A gust of wind made the boat sway. Franca, who was still standing at the mast, counterbalanced the movement, gazing silently landward. The HK swung from her shoulder.

Waltraud and Jens had packed up their things neatly. They were waiting on the port side for us to dock. We sailed past the south pier into the deserted harbor. Some of the boats left there had capsized. The Dutchman jumped onto the wobbly quayside and secured the hawser I threw to him. Waltraud then handed him the two backpacks and a smaller sub-machine gun that Patrick had taken from the yellow e-pickup at the villa. The ammunition was stowed in their bags.

"That's everything," she whispered and left the boat.

Yielding to my grief, I jumped over the railing too, onto the unsteady jetty. Tears burned my eyes. Stiffly, I walked up to them and took each of them in my arms.

Suppressing a sob, I heard myself say to Jens, "Damn, I'm going to miss you. And eat something, will you, so you don't disappear altogether."

Laughing and crying at the same time, he replied, "And you take care you don't cut your ear off with that spear." I heard the stomping of feet and realized the others were joining us. Then I buried my face in Waltraud's shoulder.

She squeezed me tightly before beginning to muse, "Well friends, here at last, on the shores of the sea, comes the end of our Zombie Earth fellowship. Go in peace. I will not say do not weep, for not all tears are an evil."

It took a while for them to detach themselves and disappear from view landward. Patrick immediately turned his attention to the boats moored around us, inspecting some of them and then returning to Franca and me.

"The yacht has too big a draft for your route, I think. I found two or three other boats here. They're much smaller, but they're in good shape and suitable for inland waters. And they'll take five people, no problem."

Franca frowned. "Hmm, there's something in that," she replied. "How long do you think it'll take us to get from here to Hamburg? A week? Ten days?"

"Something like that, depending on the wind. You'll be sailing relatively close to the coast. A small boat will definitely be better for the Wadden Sea area."

"Okay. But it's already too late to move on today. We'll spend the night here. We'll move our things right away."

"All right. Then come and choose a boat!"

"Fine. Backup, can you bring our luggage?" Franca asked.

I nodded, and they trudged off.

The young people pitched in. I hadn't yet mustered the enthusiasm to get to know them. I realized this would have to change, but I pushed the thought aside. I'd have plenty of time to get onto it tomorrow. Within half an hour we had emptied the big yacht, leaving Eva and Patrick's share of the supplies and weapons. In the meantime, Franca had arrived with the smaller boat, anchoring it next to us. She had also found two canisters of reserve diesel. The engine was sound. Unlike the other sloops, which had outboard motors, it was built into the hull, which meant it ran much more quietly. Once we were on the Elbe, I thought, we would have to resort to it more often. I was pleased with our new craft, even though it marked the start of the last leg of our journey.

Meanwhile, my biggest concern was navigating the locks on the Elbe. How many were working? I was not so foolish as to believe that someone would be on-site to operate them. Would we be able to do it ourselves? According to my research, there was just one, shortly after Hamburg. But what if there were other, smaller locks I didn't know about? That weren't marked on the map, which scarcely showed waterways anyway. Patrick wasn't much help on this score, either.

The new vessel was much less comfortable than the big yacht. It had only one berth, at the front, and we assigned this to the youngsters. Franca and I would have to make do with the fold-down seating. We stowed our tools as best we could, while Patrick checked and oiled the engine.

Back on the yacht, we prepared our last meal together. No one felt like talking. We sat quietly on deck, picking at our plates. Now and again, Patrick tried to lighten the mood with remarks that we'd have found funny any other time.

Today he was unsuccessful.

The daylight was gradually fading. We assigned the watches, but this proved unnecessary. We spent the whole of the night as a group, clinging to our disintegrating friendship. No one slept.

Shortly before sunrise, the clouds dispersed. It looked like it would be a bright and beautiful day.

"Well, I guess that's it," Patrick growled. "Luckily, Iceland is so far away, there's no risk we'll run into each other again." He grinned, revealing his crooked teeth. I wonder if I would miss that grin. Probably not, but I would miss the guy behind it very much. We clutched each other's forearms in a parody of warriors.

"I'll miss your stupid ramblings. I hope your arrogance doesn't cost you your head," I said.

"Don't worry. I've copied so many other things from you that those are the real dangers to my life."

With a heavy heart, I let go of him and hugged Eva. Franca and the young people hugged them, too. Our friends got onto the yacht, and I cast off for them. Patrick started the engine and chugged out of the harbor toward the open sea. We watched as they hoisted the sails. They flapped loosely in the wind for a moment, then filled. Everyone waved. Then they passed the north pier and disappeared.

# CHAPTER 3

# ELBE

We sailed close to the wind. Our small nutshell held its own against the high waves in exemplary fashion. Two days after the breakup of our community, we sighted the North German coast on the horizon. We swiftly passed the archipelago between Juist and Wangerooge. As we sailed into the mouth of the Elbe River, we saw Cuxhaven.

I wasn't sure what I was expecting. Burned-out ruins? Streets destroyed beyond recognition? Hordes of zombies screaming at us from the beach? We passed the small harbor town from only a few hundred meters away. It seemed untouched. All we could see were some abandoned vehicles rusting away. Birds flew in and out of the open windows of the houses. Two stray dogs barked at us from a distance.

I was finding it difficult to pin down my emotions. Being on the boat gave me the time to mull it over. The fear, the uncertainty, the constant vigilance—they all stalked me, and I couldn't shake them off. The separation of our Mallorca team weighed heavily on me. At night, before I fell asleep, I kept thinking about how much I missed Patrick's teasing, Waltraud's film quotes in the most inappropriate situations, Nils's grumpiness, Eva's cool head, and Jens's gluttony. Hoping for a reunion was futile. I was just happy to survive each day. I could count my life goals on the fingers of one hand: a safe and dry place to sleep at night, food and water for two to three days, and a weapon to defend myself with. Except for a few moments when they flared briefly, needs for things like physical closeness and the comfort of another human being were noticeably wasting away, like an animal that gradually starved to death if it wasn't fed. The nighttime hours I spent back-to-back with Franca on the narrow couch were the crumbs that saved me from dying of emotional malnutrition.

The young people, on the other hand, were friendly and open. They were dealing with the apocalypse far more calmly than my prejudice and ego had led me to expect. I wondered how I had managed to ignore them for so long on our journey. I quickly made friends with the older members of the group. Even Hanna signaled a certain openness toward me. Franca remained distant in her strange way, and generally spoke only when necessary.

Standing next to me at the main mast, she scanned the coast off Cuxhaven. "Hmm, at first glance it seems deserted. No wandering corpses so far. Let's hope it's just as peaceful when we get to Hamburg."

"Oh," I objected, "there are bound to be survivors here, too. They might be watching us right now. But I can understand if they don't make themselves known. We'll be lucky if they don't decide we're sitting ducks and attack."

"If that happens, luck will be on the side of this." She put a hand on the HK that dangled permanently from her shoulder. Then she changed the subject. "Have you found somewhere suitable for us to land before Hamburg?"

"There was an island marked on the map, about thirty clicks from the city. The wind's in our favor. We'll need to sail another eighty kilometers. If it's uninhabited, we can spend the night there and stretch our legs for a change."

"That would be good. I'm getting sick of boats."

For the rest of the day, I thought about what Eva and Patrick and Waltraud and Jens might be doing right then.

The sun was constantly behind a gray veil. The river below us was more than three kilometers in places. The lack of sunlight made the water appear brown and murky. Where the river grew narrower, we saw settlements and isolated houses. But nothing moved.

In between, Franca went through drills with Hanna on the bow, as she had once done with me in the cellar. Around noon, Verena relieved Marcus at the tiller. He went below to prepare food. I lent a hand. In the early afternoon, we ate rice with black olives.

"Remember how Waltraud told us they had shut down most of the world's nuclear plants?" I said as we sailed past one. "Because there was no one to maintain them and keep them running? I wonder what's going on with that one."

"I guess some of them will have had meltdowns," Marcus responded. "So the areas around them will be uninhabitable for centuries," he said, adding more pensively, "as if that matters now. But this one seems okay still."

"Yes, the dome doesn't look damaged. But we should still get out of here as fast as possible. No one knows whether we're being exposed to radiation or not."

An hour before sunset, we reached the island, which a block of stone painted with red letters identified as Black Clay Sand. We spotted a beach on the north side and headed for it. A large fallen pine tree jutted out into the river there, and we moored to starboard, using the trunk as a jetty. The minute my feet touched solid ground, I was gripped by land sickness, just as I had been in the harbor on St. Anne. I staggered slightly, trying to offset the lack of a swaying boat. The others had the same problem.

"Whoa, what's going on now?" Marcus asked. Hanna grinned, spreading out her arms to regain her balance.

Verena laughed out loud. "The last time I felt like this, I was drunk," she exulted.

Franca confirmed what I was thinking. "You've got so used to the rocking of the ship, which is now gone, that you'll need to get used to solid ground again. But don't worry, the fun will be over in two hours at most."

I grabbed the spear. "Marcus and I will check the terrain." Franca nodded. She tossed the boy a pistol, which he tucked into his waistband.

The island was a sandbank, lined by a strip of trees. We jogged in parallel to each other, about a hundred and fifty meters apart, so as to have both shores in view. It felt good to run freely again after so much time on the boat. Soon I was sweating profusely. My spirits slowly revived, and my body began to release endorphins. After three kilometers—at the end of the islet—we turned around. We were back within half an hour. A campfire was blazing, and steam was rising from two cooking pots above it.

"It seems safe," I reported. "The island is uninhabited."

"We'll still post guards." Franca wasn't taking any chances. "As soon as it gets dark, we'll head back to the boat. We could think about spending the night on land if the island were smaller. If we could see all of it at night. But with this one we can't. I don't want us to be surprised in our sleep by a wandering corpse that's washed ashore." We nodded, assenting to her suggestion as if we had any say in the matter.

Verena passed the info on to her sister using finger gestures. Hanna agreed. The siblings didn't know sign language, so they had developed their own system for communicating. At the moment it was rudimentary, but it did the job.

Sitting on the fine sand, we devoured the canned food. Everyone got an orange, too. We had one last box of fresh fruit, which would be gone in six days. The cans would last another three weeks. By then we hoped to be in Berlin.

Later in the evening, we heard thunder rumbling and watched the sheet lightning in the distance together. The only sounds any of us made were occasional cries of surprise when the lightning flashed particularly bright.

Franca and I were assigned the last two shifts and went below around midnight. Uncertainty and tension were an everyday experience for me now, so I was asleep within ten minutes.

After a breakfast of coffee and rusks, we spread out on the beach to wash, with one of us keeping an eye on the surrounding area at all times. I cleaned the dishes with sand and set about washing my socks and underwear. Refreshed by the morning bath, we boarded the boat and let the current carry it to the middle of the river. The wind had weakened, but it was blowing in our favor. The sun even came out occasionally. We hoisted the sails and braved the drift. Conversation dropped away as the journey progressed, and around noon we caught sight of Hamburg.

The rain had done its best to extinguish the fires that had ravaged the city. From a distance, we could see blackened concrete towers that had once served as apartment complexes or offices.

The sides of some of them had crumbled away, and they rose out of the earth like broken swords. The deeper we sailed into the city, the more burned out areas were revealed. A gigantic soot-covered area stretched out to port. There were homes burned to the ground as far as the eye could see.

This was the apocalyptic landscape I had expected.

"Where are all the people? There must be survivors," Verena murmured, without expecting an answer. She held her sister in her arms.

Stunned, we gawked at a passenger plane on the right that had burned out on the runway. A little farther on were thousands of shipping containers, rotting away in abandoned storage yards. Not a seagull could be heard. The air smelled pungently of burned rubber.

We looked around continuously, not daring to speak. The plan was to stay on the branch of the river that—if the way was clear—would bend southward and take us out of the city. We passed wrecked supertankers and dodged one blocking half the river.

"Just look at that," Marcus whispered. Verena nodded, massaging the back of her neck with one hand. We sailed past a tall building on a corner. Like the other buildings, this one was almost completely burned out. The lower third was made of red brick. The upper floors had once been glazed, but the glass had melted and solidified into long columns as it flowed.

"What is it?" I asked.

Marcus grinned gleefully. "It's one of those prestigious properties that cost millions and would never have made a profit. Seeing it like this . . ." He looked over again, shaking his head disapprovingly. We sailed silently on.

Upstream, we saw an impressive bridge. It was over fifteen meters high and held up by three elongated arches made of gray steel girders.

My hackles rose a moment before I smelled them. They arrived in their hundreds on both sides of the river, watching us from the banks without making a sound. Fear and the desire to fight flared simultaneously in my veins. Silently, the zombies followed our journey. Could they see now, or were they merely sensing the sails? Then their ranks began to move. As one, they marched upstream toward the bridge.

"Oh, shit!" Franca thundered as she registered what they were about to do. "Backup, start the engine now! Verena, we're going to need something large caliber for this, right now!"

"Okay," I said.

"On it," replied Verena at the same time.

The two of us crashed around below deck. Verena took a pump-action shotgun, a Beretta, and the bag with the ammunition and went back on deck.

I knelt, opened the hatch to the transmission, and fiddled with the ignition.

Meanwhile, Franca gave instructions. "Verena, tell Hanna to head for the center of the bridge—no matter what." I heard her release the safety catch of her HK. "We'll focus only on the ones that get too close. Backup, everything all right down there?"

"I'm ready." The engine spluttered once and roared to life.

"Full speed ahead!" bellowed Franca.

The boat leapt forward, sedately gaining speed. "Backup, grab your weapon!"

I rushed up the stairs to the main mast and grabbed my spear.

As soon as the undead heard the engine, they collectively let out a loud groan.

Franca put the magazines in both of her trouser pockets. I positioned myself behind her while simultaneously keeping an eye on Hanna at the helm.

"Right, thirty seconds to go. Haul in the sails! I don't want a zombie to get caught in them or even tear one."

We were two hundred meters from the bridge. The first wandering corpses were climbing some stairs on the left bank. A few moments later, they were pouring into the street and hurrying to the middle of the bridge. I saw a similar scenario was playing out on the other bank. Silently, I calculated that we might have enough time—that we would pass under the bridge just before they rained down on us.

"Listen carefully, all of you!" thundered Franca. "I'll take care of the ones on the bridge, but the minute one of those stinkers jumps down, he's yours. Got it?"

Verena and Marcus nodded. They stationed themselves three steps behind and to the side of Franca, who had taken up position by the main mast. "And try not to shoot each other—or me!"

Now we were a hundred meters away. The zombies above us reached the two pillars that separated the bridge into three sections. Franca took aim and fired a short volley as soon as the first flesh eaters entered the middle section. Some fell, some stumbled, but most of them kept on coming. I rolled the shaft of the spear between my sweating hands to unclench my fingers.

Franca fired to left and right. "Can't we go any faster?" she yelled, glancing at Hanna. The girl indicated that she didn't understand. I signaled her to give it more gas.

On the bridge, the first of them were already climbing over the parapet. Franca emptied a magazine, replacing it immediately.

The HK rattled almost unceasingly.

Less than thirty meters separated us from the landing stage. An emaciated zombie occasionally fell into the water, but there was no imminent danger yet.

When one of them splatted into the water ten meters ahead of us, Franca roared: "Guys, it's your turn now! Always aim for their heads! And watch out for their bodily fluids!" The other two didn't need to be told twice.

The Glock cracked; the shotgun thundered. The trio fired vertically upward. I saw wandering corpses losing limbs as they flew through the air. Three zombies slammed onto the deck one after another. They were killed instantly. Another hit the deck next to Hanna: I killed him with a spear thrust through the temple into his brain.

In the shadow of the bridge, it was darker. Franca was in her element. "Okay, reload quickly! The second round is about to start."

Marcus and Verena did as they were told. I looked at Hanna questioningly. She gave me a thumbs-up. Then I shoved the bodies into the water. They were frighteningly light.

The upstream edge of the bridge was directly in front of us. We heard the undead one floor up, roaring and switching to the other side of the street.

"Now we all shoot at anything that moves!" shouted Franca.

The first shots echoed brutally and loudly. More stinkers slammed onto the boat. One almost landed on me. I dodged it, speared it while it was still falling, and sent it into the river before it even touched the deck. Then we chugged out of the danger zone. Behind us, dozens of wandering corpses plunged into the water. The current pulled them away. Hanna kept the boat on course at full power.

"Did they get anyone?" Franca looked at us one by one, keeping the gun trained on us. Shaking our heads, we indicated that they hadn't. She waited a few seconds. No one showed signs of infection. Glancing at the soiled deck, she said, "Backup, hand me that bucket."

I stepped to the back, filled the water bucket, and passed it to her. She splashed away the stinking mucus, which had begun to clot. Once we passed the second bridge, Franca indicated to the helmswoman that she could slow down.

It was important not to put too much strain on the engine. In addition, we needed to conserve fuel. The roaring died away to a monotonous gurgle. Verena sat down with her sister to make sure she was okay. Marcus collected the rifles. I took the bag of ammunition.

"We'd better clean and reload the guns right away," I suggested. "Who knows when we'll get another chance."

"I'll do Franca's HK," he replied, but she wasn't ready to part with her machine gun for the time being. I nodded and went below with Verena's pump-action shotgun. A little later, we set to work.

By the afternoon, we had passed Hamburg without further incident. The industrial and port architecture had given way to agriculture. A brisk north wind helped us to make rapid progress against the current. But then, after twenty kilometers, we were faced with a huge problem. Our boat had reached the place I had marked on the map, where the river divided into two branches. The southern one ended at a dam, the other at a ship lift.

The dam had been breached by a Polish cargo vessel, a third of which now towered above it, the bow hovering five or six meters up in the air. Beneath it, the water was shooting out in a great jet. Three more tankers were bobbing on either side of the Eastern European one. Between them I saw isolated sails, not unlike ours.

From a distance, the lock looked deserted. Dozens of ships of all sizes were waiting in vain to descend.

"Go into that little bay," Franca ordered. Verena, who had relieved Hanna at the helm, obeyed. She steered the boat to the north shore, a hundred meters ahead of the dam. The Italian added, "Marcus and I will check the lock. Maybe there's a way to get it working."

She didn't sound convinced.

"I'd like to take a look at what's going on at the bridge. We might be able to commandeer one of the boats that is caught between the tankers," Verena said, gesturing over at the jammed vessels.

Franca nodded. "Okay, you do that. But you are not to enter any of the ships. And at the first sign of danger, you run away!"

"Yes, ma'am," said the young woman, saluting with two fingers. She brought our boat as close to shore as she could. Marcus, meanwhile, had retrieved and distributed the weapons. They jumped ashore from the stern and left Hanna and me aboard. We watched them as they crept part of the way together, crouching as they crossed the field. Then they climbed up a small embankment to the road and separated.

Franca and Marcus ran left and northward and soon disappeared. So we watched Hanna's sister on the ruptured bridge.

Verena went over to the tanker and looked upstream for a minute. Every now and then she changed position, probably to get a better view of her surroundings. She turned to us once and shook her head. She waited another twenty minutes until Franca and Marcus returned. Just before they reached the bridge, they separated, him joining us on the boat and her trudging over to Verena. They spoke together, and then Franca climbed onto the tanker and disappeared onto the deck. Meanwhile, Marcus climbed aboard the nutshell. I could tell by the look on his face that the lock was not an option.

"It's all closed up there." He spoke slowly and over-enunciated so Hanna could read his lips. "We couldn't find any way in. We'll have to think of something else if we want to keep following the river."

"We've been doing pretty well by water so far. I'd be reluctant to go on land." My gaze drifted over to the tanker, where Franca had come back and was climbing down. She conferred with Verena again. Ten minutes later, we were all back together.

"Did Marcus tell you it was a no-go at the lock?" asked Franca. We nodded gloomily. "Even the individual boats beyond the dam can't be used. They've been damaged by the tankers. We have no choice but to continue on foot. Unless . . ." She left a meaningful pause. "Yes, that might work. Listen, I have an idea . . ."

An hour later, we had traveled back a kilometer and a half and stopped in the approach channel to the lock. The sun had strengthened again—a welcome change from the autumn chill—and was now descending to the horizon. I stood upright and looked westward over the artificial island. Tensely, I watched for Franca's form.

According to my wristwatch, she had exceeded the upon agreed time by three minutes. My knuckles turned white every time I squeezed the spear shaft. *Four minutes.* The youngsters stood holding their breath alongside me. *Five minutes.* When we reached six, I was going to go in search of her. But then we saw her. She was running. I wished she was going faster. Thirty seconds later, she jumped onto the boat to join us.

"Did it all go okay?" I asked.

She raised a hand, indicating that I should wait until she caught her breath. "I . . . attached . . . everything . . . as far as . . . It took . . . longer . . . to find . . . a suitable . . . place." She looked at her watch. "Hmm. I'm just . . . wondering . . . why nothing . . . has happened . . . yet?"

A bright flash to the right, which mutated into a deafening explosion within milliseconds, blinded me briefly. Seconds later, the shock wave rolled down the island's withered grasses and rippled the surface of the water. There was a popping sound in my ears. I didn't see the two detonations that followed, but that just meant I heard them all the better.

"TAKE COVER!" yelled someone who was lucky enough not to have been staring directly at one of the fireballs. I was yanked from the boat into the water.

The sudden shock of cold made me wince. Objects crashed down around me, disappearing, hissing, into the depths. I sensed the elongated shadow of the ship's hull and dove toward it. As soon as the splashing stopped, I ventured back to the surface. Snorting out water, I greeted the others. "It worked out after all," I said.

Franca laughed, for the first time in a long time. "Not quite yet. We don't know if the discharge has loosened enough subsoil. But now more than ever, we must be on our guard. The stinkers are bound to have heard the explosion. They'll show up soon."

Her concerns about the blast not having been big enough were groundless. At the sight of the destroyed dam, we cheered for joy. The explosions had almost completely destroyed the three-hundred-meter bridge. The river was flowing more strongly, which was making our ascent more difficult. We would have to wait until the flow had diminished somewhat.

"How did you do that?" asked Verena. Her expression showed how impressed she was. Hanna's eyes were wide under her wet turban.

"Here's what I want to know," Marcus interjected, pointing at the demolished bridge. "There were three cargo ships there—and now they're all gone."

Franca grinned and was silent for a few moments. Then she began to explain.

While the crew was moving the boat to safety, Franca had run to the tanker. The vessel, which she discovered had rungs embedded in the hull, was loaded to the brim with propane. There were pipes and lines everywhere. Once on deck, she pulled out her Glock. The hard soles of her combat boots thudded on the thick steel, emphasizing her every step. Her attention was caught by a staircase leading down into the darkness. She checked the smell of the air flowing up to her. No stench of decay, no smell of gas. It grew darker with every downward step she took. Breathing deeply, she walked the narrow corridors, flashlight in hand. Dust motes flickered in the beam of light in front of her. She looked around nervously at each crack that came from the thousands of tons of metal around her. The pipes gurgled occasionally. She kept needing to wipe the sweat away with the back of her hand as she inspected the lower deck.

Behind a door marked with danger signs, she found a room with shelves full of tools. There were tape and cable ties on the workbench. In the right-hand corner was an oxyacetylene welder. Franca checked the pressure regulator and was relieved to find that the two one-and-a-half-meter gas cylinders could withstand nearly two hundred bars of pressure. That was more than she needed.

Before leaving the room, she checked carefully to see if she could find anything else that might be useful. But everything was too heavy or too unwieldy. So, she went for the tape and cable ties and grabbed the trolley. Inside it, the gas cylinders, secured with chains, clanged against each other as she left the workroom.

With the beam of her flashlight, she traced a pipe as thick as her arm. She found a red valve and positioned the trolley beneath it. Using the cable ties and tape, she fixed the burner head so that it was pointing at the T-piece with the pressure relief valve. Determinedly, she tried to remember the Special Forces Unit workshop where years ago they had taught her to break open chains and locks this way. Then she turned the valves on the gas cylinders halfway around. She carefully opened the gas supply on the handpiece. As soon as the gas hissed from the burner head, she activated the piezo igniter. A bright yellow flame flickered. She then added oxygen.

The fire went out with a loud bang. Since she had half expected this, she didn't faint with fright on the spot. On the next try, she adjusted the control dial much more carefully until she produced a sharp, hissing flame whose tip touched the copper of the connector. She brought the burner head closer and increased the temperature by adding a little more oxygen. She felt the intense heat of the blue flame on her face. Then she took to her heels.

"That was a good loud bang. My ears are still ringing." Marcus opened his mouth wide to dispel the ringing in his ears.

In the middle of the river, the mass of retained water flowed over a deep channel, forming rapids. At the current's present speed, we couldn't even think about trying to get upriver—even under full sail.

But this was precisely what we had been planning for. It was the end of summer, and the Elbe was at its lowest. The breadth of the channel now available to the water meant it would not be long before some of it ran off. Then we would risk heading upstream, hoping that the commotion had not attracted all the zombies in the area.

Thirty, forty meters from the banks, the first wrecks soon loomed out of the reservoir. A handful of cutters that had been moored farther back from the lock had been released by the detonations. Now they were drifting between us and it.

We watched tensely as the thundering river slowly abated. The shadows lengthened. The wind picked up as evening fell.

Franca got us moving in one bound and sat down at the tiller. "So, let's give it a go now. If it doesn't work, we'll try again in the morning."

I started the engine. The acrid smell of burned diesel rose into my nostrils. The crew cast off, and the former elite policewoman steered the boat upstream along the strongest current.

Just before we reached the place where the dam had been a few hours ago, she moved to the middle of the rapids. We immediately lost speed. But Franca opened the throttle and set the boat even more into the breeze. The engine howled at maximum power. Centimeter by centimeter, we fought our way up. At one point it seemed as though we were standing still. Then Franca pushed the rudder to the left, the breeze filled the sails, and we bobbed jubilantly into the gentler waters beyond the dam.

We spent the night seven kilometers farther on, in the bay of a small island, which seemed to be made for our craft. After taking the first watch, I went below and slept dreamlessly until sunrise.

I was woken by the soft clatter of cutlery. Franca was making coffee and a watery porridge from the leftover oatmeal. We didn't speak. I got up and carried the coffeepot and cups up to the deck after her. The others soon joined us. The young people immediately started talking among themselves but respected our silence.

Meanwhile, I spooned the bland porridge into my mouth, scanning our surroundings. Judging from the mobile homes along the bank on the other side, that area had been a campsite. Not a soul was stirring. My mouth full, I jerked my chin toward the twenty or so camper vans that were strewn about and said, "Let's check out those trailers over there." Marcus looked at me questioningly. "Our supplies won't last forever," I explained. "It looks like a reasonable risk to me, and people always leave food behind in campers like that."

Behind me I heard Franca say, "Yeah, we should do that. Marcus, take the boat as close as you can to that spot there." She pointed over my shoulder.

Ten minutes later, we were ready and jumped from the stern to the mainland. I had swapped my spear for a handy pistol this time. Franca and I ran to the southernmost corner of the site.

"You open the door, and I'll check the interior. When I call, come in and get to work. While you do that, I'll get out and cover your back. Got it?" she whispered without looking at me.

"Okay, got it," I confirmed.

The caravan was an older model that had neither been moved for decades nor entered for months. The grass strip in front of it had been overgrown in the spring. In summer, thistles and chamomile bushes had seeded. We had to climb over them to get to the door. Franca stood right in front of it and signaled to me to open it. I grabbed the handle, which was set into black plastic, and turned it clockwise. Barely a quarter turn later, it stopped. The door was locked. "Fuck!" I cursed softly.

"Check under the car and see if you can find anything we can use to break it open," the Italian recommended, setting off in turn to hunt for something herself. The pistol in my hand, I first looked at my immediate surroundings. Then I looked under the trailer, pushing the grasses away with my foot. In a bucket of gardening equipment, I discovered some tools. Quietly, I whistled for Franca. Seconds later, she was standing next to me, grinning, as I showed her my find. She took a small trowel and ran back to the door, stuck the tip in the crack at the bottom corner, and levered the door up and down. I assisted her with the miniature rake. We wiggled it back and forth a few more times until the simple plastic lock gave way with a loud crack. The door burst open. Immediately we reached for our weapons, me aiming into the trailer, and Franca scanning the area behind us. Nothing happened. We exhaled in relief and grinned briefly at each other.

"My turn," she said, climbing inside and examining the interior. "All clear. You can come in."

I looked around again, went into the trailer and started rummaging through the cabinets.

"How does it look?" asked Franca from outside.

"There's not that much here; just a few spices and some clothes. Nothing we really need. But I've found a grocery bag, candles, and a lighter. And toilet paper."

"Good. By all means, bring them with you. If you see any salt, bring that, too. You can leave the rest."

I obeyed and left the camper. We took the garden tools with us. At the campsite, we checked a good fifteen properties, and to our amazement, rustled up quite a bit of food. Six packets of pasta, and a total of nine cans and jars of tomato sauce in various forms. Basics that campers love. But we also found canned peaches, four kilograms of rice, two liters of oil, as well as nine rolls of toilet paper. Underneath one motor home, we discovered a thirty-liter jerrican filled to the brim with diesel, the contents of which we poured into the boat tank. We had a hundred and fifty kilometers of waterway ahead of us before the last part of the journey, where we'd be traveling by road. We had burned through quite a few liters on the way upriver, so this could only be useful. After an hour—once we had stowed our looted products—we were on the river again.

The landscape was disappointingly monotonous. Now and again, we passed a town or settlement or saw the occasional forest, but mostly it was one uncultivated field after the next. Neither zombies nor living people were to be seen. At night, we found shelter in one of the countless artificial bays or sought out islands that proved safe. Once we ventured into a neighboring village but came back empty-handed. We had at least hoped for drinking water. But someone had looted it before us, and the water supply had long since dried up. Two days later, as our drinking water reserves dwindled, we were forced to boil filtered river water.

After breakfast, we usually exercised. Franca now had us doing push-ups until we dropped. I managed four rounds of thirty and then ignored the drill. I missed endurance training. Our cruising speed leveled off at fifteen kilometers per hour. The zigzag course the wind direction often forced on us meant we were traveling nearly twice the distance.

The narrowness of the boat left little room for privacy, which led to at least one heated debate every day. We seemed to be taking turns in having our nerves on edge. During the last few hours of the day, we pulled our socks up, put our heads together, and went over our itinerary. Verena and Hanna knew their way around Berlin, but none of us had any idea of how to get there.

And then, a week after leaving Hamburg, we reached Havelberg.

# CHAPTER 4

# AMSTERDAM

Jens tightens the shoulder strap of his backpack. A brief spasm of pain reminds him of his healed wound—and a summer he wishes had been different. Reality still seems unreal to him. Across his chest hangs the light MP5 they had acquired from the police station in Mallorca. He's carrying three hundred rounds and three spare magazines. Waltraud is walking alongside him, her hair tousled by the wind. Looking at her in her hiking gear and ignoring the matte black pistols at her hips, he might imagine that they had just returned from their sabbatical without the world having been turned upside down while they were away. The colors of the fabrics she's wearing are lightly faded and worn, and her hiking boots now fit perfectly, having been thoroughly broken in, but they're all made of sturdy materials and functioning well.

Mentally, Jens goes through the list of what they still have: food for a week, a hundred and eighty cartridges for their pistols, and two spare magazines. He himself has four liters of water in his backpack. No one can say when or if they will have the opportunity to replenish their supplies. But after the experience of the last few months, he is confident that they would know how to survive here—at least as far as getting ahold of food is concerned. Like Backup had to do in Mallorca, they'd have to scavenge to get by if it came to it.

A few minutes later, they are standing on the sand dune above a deserted campsite and between the ruins of spray-painted World War II concrete bunkers. A couple of rabbits romping around in the low-lying bushes may be the only other living creatures besides them.

"So, you know your way around from here?" asks Waltraud, her gaze roaming searchingly over the flat wasteland.

"Yes, this is my old stomping ground, so to speak. When I was a teenager, my sisters and I used to take bike rides here in the summer. That's where we used to camp." He points at the haphazard bungalows and trailers, which look like shipping containers in disguise. A large area around them has pitches for tents. Jens needs to swallow as he is seized by melancholy and longing for his family. Not knowing their whereabouts makes his heart beat unpleasantly fast.

"We should stay away from the residential areas. There's a bicycle path that leads across open fields. On one hand, we'll be visible from a distance, but on the other hand, we'll be able to spot anyone approaching in good time. And let's keep our eyes peeled for bicycles. After all, we're in Holland now." He looks anxiously at his watch. "Hmm, we still have a good six hours of daylight. We could make it halfway in that time. It's roughly that way," he says, gesturing inland with his arm. "Or we could bunk down there for the night," pointing to the campsite, "and try to do the whole thing in one go in the morning."

Waltraud shakes her head. "I'd also favor moving on today—and as fast as we can." She cracks the back of her neck. "Right now, the weather's still holding. Who knows; tomorrow it might rain. That would not be ideal. And if we split the distance over two days, I won't feel it's too far to manage."

They look out over their shoulders at the sea one last time, and then start walking. Sharp grasses, a meter high, whip against their legs as they tread the paths between the dunes. Sand crackles under the soles of Jens's feet. Now that no one is walking on the delicate flora, nature is reasserting itself.

"I don't know if it's the right time to say this," Waltraud says to him, watching where she puts her feet, "but what if we don't find them?"

He takes his time over the answer. "I don't know," he replies finally. "They're close to eighty and wouldn't be likely to travel far. Certainly not to my sisters in the States. Besides, my father worked his entire life to pay off the house we grew up in. He's so attached to it that he's become a part of it—literally. All his free time has been spent working on the house or in the garden. All of it! That was his whole life. He would never leave it! And my mother . . ." Jens stops and looks Waltraud in the eye. "I know that's not an answer to your question." Taking a deep breath, he runs his fingers through his hair. "If they're not there . . . then we'll head for Norway . . . If you like."

"Hmm," says Waltraud, unsure how to respond. "But would you be at ease there?"

"At ease?" Jens thinks for a moment, as if he has forgotten what the phrase means in this day and age. Then he speaks, "I don't care where I live, as long as I'm by your side."

She just nods, as if it were the most natural thing in the world. Now that they are really alone for the first time in months, the familiar ardor rises in him. He puts a hand on the back of her neck, pulls her close, and kisses her gently.

"I've missed this," she murmurs, her eyes closed.

"I've missed it more," he replies. His whole body is vibrating with emotion. But they still have a long way to go.

The sand beneath their feet soon gives way to solid ground. After twenty minutes, they reach a tiny, long-abandoned pool of water in the forest, the first harbinger of the demise of civilization. It is full of rain from recent days. Its edges are mossy. All around it are tracks indicating that for some time now it's been serving as a watering hole for wild animals. They carefully skirt the ruins of an old hunting lodge and soon reach Haarlem. In the once well-heeled northern quarter of the city, they are greeted by the familiar picture of desolation, only this time with a Dutch backdrop. Thatched red-brick houses, with seemingly ends rows of apartment buildings between them, tidily divided into even rectangles. A number of vehicles parked neatly in parking bays. Miniature front yards, now gloriously overgrown, full of insects and small animals. Everything buzzes with life; the absence of humans goes unlamented.

Waltraud and Jens keep to the southern edge of the settlement, which they leave at a traffic circle. Jens points across it: "We have to take that underpass there. The bike path takes us directly to Amsterdam. It's astonishing to see everything so empty. You can't imagine how many bikes used to be here."

Silently, they cross the street.

The wind has blown some garbage into the tunnel. Scraps of paper and plastic cups scrunch underfoot. He would have thought he would have gotten used to the sight of deserted cities, but the lack of any human activity—except their own—disquiets him. Or maybe it's because this is a place he knows so well, and now he must see it so deserted and desolate.

He always tries to approach things in a cool and confident manner. But he's very worried. He hasn't heard from his sisters in a long time, and he doesn't know what the situation is on the other continents. How have his parents fared—and what will happen if he finds them alive? *When*, he corrects himself. He still has no answers to all these questions. How could he have? He's never had to deal with an apocalypse before. He'll probably have to fall back on his experience of Mallorca. His imagination doesn't extend to anything else.

Fields—which have now degenerated into meadows—stretch away to the left, and a cemetery comes into view on the right. Involuntarily, they quicken their pace. In Spaarndam, half an hour later, with only the wind for company, Jens discovers something he had been secretly hoping to find.

"There! There, in the garage!" he exclaims delightedly.

"Oh, good!" Waltraud says in surprise. "I was wondering where all the bikes had gone."

They approach the garage, whose door is folded upward. The family that once owned it is long gone. The floor is covered with scraps of newspaper, plastic bags, and leaves that the wind has blown in. Inside, behind a stroller and a surfboard, they discover four bicycles that appear roadworthy. Jens inspects them closely. "The tires are flat," he announces. "We need a bicycle pump."

He looks around and finds one fitted to one of the frames. Waltraud picks out two of the larger bikes and helps him get access to the valves. While he gets the bikes into shape, she secures the surrounding area.

Ten minutes later, they are bowling toward Amsterdam, through endless meadows. They have strapped their backpacks to the pannier racks. It's fun to ride a bike again after such a long time. The breeze blows into his jacket collar, cooling his sweaty back.

"Now we only have two hours to go," he calls out to Waltraud. Every now and then they pass a farmhouse. One is completely burned out; the others look lonely and run-down. There's a hostile atmosphere everywhere.

"Look, there's the airport on the right. Now we're not far from the city. From there it's about another three or four kilometers. But we can take the freeway."

"After everything that happened in Barcelona, you still want to take the freeway? On a bike?" Waltraud's blunt sarcasm makes him think again.

"Hmm, there's something to that. We'll take a quick look at it and then decide, okay?"

She nods. "Can we make it all the way before sunset? Now that we have the bikes?"

"If we go on like this, then yes."

The rest of the way into the city is clear. In the ditch to their left, they occasionally spot human remains floating on the surface of the water.

In order to at least have the guardrail as a barrier between them and the forest on the right, they decide to take the opposite lane. As soon as they draw level with the first high-rise buildings on the periphery, they start having to weave past broken-down vehicles.

"I'd be okay staying on this road," Jens suggests.

"Yes, it looks better than I feared. Let's keep going!" The cars they pass are unusable. Often the keys are missing, and the doors of most vehicles have probably been standing open for months, the batteries long dead. A kilometer farther on, they jump out of their skins with fright when they hear a rustling in the trees on their right. They stop abruptly, silently put down their bikes, and draw their weapons. Jens's sense of smell is on high alert and Waltraud wrinkles her nose, too.

"Where did that come from?" she hisses.

For a moment, he thinks he has seen a chimpanzee in the treetops. But that would be nonsense, of course.

"Can you see anything?" he whispers. Standing back-to-back, they turn nervously in a circle.

"No, I can just smell them," she replies. The rustling in the trees quickly recedes. But their hearts are beating wildly with stress, pumping vast amounts of blood past their ear canals.

The sound of many footsteps reaches them, tramping quickly up from the lower highway, which crosses the road they're standing on. They hold their breath and move cautiously to the edge of the overpass. The sound-proofing here is made of transparent Plexiglas.

Through it they see ten, maybe twelve people running as a unit in their direction. Living people!

"Oh, fuck!" Waltraud exclaims. Three seconds later she says, "They're coming!"

A superior force of gray-and-white figures stomps around the corner, pursuing the runners, who are just fifteen meters ahead. Waltraud and Jens duck down instinctively and creep back to their bicycles. Peering over the edge, they watch the chase. The fugitives disappear under the highway. Jens crosses the road to get a better view. He sees the group break up. Two of them climb over the guardrail and run up the embankment supporting the upper lane. The rest pound onward.

Jens wonders where the two are headed—his eye catches the emergency door in the soundproofing. Then it opens and the two men leap toward him. He manages to yank the gun up before the first one sees him and stops, wide-eyed. The one behind crashes into him. Both of them fall to the ground. Out of the corner of his eye, Jens notices Waltraud standing rooted to the spot with her mouth open. The first of the undead appears in the doorway—he fires a short volley directly into its eye. Half its skull becomes a geyser of black blood and gray brain matter. His next shot tears a gaping hole in the neck of the second.

Before more of them can get through, Waltraud finally acts. She grabs the round handle and throws the door shut. The wandering corpses crash against it. "Come on. Let's get out of here," she yells at the stunned arrivals, pulling one to his feet by the collar of his black leatherette jacket.

Then she turns toward her bike, gets on, and rides off. *It's fortunate zombies aren't capable of operating doorknobs*, thinks Jens, wasting no time and swinging onto his vehicle.

Fleeing eastward as fast as they can, they soon realize they're being pursued. The two whose lives they saved are keeping pace with them easily. They're waving and calling to them to stop.

Jens is astonished. "What do they want now?" There's no trace of the infected, he notes with relief.

"We'll just ask them, shall we?" Waltraud brakes sharply, pushes down her kickstand and draws her weapons.

"Wow, Tomb Raider, don't shoot!" someone shouts at her.

Both raise their hands and stop in their tracks ten meters away. "We are unarmed!"

Jens grins broadly. "Who on earth goes out on the street unarmed these days?"

"Well—us. Whenever we need to scout the area. Our strength is speed," replies the one in the faux leather jacket, pointing to his sneakers.

The young people's unabashed tone and open attitude lift Jens's spirits. They remind him of himself when he was that age.

"What did he say?" asks Waltraud.

"You'll need to speak to her in English. She doesn't understand Dutch," he explains, waving the boys closer as he translates their brief conversation for her.

The one in the leather jacket grins broadly. Dark blond hair covers half of his face.

A little out of breath, he answers, "Okay. Hi, I'm Jori." He holds out his hand. His gaze lingers on their arsenal. "Where did you guys get that?" His jeans are frayed, but his running shoes are of the best quality.

"It's a long story." Jens sighs. "Hi, I'm Jens—and this is Waltraud."

He takes the water bottle out of his backpack and passes it around. Everyone drinks greedily.

"Thank you," Jori says, wiping his mouth with his sleeve as the others shake hands. He's pleasantly hyperactive and shifts his weight from one leg to the other every two or three seconds.

"So your name is Jori," Waltraud notes. "And who's your friend?"

"That's Pepe, but we all just call him Pepsi."

"No, not all—just you," the latter contradicts in a much calmer voice.

"What are you doing out here? Where did your friends go? What about your parents?"

Pepe and Jori cast a brief glance at each other before the Pepe answers. His olive hoodie is stained with sweat. "Well, this and that. Spying and scavenging, annoying sniffers, that kind of thing . . . with friends, who are hopefully hiding from them by now. Didn't you see them earlier? And our parents are . . ." Jori gives him a warning glance and he quickly falls silent.

Jens doesn't want to put the boys in an awkward situation and steers the conversation into safer waters. "Sniffers? You mean the undead?" He's happy to finally be talking to some of his countrymen again. Suddenly, a thousand questions are buzzing around in his head. What has happened here in the last few months? How many have survived? Where are they hiding?

"Yes, sniffers," Jori replies. He lifts his nose in the air, wrinkles it, and inhales and exhales noisily a few times. "And you? What brings you here? Why are you so well armed?" He turns his head slightly from side to side with each question.

"I'm from here," Jens puts in. "That is, I was born in Rotterdam but grew up in Abcoude. Long before . . ." He can't think of a proper term to describe what has happened to the world. So he just raises his right hand

and gestures to the rusting vehicles, abandoned buildings, and nature run wild.

"I don't want to be rude," he adds, "but we need to get going now, even though I'm dying to know everything that happened here. But it's getting late, and we have a long way to go. "

"Where are you going? Maybe we can come with you? We know our way around very well here. We'll help you find a place to sleep," Jori says in a flurry.

"Thanks for the offer, but no. I'm sure there'll be somewhere we can sleep at my parents' house. And your parents must be worried sick about you."

"Nonsense, they know we can take care of ourselves. It wouldn't be the first time we've stayed out overnight. The sniffers are out and about downtown right now; it wouldn't be safe to go there. Our activities have put them on edge. And it's only two or three kilometers down the highway to Abcoude. If we come along, we can tell you all about it."

Jens looks at Waltraud. She shrugs, says, "Well, why not?" and turns to the boys, "I hope you don't mind running beside us?"

"Not at all," Pepe replies, "we're used to running long distances. To be honest, it's all we've been doing for three months," he adds with a grin.

Half an hour later, they are standing in front of Jens's parents' house in Abcoude. Waltraud watches him from a few meters away while keeping an eye on their surroundings. Behind her, Pepe and Jori are panting. Jens looks at the building from the sidewalk. It's the first in a row of identical buildings with a red brick facade. The front door is to the right of a single window, which is set deep into the building and a head taller than him. It's partially hidden behind a hedge. He enters the small front yard and knocks on the door. He knocks again. And again. The tension makes Waltraud's breath quicken. Jens looks at her over his shoulder and shakes his head. The disappointment in his eyes is huge. She swallows hard. He bends down and rummages in the bushes until he finds the key and opens the door. Before he pushes it fully open, he picks up the submachine gun.

"Okay, we're going in," she hears him call in a muffled voice. Then he enters the hallway. A moment later, he beckons her after him. The boys follow them.

The air in the house smells stale. In the hallway, she closes the door behind her and whispers to them, "Stay here until we've checked all the rooms!" They nod. Waltraud follows Jens.

They move from the small vestibule to the living room, which takes up the entire first floor. Jens checks the kitchenette and goes to the conservatory. He draws the curtains. Waltraud has taken up position by the stairs and waits for him to let her in. They communicate with hand signals. She climbs to the upper floor ahead of him. There she discovers four more doors. Two of them are standing half open.

In the first room, his grin indicates that this used to be his nursery. It's small, with just enough room for a cot and a desk. Now it's a hobby room or a study. *Or it used to be*, she corrects herself. The adjoining room is twice as big. She sees him mouth the word *sisters* and suspects that they now only occupy it when they come to visit with their families. *Came to visit.*

The bathroom behind the third door is empty. The air inside is fresher because the small window facing the street is tilted open. He hesitates in front of the last door. Waltraud waits patiently for a few minutes until he finally screws up his courage and turns the knob. Immediately, a sweet smell of decay comes out. She puts a hand to her mouth. Jens turns his head to the side and takes a deep breath before entering the room.

It is his parents' bedroom. Was. Moving past him, she identifies two shriveled, bluish bodies in bed, clinging to each other. They're holding a photo in their hands, showing Jens and his sisters as children. There are empty pill dispensers on the nightstand. Waltraud doesn't have to read what's written on them to guess the contents. At the side of the bed, Jens falls to his knees and sobs.

An hour later, they have wrapped the withered corpses in bedding and carried them out to the yard. The bundle was stiff and disconcertingly light. They also took the stained mattress out and opened the window wide. They've built a funeral pyre from garden furniture and last year's logs from the shed and laid the remains of the deceased on it. The shed also contained some gasoline that was once meant for the lawn mower. They plan to use it to light the fire tomorrow, just before they move on.

The houses around them are eerily quiet. It's a cloudless night. Carefully, they lower the shutters on the window facing the street. In the cupboards and the cellar, which they check last, they find food and drinking water.

They make pasta with tomato sauce—the gas canister in the old-fashioned stove is still half full. By the light of the candle, they all eat fruit cocktail from a can for dessert.

Waltraud feels Jens is coping far better with the horrific discovery than she might have expected him to. He had probably secretly prepared himself for it, she speculates. Now she's waiting until they're alone. They can talk then.

"Boys," he says after dinner, "you're welcome to use my old bedroom for the night. But we'll have to lock you in."

Jori and Pepe look at each other in surprise, but nod. "That's all right. I'd do the same in your position. Not that you have anything to fear from us, of course, but in principle, it's understandable," Pepe says reasonably.

"Aren't you guys afraid something might happen to you? I mean, you don't know us any more than we know you. Who says we won't screw you over?" Waltraud wants to know.

"Nobody says so. But if you were some kind of freaks, you wouldn't have saved us on the highway," Pepe explains.

"And you wouldn't have shared your *super* delicious fruit cocktail with us," Jori jokes. "Don't worry about it. We'll be happy to sleep in the children's room."

"Good," the Norwegian says with a smile. "Then let's put one of the mattresses from the sisters' room in there later. We'll keep the other one."

"But I'm still dying to know all about what happened here after the fungus spread." says Jens.

"Fungus? What fungus?" The young people look at him uncomprehendingly.

"The fungus that turns people into zombies," Waltraud explains.

"It's a fungus? We always thought it was a virus."

"No, though it does behave like one. It's a mutated fungus species that has reached humans in a roundabout way. And now it's doing what it normally does to ants. The difference is that the infected turn rabid and . . . Well, you know what they do."

"Oh," says Jori. "And how do you stop it?"

"We don't know. In Berlin, they were working on a treatment until recently. We were in touch with someone there who explained it all to us. But we lost contact some time ago." She shrugs. "And what happened here?"

"As you saw this afternoon. Sniffers everywhere. It has"—he pauses briefly—"modified almost seventy percent of the population. Right at the beginning, they thought the army and the police might be able to defend us, but when you're fighting an opponent who doesn't feel pain and doesn't care about dying, you just don't stand a chance. Of the remaining thirty percent, barely half have survived. And they formed smaller groups on homesteads and the like, all over the Netherlands."

"How can you know all that? Are you in contact with each other?" Waltraud suddenly sits upright.

"Yes, we have contact with other communities. That's another reason we travel so much. My father is—was—a helicopter pilot for an energy company; he flew personnel to and from oil rigs in the North Sea. He also worked as an emergency paramedic, and he knew his way around the medical sector—until it all came crashing down, of course. He was able to get some equipment just in time. Radios, world receivers, antennae, all that kind of stuff. He got it wherever he could. He often sends us out to find other groups and let them use it—when we're not looking for food, that is."

"Where is your father now?"

The question seems to make Jori uncomfortable. He squirms in his chair and looks furtively at Pepe. Pepe just shrugs and says, "I think these two are cool. We can take them to Twiske tomorrow if you want. Your dad will grumble at first, but when he meets them . . . You know how he is. And we'll all be happy to have a few extra guns, won't we?"

"You're probably right," Jori says after thinking for a minute, and in which Waltraud waits like a cat on hot bricks to see where the discussion will lead. "My father has housed a group of survivors in a large city park to the north. We're holed up there and are trying to make ends meet. You'll like it." He grins. Then he announces almost solemnly, "We'll take you to Twiske tomorrow, if you're up for it."

Jens and Waltraud look at each other—and nod. "Then we'll go to Twiske tomorrow—whatever that may be," she murmurs skeptically.

At midnight, Waltraud and Jens are still awake. He has put his head on her shoulder. She hears him saying, "I was afraid we wouldn't find them alive. But not like this. They must have been desperate beyond all measure. They must have been so afraid in their final hours. It kills me."

"I know, my love. But there's nothing you could have done."

"If only we hadn't packed the cell phones away . . ." he continues.

Immediately she interrupts him, "Shh, stop it! It's not your fault. Listen, there was no way you could have done anything from so far away."

He clings to her like a drowning man. Long, tearless sobs escape his throat. When they abate, Waltraud whispers, "Sleep now, darling. Tomorrow is another day." But he has already fallen asleep and doesn't hear her words.

The next morning, as agreed, she unlocks the nursery door. Jori and Pepe are awake and eager to go to the toilet. There is a pitiful amount of water left in the cistern, which Waltraud only flushes after she—the last person to use it—has done her business.

In the bathroom cabinet, she discovers unused toothbrushes, which she takes, along with toothpaste and soap. She brushes her teeth and rinses her mouth with a small sip of drinking water they have brought upstairs from the cellar.

It is cool in the backyard, and there's the acrid smell of gasoline. When she appears, Jens has just finished soaking the wood with it. Heedlessly, he hurls the canister away into the tall grass. He takes one of the matches out of the box he found in the kitchen drawer. Then he looks around him. His anguished expression breaks her heart. He drags the red phosphorus tip over the rough side of the small box and waits until the crackling flame is burning steadily. Only then does he drop the little stick onto the soaked woodpile. Tongues of fire blaze up instantly, licking at the bundle of bedding. Waltraud watches him as he stands by the fire for a long time, his head bowed.

When the heat becomes unbearable—in the small yard, they are barely ten feet from the pyre—he turns around and says calmly, "Let's go."

They've already taken two ancient bicycles, which used to belong to his sisters, from the shed, pumped up the tires, and cleaned the dust and cobwebs from them. They have divided the last food they could find in the house between them and loaded it into the bike baskets.

The four of them cycle through the deserted village toward the A2. The sun is shining in a cloudless sky. To minimize the risk of running into the undead, they intend to stay on the freeway until they reach the Amstel junction.

Their eyes scan the area nervously until Pepe comes to an abrupt halt. Breathlessly, he whispers, "There! Look!" and points westward toward the overgrown fields. Clouds of water vapor are billowing upward.

Jori whoops. "There they are!"

Waltraud's gaze follows his extended finger, and she lets out a yelp of surprise. "You're kidding?"

Jori is fascinated by what's happening in the fields and, without looking at them, replies, "No. If I was joking, I'd say something like: A horse walks into a bar. And the bartender says: Why the long face?"

Stunned, she looks over at Jens, who is barely holding back his laughter. "Why should your life be any easier than mine?" He chuckles.

She knows it's a rhetorical question, so she doesn't answer. Then she hears him say enthusiastically, "What are *they* doing here?" Four pairs of eyes turn westward.

A herd of antelope is grazing comfortably at a safe distance. Far away, two giraffes are swaying through the marshes. A little farther north, she spots a herd of zebra drinking from the ditch. A hippo rises from the water, tearing its enormous mouth open so that she can see the pink mucous membrane even from here. A flock of cranes lands in the adjacent thicket. One of them jumps onto the back of a crocodile that is making its leisurely way through the still waters. Waltraud breathes in with a hissing sound as she hears the trumpeting of an elephant. A pair of pachyderms and their offspring are disappearing behind a patch of woodland to the south. The extensive area resembles the vastness of the savanna; that's why the animals must be congregating here.

Waltraud forces herself to drag her eyes away from this idyll. "Where did all these animals come from?" she asks hoarsely. The boys look at her, their faces glowing with pride. Pepe replies, "We liberated them from the zoos."

"You what?"

"Yes—with a little help from our friends. Freeing the fish and penguins from Sea Life near The Hague was relatively easy, but my father had to help us with the dolphins, manatees, and walruses from Harderwijk. Oh yes, there's another thing we didn't tell you . . ." he suddenly blurts out.

The hairs on the back of Waltraud's neck stand up. "What?"

"Well, the wild cats . . . are out there somewhere, too."

"You released the wild cats?"

"Lions, panthers, leopards, cheetahs. Even jackals, hyenas . . . And we need to be wary of them."

"But there are chimpanzees, baboons, camels, and dromedaries, too. You've no idea how many animals locked up there were being exploited," Pepe adds indignantly. "That's why we should move on now before they realize we're here."

"So, I did see monkeys making a racket in the trees yesterday." Jens is almost euphoric.

"You're out of your minds," is the only thing Waltraud can think of to say before she gets on her bike. But secretly she admires the boys for what they have done.

At the junction, they switch to the A10. Six kilometers on, they have to decide whether to take the tunnel under the water or take the federal highway bypass.

Waltraud makes the decision for all of them. "With all the wild animals and stinkers that could be holed up in there, I'd be delighted to take the detour, thank you very much. I don't want to break down and have to change a tire halfway through." Three kilometers later, they are back on the A10, which they leave directly above the Twiske Canal. Although sound barriers have been installed here, beneath the highway sign the individual segments are set in staggers, one behind the other, providing direct access to the Luijendijkje.

"Now we're pretty much there," Pepe announces, pedaling away.

The path leads them along the canal, skirting the village of Landmeer and some of the sailing clubs around it. Barely five minutes later, they find themselves in front of a lift bridge. On the other side are armed men, who wave to Pepe and Jori.

"What have you two done now?" roars a full-bearded man. They lower the bridge with a rattle. "Aha, guests," growls the guy as they approach him. "Leave your weapons here with me," he says, pointing the muzzle of his rifle at Jens.

"Cut the crap, Simon. I'll vouch for them," Pepe interjects, placing himself between them. "Where's Immo?"

"Oh-ho, you'll vouch for them, will you? Jeez, you're getting smarter all the time. Hmm, as far as I know Immo's in the greenhouse, as usual," he growls, lowering his gun. "Young sir," he adds, feigning a bow and waving them through. Then he takes out his radio and whispers a message into it.

"Hi, Dad," Jori calls excitedly. He has led them through a maze of paths, asphalt walkways, and dozens of small islands to the center of what was once a park. Countless houseboats are bobbing in the still waters of the canals, and close to a hundred different caravans are dotted around the grounds.

"What are those pallets and plastic barrels down there?" asks Waltraud curiously, pointing to the bases of the mobile homes. "Are you expecting a tsunami?"

Jens laughs. He hadn't noticed them to begin with, but as soon as he sees the improvised rafts beneath the caravans, he knows the answer.

"We're in the Netherlands. About a quarter of the country . . ."

"Twenty-six percent, to be exact," Jori corrects him.

"Thanks a lot, wise guy," Jens says. "So, twenty-six percent of the land is below sea level. Constant pumping in Western Holland ensures that the inland regions remain dry. But if the pumps fail . . ."

"The water level rises," adds Pepe. "Here in Twiske, fortunately, the local pumps are run by wind-powered mills—the Twiskemolen. But they can't help all the time. So, the caravans will automatically rise with the water level . . . if it comes to that. And it will, sooner or later."

"And that's why there are so many houseboats," the Norwegian adds, as everything becomes clear to her.

"Correctomundo," Jori says.

Waltraud closes her eyes, sighs, and rubs the bridge of her nose. But that's not the only amazing thing about Twiske. It's a shock to see so many two-legged creatures who don't consider them a food source. Small groups of people are pushing wheelbarrows with fresh vegetables. Others look equally busy, though it's not immediately obvious what they're doing. In the adventure playground are dozens of children romping around. Adults stand right next to them, supervising them. A little farther on, armed men are keeping watch over the area.

The boys lead them across a footbridge to a larger island in the middle of the park. Countless smaller greenhouses stand guard around a giant one that rises six meters into the air. Jori tells them a bit about it. The greenhouses contain different types of plants—beans, tomatoes, peppers, cucumbers, zucchini, pumpkins, onions, carrots—growing in rows upon rows that rotate on shelves from bottom to top. Photovoltaic panels stand around the glass houses.

"Look over there!" calls Pepe, pointing to an expanse of water the size of a soccer field, from which a lot of little tufts are protruding. "We're trying our hand at rice growing there. And over there," he says, indicating the small lake behind it and a large pontoon bridge made of interconnected pallets and blue plastic barrels, "we're building a floating greenhouse that will be twice as big as this one. But that won't be finished till next year." Jori opens the double doors and steps into the space, where the temperature is almost tropical.

In the middle of the huge greenhouse, which Jori tells them the survivors built within a few weeks, stands his father, his three-day beard peppered with gray stubble. Wearing a short-sleeved green-and-white plaid shirt, he resembles a modern-day archaeologist. His dark blond hair is tied in a ponytail. His worn olive corduroy pants and the sandals on his feet reinforce this impression. He controls the mechanisms that keep the hundreds of racks moving slowly, following a secret logic. Between the racks, people are at work, harvesting and weeding.

At Jori's greeting, his father turns and smiles, "Hey, Jori! Where have you been? The others got back last night."

"Yes, sorry, we had to split up. Waltraud and Jens gave us a place to sleep for the night." Jori steps closer to him and says—a little more quietly, but still loud enough for everyone to hear clearly—"They're pretty cool."

His father disregards the words, looking at the newcomers. His expression darkens a little. "And who are you?" he asks them.

Without hesitation, Jens steps forward, putting out his hand. "Goedemiddag. Jori and Pepe were kind enough to bring us here."

"They're okay, Dad," Jori interjects defensively. But the adults ignore him.

"I'm Jens, and this is my girlfriend, Waltraud. She's from Norway," he explains, adding almost apologetically, "It would be kind if we could speak English in front of her. That is, of course, if it's okay with you."

Immo purses his lips and blinks in surprise. "Yes, of course we can do that. I'm Immo—now that I at least know your name. But first you need to tell me who you are and what you're doing here. And why you've been allowed to strut around the facility armed."

"They are trustworthy. We have nothing to fear from them," Pepe explains. "The thing with the guns is on me."

"I've heard that before," Immo says. "Brave of you to take responsibility for that. But now you two should let your mothers know you're back. I need to talk to our guests."

The teenagers nod and turn to Jens and Waltraud. "All right, I'll see you later, okay?" says Jori.

"Let's hope so," she replies.

Laughing, they bump fists, and the boys disappear.

"Right then; what's your story?" asks Immo.

"I'm from Abcoude, and I was aiming to get to my parents," Jens explains. "A few weeks ago, we were still stuck in Spain. It took months to get the opportunity to escape. Sadly, I found out yesterday that they . . . passed away." He lowers his eyes and takes a deep breath. Then he looks Immo in the eye. "Now we're at a bit of a loss about what to do next. However, in the long run, we'd like to get to Norway. If you could let us stay here for a few days until we work out a new plan, we'd be very grateful. We'd be happy to pitch in and help out wherever we can."

Immo scrutinizes them. Finally he says, "We have more than enough work here. But the question is, what can you do?"

A little later—after having been provided with a small trailer where they immediately put down their gear—they follow Immo into the canteen. They're still carrying their weapons, but not openly.

The canteen is located in what used to be the facility's café. Everyone they pass greets Immo. He returns the greetings in a friendly voice. He calls everyone by name.

"We don't have any hierarchies here, but everyone has a job."

Jens says, "Could I ask a question? You say there's no pecking order, but it's down to you to single-handedly decide whether or not we can stay here—without consulting the others?"

"Oh, that's an easy one. The tasks here are allocated on the basis of personal interests as well as individual expertise—and not on any social elitism. No matter what job you do, you're equally valued. Whether you're taking out the trash or standing guard. At least, that's what we agreed in the beginning, and that's how it's been so far without any disputes. But no one sits back and does nothing. Everyone pitches in because they know that it's about the survival of all of us. Apparently, this kind of emergency leads to great solidarity," he says with a shrug, as if he's surprised by the realization.

"I was assigned to overall organization," Immo continues, "because I held a similar position—before I was a pilot—on an oil rig. On a much smaller scale, but in principle it was the same work." He stretches out his arm and gestures around him. "People trust me blindly, just as I trust them. That's why I do what I do. So, me deciding whether you stay or go is nothing to do with my social status; it's to do with my abilities."

"Is that also the reason children are allowed to roam free in the city? And why you've freed predatory cats and game from the zoos?"

Immo laughs. "Oh, that! Jori was an animal rights activist even as a child. I could tell you hundreds of stories. He was horrified, for example, when he learned that a hardware store used electric fly swatters. He made a huge scene. He was six years old at the time. Well, he hasn't changed to this day. You should have seen him crying with happiness when we released the dolphins. Or the manatees." Immo shakes his head, amused. "We also give youngsters the freedom to go outside the facility. At the end of the day, it's their world and they'll have to navigate it in the future. We trust them to take good care of themselves—even if we know they'll get into mischief here and there."

They enter the remodeled café, each grab a tray with prefabricated indentations in it, and get in line.

It's around lunchtime, and the room is nearly full. Meanwhile, over the murmur of conversation, Immo continues, "As far as catering is concerned, we have two options here. You can cook for yourself in your trailer or come here to eat at the designated times. However, you need to let us know what you've decided to do a week in advance so we can allocate food and staff accordingly. We haven't planned for you two, but it'll be fine. Most of the time we have a little surplus that we take to older people in the evenings—people who find it harder to get out of their trailers."

"And you really grow everything yourselves here?" asks Waltraud, almost in awe.

"Well, in the beginning we were forced to do a lot of looting. That changed quickly once we harvested the first crop. The greenhouse actually produces all the food we need. Many of the survivors used to run greenhouses themselves. We are benefiting from that now. The van Dykes had planned to build a new one in the spring. The shipment arrived the week when . . . well—everything went down the pan. We ran into each other on one of our looting trips. When they heard about the project, they came here right away. Bringing a truck with the assembly kit. We got soil, fertilizer, and the materials we needed from the local hardware stores." Immo asks the person behind the counter for a ladle of small unpeeled fried potatoes, baked carrots, and steamed broccoli. She hands him a plate of salad with lamb's lettuce, arugula, tomatoes, and smoked tofu. He accepts with thanks. At the end of the counter, he grabs a thick slice of whole wheat bread and a small glass bowl of greenish set custard. He holds the dessert out to them: "We make oat milk, and we use fresh stevia leaves to sweeten it. Hence the color. You don't want to miss this."

Impressed, Waltraud and Jens comply. They find three empty seats at one of the tables.

"And you guys have to see how we grow potatoes. It's fascinating. Not because the technology behind it is so phenomenal. On the contrary, in fact. It's so simple, but you have to come up with it." Immo cuts the vegetables into bite-size pieces, spears two, and eats. His mouth half full, he continues, "We plant forty potatoes near the bottom of a raised bed made of ordinary pallets and lined with plastic film. As soon as the shoots are ten centimeters high, we cover them carefully with soil, again and again—all the way to the top. After three months, we harvest about sixty kilos from a single square meter. Just last week, we emptied twenty raised beds. And now, for a few days, we can finally taste the other fruits of our labor, as they're slowly beginning to ripen. But I don't know as much about plants as the others here. I'm just in charge of the technical stuff."

"The problem will be storing them over the winter," Jens muses. "Have you thought about that, too?"

"Mm-hmm, sure." Immo goes on, "We're using the basement of what used to be the soccer club. It's nice and cool in there in the summer and not too cold in winter. And we're gradually starting to ferment and preserve food.

But that's not the real problem. The problem is elsewhere: We now have almost too many people here to feed—don't worry, I'm not talking about you.

Take the racks, for example, which rotate like giant wheels to ensure all the plants get the same exposure to UV radiation. If we could optimize the rotation intervals, we could increase the yield by a few percent. But I can't figure out how to adapt the algorithm that controls the machines to the daylight, which varies with the seasons."

"Hmm, I might be able to help there," Waltraud interjects with her mouth full. "I'm a computer scientist by profession."

"And I could think of a few ways to redesign the whole process to make it more user-friendly and efficient," Jens offers.

Immo looks at them both and nods, stuffing a forkful of fried potatoes into his mouth at the same time.

Then he pulls out his radio. "Sander, it's Immo. Are you in the greenhouse? Over."

"Hi, Sander here. Yes, in the control room. Over."

"I'm sending two new people over to you right away. Find out what they can do and see if you can give them something useful to do, okay? Over."

"Roger that. Over and out."

"Can you make your own way back to the big greenhouse?" Immo asks, turning his attention to his dessert.

"Yes, that shouldn't be a problem. You can't miss it," Waltraud replies with a smile.

"Great. Sander will be waiting for you there. One thing you should know, though: He's a little—how shall I put it—headstrong! He tries hard, but sometimes a bit too hard. So don't let him discourage or provoke you. He's basically a good guy, but sometimes he oversteps the mark. His whole family died right at the beginning, and I think that might have changed him."

"Damn," Jens says. "Who wouldn't be affected by that?"

"I have to take care of the communication systems in the afternoon and maintain contact with the other survivor enclaves." Immo scrapes together the remnants of his dessert. "Mmm. I love this pudding. So, you guys are free to move around. But remember, everyone here is authorized to challenge strangers. If this happens, refer them to me. You can always radio me. But finish eating first. I'm afraid I must go. Oh, and one more thing: Dinner is at half past five. It would be nice if we could get together again then. After all, you haven't told me anything about yourselves yet. Okay?"

Waltraud and Jens look at each other and reply, grinning, "Okay!"

"Well then—see you later." Immo stands up, takes his empty tray to the drop-off point, and disappears from the café in an instant.

"What d'you think?" asks Jens as she tastes the dessert.

"Whoa, that's incredibly good," she replies, shoveling in the next spoonful.

"I mean the whole setup here, not your dessert."

"Oh, that. I'm really impressed. Holing up on an island in the middle of the mainland is a fantastic idea," she replies. "I keep thinking back to Mallorca! But I have to admit that they could hardly have found a better place, and they're making a decent effort to keep the place running. Adventure playground for the kids. A handful of bridges that can be monitored with minimal oversight. And then there are all those little islets to retreat to if there's an attack, and you only have to defend a single crossing point. The greenhouse is brilliant, and they seem like good people. So far, I think it's great. What about you?"

"Hmm." He shrugs. "I think pretty much the same thing. And the pudding—it's damn tasty!"

"This greenhouse has enough height to allow us to use automated high racks. This row," Sander says, guiding them between the rotating racks, "has more shelves because the carrots don't grow as high as the beans over there." He points across the room. "The trouble is that the carrots could benefit from being rotated a little faster, but we don't know how to adjust for that.

The machines do everything at the same speed. And we often have to re-water some varieties manually . . ."

Waltraud bends down and inspects the motor mounted beneath the carrot rack. "Hmm . . . The way I see it, we should be able to control each drive individually."

"I'm not sure that's possible," Sander comments.

"What? Oh, I was just thinking out loud. I meant, can all the motors be operated individually?"

"Yes. But as I said, we don't know exactly how . . ."

"I'm not a botanist, but don't the plants need to be fertilized from time to time?" asks Waltraud.

"Yes, they do. We have a three-chamber sewage treatment plant below the public toilets. We make the fertilizer using some of the purified water. Hmm, I wonder. Maybe you could also work out how to mix the sewage water solution in at different rates depending on the plant?"

"I get it. Hmm . . . I need something to write with."

Sander hands her a pen and the notepad in which he has meticulously entered the room temperature and soil moisture figures. Armed with this, she moves to the center of the room and begins to sketch. Then she goes to each of the racks and writes down the numbers on the rotator machines. "Can you please make me a list of the plants being grown here?"

"I think so. By when?"

"Tomorrow evening?"

"Yes, that should be fine," Sander replies.

"And where are the controls?"

"Back there. Just follow me!" In a somewhat cooler annex to the greenhouse, Sander shows her the computer. It's a traditional PC and is standing next to a server rack.

"And you really know what you're doing?" he checks.

"I wouldn't have offered to help otherwise."

"Well, in that case. I'll create an account for you so that you can play around."

"Play around? Do I look like a gamer to you, or what?"

"No, but I don't want you to break anything."

He receives a smile of consummate smugness in return.

"I'll leave you a radio, too. Just call if you can't handle it." He winks at her before leaving her alone.

"En slik drittsekk," she whispers after him. Two seconds later, she's accessed the system. First, she checks the current processes. CPU utilization is low, she notes with satisfaction. Next, she calls up the service program that controls the date and time displays. There is no internet connection, so it's no longer receiving updates from the global servers.

Her fingers long to pound the keys again at last, constructing commands and queries, but an impulse holds her back. She thinks of something that has been bugging and irritating her ever since she learned about it. Her latent perfectionism forces her to take her thoughts one step back. She realizes that she has a unique opportunity to fix a minor but serious imperfection: the one-second divergence, which becomes noticeable every four years and must be corrected every hundred years. Now she can correct it. But before identifying even one variable, she chews it over for a long time. And then her brain sets to work on her idea, modelling a new time calculation and sending impulses to her fingertips.

Two hours later, her code is ready. It was ready an hour ago, but she's trimmed it to perfection. It's not only efficient, it's also beautiful to look at. The lines are impeccably indented, and the variables are laid out in a comprehensible way. To top it off, she has taken the trouble to annotate each line of text—where necessary—for the coders who will follow her. Satisfied, she looks at her work. From today, there will be no more leap years. There'll never be another February 29. At least as long as you tap into the source code of this server.

Over the next few days, she focuses on rack controls. First, she creates a table, setting out the times of sunrises and sunsets.

Since she doesn't know these, she creates three input fields where values can be entered manually without having to mess around with the source code. One for the date, the others for the times.

After that, she plans to store more text fields with empirical data about various plant species in a new table. On this basis, anyone who's operating the program can access the current info.

She and Sander spend the subsequent day entering the values. The interfaces she has created now enable operators to combine the racks and the varieties planted in them via a few dropdown menus.

Over lunch in the cafeteria, they discuss the individual stages, as usual.

"And if you could determine the times for which the plants in question need to be exposed to UV radiation in order to thrive, yields would certainly grow by another five to eight percent. But first we need empirical data. Oh yes, we can even control the percentage of irrigation now. One hundred percent equals one liter per hour per shelf. It's the same with the sewage water."

Waltraud eats the last of her carrot and hazelnut salad. "I've set up all the input screens for you. For each type of plant, you need to enter values for when the sun rises and sets, how much water it needs, how much fertilizer to apply—then you're on your way."

"I don't have the data, but there are people here who can answer those questions for me. With fertilizer, I guess we're going to have to use the empirical data we get from your software."

"Perfect! Then ultimately it won't matter what you're cultivating in which rack. Once all the details are entered and activated for each one, the system will immediately know what to do."

Sander is almost struck dumb with amazement. Waltraud puts her empty dishes onto her tray.

"And Jens has come up with a few things, too. Come on, let's see where he's up to."

The list of potential optimizations Jens was immediately able to identify has become endless. He has been going up and down between the racks in the huge greenhouse for days, weighing up alternative structures. He watches the harvesters and weeders, talks to them. They work together to move the racks under Waltraud's guidance. Of course, if he had been there from the beginning, he would have done it all differently, but at least now he can rework it a bit.

The racks can be rotated by ninety degrees, and the clearances between them can be reduced by fifty percent. This means that weeding and harvesting only have to be done from one side—which isn't a problem with the flexible racks. So, he gains a third more cultivation space. They even have to hire people to put up new racks and plant them out. Whether the solar panels will be able to provide enough electricity to power the machines, he's not sure. But that's for Waltraud and Sander to worry about.

"You increased our yield by twenty-three percent in six days?" Immo has completely forgotten about the dessert in his hand.

"If our projections are to be believed . . ." says Waltraud, without taking her eyes off her chili.

"Then yes," adds Sander. "We gained more space and have optimized the turning intervals and fertilizer output."

Jens interjects with one last question. "Can we get more power? We need additional power for more racks."

Immo stands and asks them to follow him. "I want to show you something. Come with me." He leaves his food on the table and heads outside. Past the tennis court and across the parking lot, they come to a spot where ten blue overseas containers are stacked in five rows. Immo walks to the one on the right and opens the doors. "More electricity won't be a problem," he says, showing them the inside. The container is filled to bursting with solar panels, transformers, and lithium-ion batteries.

"That should be enough," Jens confirms.

Immo grins with satisfaction. "We have three more containers with the same contents," he says. "You've done us a great service. In return, I'm assigning you a larger trailer. The twenty-three percent increase is—to put it mildly—impressive."

"Now you're talking like the Wolf of Wall Street," Waltraud quips.

Immo snorts and raises his index finger in mock warning. "That's as much promotion as you could achieve here. But if you accomplish something," he says conspiratorially, "that benefits society in the long run, you deserve a little reward. And believe me, almost everyone here thinks so."

Two months pass in which they become actively involved in the community. They are welcomed with open arms, and not only because of their initial success with the greenhouses. They are among the few who have combat knowledge and experience.

Every day they put volunteers through the drills that Franca used to subject them to. The sports field makes an ideal training ground.

Since firearms are scarce, they also help manufacture combat equipment. They take old bicycle parts—of which there is an almost limitless supply in the Netherlands—and weld and hammer them into instruments of war.

Necessity is the mother of invention. Spears up to three meters long are produced by fixing half a dozen spokes into saddle posts, which can be extended on the other side as desired using wooden sticks. They could be used to stab attackers from a safe distance—preferably through the eye socket, because the sharpened middle wire protrudes by ten centimeters.

They grind the larger gears sharp and fix them in columns created from straight sections of frame. This creates two-sided axes. Sometimes they combine the two types of weapons into halberds. To improve the grip, they wrap the end with wide strips of adhesive tape, stretching two layers of medical tape over it.

One day Jens visits Waltraud in the armory. He finds her at her workbench, filing away at an item. "What are you doing?" he asks, puzzled.

She turns around, holding out something jagged. "Shuriken!" In her palm, he sees the star-shaped remnant of a medium-size gear.

"Shuri—what?"

"Shuriken! Throwing stars. Didn't you ever watch ninja movies as a kid?" She takes a swing and sinks one into the fifty-centimeter support beam seven meters away. "I filed down the outermost ring of a gear and sharpened the six radial spokes."

"And you think that's a useful weapon?"

"Zombie bones are becoming more porous now. The fungus seems to be tapping into all the sources of food it can find in the bodies of the undead. Haven't you noticed?"

"No, I haven't," Jens replies, aghast. "But I won't be finishing them off with throwing weapons, either."

"I think the fungus is extracting minerals or whatever from the bones, and that makes them brittle. Throwing stars are easier to use than throwing knives. The younger ones who don't have any weapons yet will love them."

A few days later, Waltraud and Jens are each given command of four groups of twelve people. From then on, each morning she trains half of them in hand-to-hand combat and the use of throwing weapons while

Jens instructs the other half in the use of axes, lances, and halberds. With every session, they miss their old crew anew.

At least once a week all this pays off, because now and then undead stray into their area. The well-trained guards have no problem eliminating the danger.

With Jori and Pepe, Waltraud and Jens go on weekly scouting trips on e-bikes. They can't keep up with the agile youngsters on foot for long. Autumn passes—they bring in a gigantic harvest and everything relaxes a bit. But winter brings new challenges.

On a day in late December, when the air is cool and the sky overcast, they take an exploratory trip to Doesburg. There's an enclave in the north of the city, similar to the one in Amsterdam, but without their many strongholds. Last night, Doesburg sent out a frantic distress call. The undead were besieging it and had gained access to the island, it said. Only a few seconds later the connection was cut and could not be restored.

Waltraud and Jens had volunteered for the rescue mission, and they set off at first light with half a dozen armed men. In two of the Citigos they had lifted from the car dealer in Keienbergweg at the end of fall, and whose range Waltraud had extended by thirty percent with a simple hack, they sped through half-blocked streets at dawn. Together with the female soldiers crammed into the confines of the small cars with them, they made up the elite unit: the fast in-and-out squad. But in the enclave, there was no one to be seen.

Waltraud speaks into the headset. "I can't see a soul, Immo. Over." Her ear crackles.

A second later, she hears his voice: "What about bodies? Any clues as to what may have happened? Over."

"Nothing conclusive, and definitely no bodies," she replies. "I can only guess from a few clues."

She holds the pistol in both hands at an angle to the ground. Her fingertips protrude from cut-off gloves. Carefully, she moves from trailer to trailer in the probably futile hope of finding survivors.

"Take a guess, then!" says Immo.

She goes over the images of the last half hour in her head before beginning. "On the north shore, I found scraps of textiles and a lot of tracks next to them. It looks like several hundred pairs of feet and shoes came ashore there. Are you sure they reported a zombie attack and not one of the gangs from the area?"

"This was a zombie attack. We know that much for sure." The tension in Immo's voice is palpable.

"But that doesn't make sense," she objects. "The water is bitterly cold. Zombies can't swim. And there are scarcely any traces of a struggle. I don't understand why there are no human or at least zombie corpses. On the spur connecting the island to the mainland, the trees and bushes are covered in fibers. It's as if the survivors fled together. The tracks lead south from there."

Immo thinks aloud. "Could this somehow be related to the movements of the undead around Amsterdam . . . ? Okay, abort the mission and get back as soon as you can. We'll meet in the refectory in two hours for a briefing."

"Roger, roger. And Immo . . . Evacuate the northern islands! We don't have enough willing fighters to defend the whole shoreline."

"Hmm." He growls. "Are you trying to tell me something?"

"I don't know. I just have a really bad feeling right now. And double the guards, okay? Over . . . and out."

"All right; I'll do that. Over and out."

Waltraud changes the channel and rounds up the troops. "Mission accomplished; meet back in the parking lot in two minutes." She waits for both groups to call in and moves briskly to the assembly point. Jens is already there with his unit. Before he gets into the car, she pulls him out of earshot of the others.

"I can't make sense of it," she admits.

"The stinkers aren't capable of making such a collective, coordinated attack. Are they?"

"What do we know about them? It's been three quarters of a year since the outbreak, and we've learned very little about them. But either way—this looks pretty scary."

"As if a rabid fungus that can control people wasn't scary enough."

She has no reply to that. She puts a hand on his chest and kisses him gently before they get into the Škodas. The drivers start the silent engines, and the cars accelerate swiftly away from the deserted enclave.

As the final dust particles swirl back to the ground, the first snowflakes float down from the gray sky.

* * *

To begin with, no one says a word. Waltraud appreciates that everyone is racking their brains, trying to work out what happened. She can't help doing it herself.

"What do you think happened back there?" asks the driver curiously, ten kilometers later. Even though Waltraud's Dutch is passable now, everyone speaks English to her. Especially in stressful situations.

"Not a clue," Waltraud replies, looking over her shoulder for the tenth time since Doesburg. Jens and his team are in the car behind them.

She doesn't want wild speculation to sap her people's morale, so she continues thoughtfully, "It looked like a coordinated attack. I can't believe it was sniffers." *Wrong,* she corrects herself, *I don't WANT TO believe they're capable of that. Because then we'd really be screwed.* "There was one time I did experience something a bit similar. But then it was two groups trying to sneak up on a single person."

At the Amsterdam-Tuindorp junction, they exit the freeway. Two minutes later, they are quickly waved through the bridge checkpoint.

Immo is already sitting in the cafeteria, where operations have been temporarily suspended. Waltraud and Jens leave their vehicles at almost the same time and enter together. Only people taking part in combat operations are allowed through.

Even from a distance, she recognizes Sander's grumpy voice. Since the harvests have multiplied many times over and his expertise in food cultivation is no longer in demand, he has devoted himself to controlling and defending the northern territories.

"I think it's a little premature to put everything on Code Red. I mean, when was the last time we saw a zombie?"

"Not directly in the vicinity. But for the last week, there've been reports that they're being . . . formed in the north. And that there's increased traffic on the N307." Someone hands Immo a cup of steaming liquid. As he says thank you, Sander turns to look at the newcomers. She'd like to knock that cocky smile off his face. Or kick his teeth in.

"Oh—Waltraud, Jens—good, you're here." The tiredness is written all over Immo's face. He lifts the teacup to his mouth and takes a sip as they sit down at the table. "Shit, it's hot," he curses, setting the cup down in front of him and using his hand to wipe the spilled liquid from the smooth surface. "I've spent the last hour contacting the surrounding enclaves."

Waltraud can't help thinking that he's trying to avoid giving them bad news.

He forces himself to continue. "Out of a total of six, I've only been able to reach four. And out of those four, three are reporting a sudden increase in zombie activity in the area. All agree that something nasty's about to happen." He massages his tired eyes with his thumb and forefinger. "Waltraud and Jens are just back from Doesburg with their teams," he explains to those around the table. "Doesburg reported a surprise attack last night and went dark shortly after," he says. She avoids his gaze. "Tell us everything you told me over the radio earlier."

Now she purses her lips and blows through them. She becomes aware of the fear of uncertainty that has haunted her since the morning. "The camp at Doesburg is empty." Looking down at her fingertips, she continues, "No traces of fighting, no bodies, no nothing. The trailers were open . . . and abandoned." Then, trying to remember all the details, she describes the crossing to the mainland in as much detail as possible.

Until Sander interrupts her. "That's alarming," he says, but there's nothing in his voice to indicate that's what he actually feels. "What do you think might have happened there? Was everyone beamed away? Summoned to the gates of Valhalla?"

In a flash, she grabs him by the hair and slams his face down onto the tabletop with full force. At least, that's what she does in her head. The imaginary sound of his nose bones breaking will have to do for the time being. In the real world, she shrugs and merely replies, "The stinkers entered via the north bank—that's why there were so many footprints there. The survivors apparently fled south." Before uttering the next sentence, she takes a deep breath. "It was as if they'd been deliberately driven out."

No one but Sander laughs. "You don't really believe that, do you?" He smacks the table with the palm of his hand.

"Yes, I do. That's exactly what I think. I've been through this before, on Mallorca." Sadly, she tells of the day they had to flee the villa and about saving Backup at literally the last second.

"And that's supposed to convince us of what?"

"Sander, please!" Immo's tone betrays his tension. The others around the table look away, embarrassed.

"What? You suddenly want us to change our daily routine just because she"—he stretches out his hand and points at Waltraud—"thinks that the zombies have gotten organized? Come on; you can't be serious!"

"It doesn't matter what I think, Sander. But until we have a more definite explanation, or an alternative one, let's play it safe." Immo looks everyone in the eye one after the other. "I suggest we triple the guards, including along the shore, not just at the bridges. The northern islands are being evacuated as we speak."

A good move on Immo's part, Waltraud realizes. Having the eviction take place at the same time as the war council deprives Sander of the opportunity to sabotage the process. Sander's mouth forms a silent O. Immo raises his hand, but that doesn't stop his counterpart from continuing, "You can propose as much as you like, but as far as I know, it needs a general vote to push through what you're planning. So I suggest we call another meeting tonight with everyone in attendance. Then we'll see who wants to change everything right now."

The person to Immo's right, a handsome man most likely in his sixties, suddenly slams his fist onto the table. Dishes clatter. Everyone flinches. He stands up, his chair squeaking as he pushes it with the backs of his knees, and leans on the table. Ice-cold eyes glitter at Sander from under bushy eyebrows.

His voice is threatening. "I'm sick of your troublemaker crap, Sander—today's the straw that breaks the camel's back. You're basically against everything we're doing, and the lame science behind your pseudo-skepticism is completely pointless. We've already spent enough energy trying to convince you. Either you comply this time without argument, or you get the hell out of here, dickhead."

Then he looks down to his left at his neighbor on the bench. "Immo, we'll triple the guards on the east bank. And don't worry about the easterners. I'll impress on them the urgency of the decision."

Immo looks at him mutely—and nods. "Anyone who is capable of carrying a weapon should get ready to fight, starting now. We have no idea what we're facing, but I don't want us to end up like Doesburg. Since we're giving up the northern areas as a precaution, it's going to be a little tighter on the main island. We've often practiced for emergencies. And now one's around the corner. We can handle it! Now—let's get going!"

The representatives of the districts stand and leave the room without a word. Waltraud watches them, fascinated. There's a tension in the air that she hasn't felt in a long time. It smells like a fight. Twenty seconds later, she is the second last to leave the common room. Only Sander is still sitting there like he's paralyzed, wondering what just happened.

The afternoon passes in an orderly bustle. In the open-plan kitchen, they prepare rations so that the first watch can eat directly after they are relieved. In the smaller restaurant at Twiske Haven, a command center is being set up to coordinate the defenses and any potential evacuation.

In addition to weapons, face coverings and protective goggles of all kinds are handed out. Headlamps, radios, and fully charged batteries are also provided to combatants.

Those who cannot fight, either because they are too frail or too young, will be taken to the southernmost island. If there is an attack and the defense lines are breached, there should be enough time to get them out of Twiske to safety. At least in theory.

The biggest problem, however, is that no one knows which direction the attack will come from. But hardly anyone doubts that one is imminent, now.

Waltraud and Jens have packed for the emergency. Their backpacks, which they haven't used in months, are loaded with essential supplies for two weeks.

Late that afternoon, they try to get some rest in their trailer, but they are so worked up that they don't get a wink of sleep. Their firearms—freshly cleaned and oiled—are ready and waiting.

"Listen," he says before they set off for guard duty, "let's stow the backpacks under the trailer. Who knows what else is going to happen today?"

She nods. "Yeah, they'll be quicker to grab there." Then she picks up hers and steps out into the cold night air.

Jens follows her and closes the door. The backpacks quickly disappear beneath the rubbery floor covering. "If it gets bad, we'll meet here and then fight our way through together," he says.

Waltraud replies, "No matter what—we wait for each other!"


Everything north of Baaiegatstrand is deserted. As they march toward it, frostbitten blades of grass crackle under their feet. Although the temperature has dropped below zero, they're not freezing. The looting during the summer has ensured they have good winter clothing.

Their troops are ranged along the last trench, looking into the moonlit night. Only some are carrying firearms. Every twenty or thirty meters, lances, halberds, and double axes are leaning against specially made beams. Waltraud takes an ax and straps it over her shoulder. She's responsible for covering the trench running southwest.

"Jens, I'm going to my post. What about you?" she asks when he makes no effort to move.

"Somehow I dislike leaving you alone."

"Do you think I can't take care of myself?"

"What makes you think that? I'm just afraid that we might get separated. And since I have no way of contacting you, I don't like the thought of it at all."

"You do have your radio," she contradicts.

"Oh man, you know what I mean."

She rolls her eyes. "Then here's what we'll do: We'll meet here every half hour. What do you think of that?"

"I still don't feel right."

"Jens, stop whining," she says, tugging lovingly on his ear, eliciting a surprised whimper. "Come on, let's go—meet back here in thirty minutes," she adds, turning on the radio. "Immo, Northwest here. We're in position. Over."

It crackles. "Immo here. Noted. Keep your eyes and ears open. Over."

"Roger. Over and out."

"Then see you again in half an hour. Over and out," replies Immo, and he clicks off.

"Do you think it'll snow soon?" asks Jens.

"I think so. Or I hope so. And I'm even keener for it to get a lot colder. I'm kind of sick of wandering corpses."

"When this is all over, would you like to take a little vacation with me?" he says, as if trying to shake off the ominous mood. "We could go to Norway, for instance. What do you reckon?"

"I don't know if that's a good idea! The last time we went on vacation together, the world ended."

"Ha-ha!" He laughs in mock horror.

"Nah, fun!"

"No kidding!" Her cheerfulness makes him smile. "Let's survive the winter. You see, I've got a plan to put a solar panel on the roof of a Citigo, so we can recharge the battery as we go. It'll take us a few days to get to Norway, but we'll have more than enough time."

She takes his hand and murmurs, "Do you really mean that?" Then she kisses him deeply and sets off. "I'll see you in half an hour," she calls over her shoulder and disappears into the darkness.

* * *

It is well past midnight. Nothing significant has happened. Jens passes her every half hour, always in the same place. She checks in regularly with Immo: "Northwest here. All quiet. Over and out."

"Okay, Northwest. Over and out."

Three hours to go until they're relieved. The moon has disappeared behind the clouds. Fatigue creeps slowly up her limbs. She yawns more and more often. Her body has long since stopped releasing the stress hormones that would have kept her awake. As she walks, she feels her eyelids getting heavier. And then she hears cries of alarm coming from the east. The cold air carries the sound. In a flash, she's wide awake and fiddling with the radio. "Immo, what's going on?" No answer. The other channels are either silent or have panicked shouts coming from of them.

There's a sudden splash in the water behind her. "West bank—stand by!" she calls into the night. "Headlamps on!" In response, the shore area is illuminated. Guns are drawn. Beams of light twitch back and forth. "Face the water!" orders Waltraud, to stop the frantic flickering, which is irritating her. She holds the double-edged ax in front of her. She strokes the handle of the weapon with both hands. For a split second, the night seems to hold its breath.

And then the wandering corpses burst up from the water. Along the entire defensive line, they rise up and rush toward the defenders. With a bloodcurdling scream, Waltraud sprints toward them, her weapon raised high above her head. All around her, the defenders recover from their initial shock and throw themselves at the zombies, roaring. The Norwegian sinks her blade into the nearest wet skull and pries the weapon out with a jerk. Her second blow decapitates another of the undead. The battle cries of the defenders mingle with the angry grunts and shrieks of the creatures still getting to their feet out of the water.

"Immo, what's going on with you?" she calls into her headset. No answer. The man next to her doesn't aim his spear in time. He is immediately buried under three stinkers. It takes her four quick blows to finish them all off. She looks around quickly. The stony embankment is paved with dead bodies. More and more undead emerge, stumbling over those that have fallen. Their defenses falter—the zombies tear large holes in their ranks.

"HOLD YOUR GROUND," she roars at the top of her lungs, splitting another skull. But all their efforts seem to be in vain. There must be hundreds. Thousands, she thinks, close to panic. We have completely underestimated the situation. She draws her pistol and shoots seven monsters at a distance of less than two meters.

In one of the three seconds that this buys her, she retrieves the empty gun and radios Jens. "Jens! Do you read me?"

"Bloody hell, there are too many of them! What's your situation?" His words are drowned out by the sound of wild fighting in the background.

"Better not ask." Quick as a flash, she drops to her knees, letting one of the undead crash into her hip. The next instant, she quickly straightens up, launching it into the air in a high arc. She feels its temporal bone give way as she kicks it, before her victim even touches the ground. "Immo's not answering, either. Over."

Then she swings the ax in a wide arc in front of her. Dark gray blood spurts from two throats as the heads roll.

"You remember what to do? Over."

"Yes," she admits. "Over and out." Without waiting for a response, she turns off the radio. Finally, the defense line backs away. Waltraud must decide, quickly. "Retreat! Pull back!"

They pass the call on, "Back! To the second line of defense!" Her people try to follow the command in an orderly fashion.

But then it all breaks down. Panic spreads through the defenders. They turn away from the fight and flee headlong. At first, it's only a few of them. But with every second that passes, more and more become aware of the hopelessness of what they're doing. Within half a minute, Waltraud is surrounded by only a handful of fierce fighters. And the number of wandering corpses seems to be increasing exponentially. Desperately, she yells her last command: "Abandon posts! ABANDON POSTS!" The ax in her hands, she brings it down in a mighty diagonal slash, splitting open the chest of an emaciated zombie. Still in motion, she turns around and sprints toward the trailer.

The last shuriken whizz past, close to his ear. Jens watches as three undead go down almost simultaneously when the throwing stars smash into their skulls. For his part, he whirls the lance above his head and shatters another. But for every zombie they finish off, ten more appear in the breach. At first they were able to hold them off, but it's been clear for a few minutes that they are far outnumbered. Waltraud's situation is no better, as he has just learned. But he has no time to think about it. With the blunt end of the lance, he pushes an attacker—who is groaning and rushing in his direction with wide, milky eyes—back into the water. They are streaming toward him from all directions. The weapon is abruptly snatched from his hand as its tip pierces two monsters running in a line, knocking them to the ground.

Before the company is overrun, he gives the order to retreat. As if this was what the troops had been waiting for, they turn and take to their heels. He stares hopelessly after them before running after them.

*What the hell just happened? How can the undead gather and organize like this? Is this what happened in Doesburg?* Question after question shoots across his mind. And again and again: *Is Waltraud all right?* All around him, fugitives are beating their way through hedges and bushes and jumping over ditches in vain attempts to escape. Those who are not fast enough are torn to pieces. Jens knows that Twiske must have fallen. To his left, he hears the shattering of glass—it must be the greenhouses. The noise is so loud he fears the entire building has collapsed. He can't make sense of why they weren't told how many zombies there were. What have the scouts been doing these last few days? If they had known, they could at least have got away in time.

He pulls out the radio and switches to Immo's channel. "Immo? Can anyone hear me? The West bank has fallen. There are thousands coming at you. Over." No response. "Godverdomme," he bellows, dialing Waltraud. "Waltraud? WALTRAUD?"

The cable catches on a low-hanging branch. Her headset is torn from her head. She gropes blindly for the radio, which is no longer there. "Shit!" she curses. Jens's worries about not being able to reach her suddenly come back to her. She wants to run back and find it, but the undead are hot on her heels. At least she can reload the pistol. Running at full tilt, she replaces the magazines. She races past the tennis courts, crosses the street, and jumps bravely over a ten-foot ditch. After putting on a burst of speed through a coppice, she arrives at the trailer. There is no trace of Jens. Without slowing down, she slides underneath. The cover falls back to the ground behind her. Screaming and screeching, hundreds of feet trample past, oblivious to her. Their backpacks are still there.

Breathing heavily, she rolls onto her stomach and aims the pistol. At that moment, the cover in front of her is jerked upward. Her trembling finger finds the trigger and her brain orders her to pull it.

*　*　*

He covers the seven hundred meters or so to the caravan in record time. Total chaos has broken out around him. At one point he had tripped over an object, rolled over it, and just kept running. The beams of countless headlamps flickering everywhere bring the extent of the disaster home to him. Everyone is trying to save themselves.

When he arrives at the trailer, he looks around. There is no sign of Waltraud. He quickly bends down and lifts the cover. When he recognizes the black muzzle in the light of his headlamp, he instinctively jerks his head up. There is a flash and a bang. A projectile misses his forehead by a few millimeters and whizzes between his legs.

"Hey, what the fuck is wrong with you?" he shouts, startled. It must be Waltraud because she's the only one who owns a Beretta like that. "It's me! Jens!"

She crawls out of hiding. "Oh shit, did I get you?"

"Full in the face! You're now talking to my ghost," he replies, panting. "Where's your radio?"

"I lost it," she admits contritely.

He shakes his head and gives her his I-told-you-so look. "Give me my backpack. We need to see where Immo's got to. He hasn't checked in once this whole time."

"Fuck it. Let's get out of here."

"No, I need to know why they dropped us," he says angrily, shouldering his bag.

"Now? Really?" she asks, horrified.

He ignores her objection. He runs purposefully back to Twiske Haven, where the command post is located. The first wave of fugitives and pursuers has just streamed past them. Jens turns off his light, signaling her to follow suit. The night is dark, but they know the way. They creep carefully from tree to tree, car to car. At the former boat rental, they can't spot any guards. Covering each other, they reach the entrance. There's a body lying in front of it. Jens cautiously feels for a pulse below the chin and shakes his head at Waltraud. She approaches the door and signals to him to open it. Weapons raised, they go inside. In the pale emergency lighting, they discover abandoned radios beeping softly.

Two corpses lie under the tables. A thin beam of light falls through the crack in the door behind the bar. Silently, they walk toward it. They hear muffled voices coming from behind it. Cautiously, Jens pushes the door open. Waltraud steps inside, Beretta drawn. He follows her a heartbeat later. Immo's family is cowering on the floor. Pepe is there too, with his mother.

They all have their hands on their heads. Immo is bleeding from a laceration above his left eye. Sander has the pistol trained on him. Then he looks at the door and sees Jens and Waltraud.

"Don't take another step," he roars.

Sander is about to say more, but Jens doesn't hesitate and puts a bullet between his eyes. The gun slips from Sander's fingers as he falls over backward.

"Is everyone all right?" Waltraud rushes to the family before his body even hits the ground. It takes a few moments before they can at least halfway shake off their shock.

"Given the circumstances, yes," Immo replies, wiping the blood from his face. "Sander sabotaged everything. He brought my family here and used them as leverage against me. He shot everyone else. But he wanted me to witness the downfall of my empire before he killed us, too. My empire—what a madman. And how's it looking out there?"

Jens just shakes his head.

"That bad?" asks Immo gloomily.

"Worse than you can imagine. The greenhouses have been destroyed; there are hundreds of zombies on the islands," Jens replies. "And now what?"

Waltraud has now helped everyone to their feet.

"Can you get us across the bridge at Twiskeweg? Preferably unharmed?"

Jens catches Waltraud's belligerent eye and rocks his head to and fro. "We can try," he replies without any real conviction.


Everyone but Waltraud and Immo, who are in the front seat, is sitting on the floor of a small removals van that Immo had parked in a side alley months ago and loaded with some nonperishable food items. Only he knows where they are headed. All summer long, he has been preparing and maintaining the vehicle in secret. For the emergency that has now come to pass, obviously.

Waltraud and Jens got them the last few meters across the bridge on foot, as Immo had intended. It had not been easy, and they had had a fierce skirmish with some zombie stragglers, but no one had been hurt. Jori and Pepe had put the last of their shuriken to good use.

But now no one is saying anything. Shortly before they left, Immo had an outburst of emotion that upended the mood.

"What, you want to escape?" Jens had asked, horrified, when they got in the van.

"It has nothing to do with wanting." He struggled to keep his voice under control. "We have to!"

"And what about the other survivors? We can't just leave them to their own devices!"

"Godverdomme, don't tell me to do!" exploded Immo. "Don't you think it's hard enough for me to leave all this behind? The people who trusted me with their lives? But we've all seen how many of the undead are out and about on Twiske. What do you think the likelihood is of finding any survivors now?"

No one answered.

"That's what I thought. Anyone who wants to go back can decide to right now. And I don't want to hear any complaints later. Yes, it breaks my heart to betray Twiske! But I'm sticking to my decision.

So, now it's your turn. Either you do what I'm doing and focus on survival. Later, if by some chance we ever feel safe again, you can give your feelings free rein. But if you want to go after that, please get out now."

No one ventured to speak, and after a while, Immo said, "Fine," started the engine, and drove off. Twenty or thirty minutes later, he said in a more conciliatory tone, "Secretly, I had long expected this kind of disaster. There were too many unknown variables we would have had to deal with. People like Sander, for example. That's why I quietly came up with this alternative rescue plan. But the biggest problem is that the pumps that keep the Netherlands dry are no longer operational," he adds, discouraged. "No electricity! So the sea will soon reclaim the land we gained by draining it anyway."

"Why did you keep this from us?" asks Jens, aghast.

"I only got the info a few days ago. I was going to tell you soon," Immo replies contritely. "The inland water level is slowly rising. We did of course take precautions. We underpinned caravans with plastic barrels and canisters, so that they'd be able to serve as rafts or temporary houseboats. Later, we would have linked them together to create an artificial island, with the greenhouses in the middle. But the undead . . . have beaten us to the punch with their attack today."

After an hour spent jolting around in the windowless cargo area between a dozen crates of food rations, they get out. They are greeted by the first rays of dawn. No one can shake the demoralizing feeling that has dogged them since Twiske fell.

Jens stretches. "Where are we?" he inquires, watching Immo tinker with the gate of a hangar as high as a house.

"About seventy kilometers north of Amsterdam," Immo explains, "on the landing field of the offshore services company I used to work for. My old workplace, so to speak."

With a click, the lock springs open. He pushes apart the rattling gates to reveal the interior. "And this is another part of my fallback plan," he says proudly, pointing to a red-and-white aircraft standing in the middle of the room. "Help me push it out, please!"

"How are you planning to push a helicopter out of there?" asks Jens incredulously. Then he realizes it has wheels and not the runners he had been expecting. Their combined strength enables them to bring the helicopter out and position it in a spray-painted circle on the asphalt.

"Have you also thought about where to go?" asks Waltraud.

Immo nods. "First, we'll fly to an oil rig on the Norwegian coast. We'll take you home from there."

"Excuse me?" She can barely keep her features under control.

"You heard right," he says, disappearing into the cockpit. While he fires up the control panel, the others carry the food from the truck to the helicopter. Waltraud and Jens secure the perimeter. Everyone is glad that nothing is moving.

As soon as the last crate is loaded, they put on yellow life jackets and climb in. The rotor blades spin faster and faster. "Everybody, buckle up," Immo says, "we're about to take off."

"What if there were some survivors on Twiske?" yells Jens over the sound of the rotors. The noise quickly becomes deafening and is only slightly mitigated by their large headphones.

"I assume," Immo replies, "that Twiske has now suffered the same fate as Doesburg. You told me that everyone there fled to the south, didn't you? As if they had been driven out by the undead?"

"Yes," Jens confirms. "But is it conceivable that exactly the same thing would happen in two places? And be so well coordinated?"

"Well, if you had asked me that question a week or two ago, I would have said no for sure. But after last night, I'm not so sure. I'm all the more certain there's no one left alive on Twiske."

"Then let's at least fly over it once. Maybe we can figure out in hindsight what happened. Where the zombies are headed or something . . ."

"And what do you expect to get out of that? It's a good hundred and fifty kilometers there and back. The helicopter is fully loaded. It'd cost us almost a third of our fuel. Refueling here is impossible because the power is out. And we can't pick up anyone anyway. We'd crash halfway across the North Sea before we reached the first production platform. Our best chance is to get to Scandinavia. We can refuel on an oil rig. They're self-sufficient, and I know what to do."

Jens clenches his right hand into a fist and brings it to his mouth in frustration. Waltraud puts a hand gently on his shoulder. Reluctantly, he leans back and buckles his seat belt.

The helicopter jolts. It takes off sluggishly, its nose sinks a few degrees, and it heads northward.


In the relative safety four thousand feet above the sea, she has time to think. Her seat by the door gives her a clear view of her companions.

Jens is stroking her left hand, seemingly absent-mindedly, and watching the sunrise through a porthole. His face is strangely expressionless. For the first time in ages, she has no idea what he might be thinking. He seems unusually relaxed. She fears he is in shock and hopes his apathy will be short-lived.

At first she wonders what Pepe and his mother were doing in the command center. But then she remembers they gave their caravan to another family and moved in temporarily with Immo, Jori, and Katja. Now they're sitting across from her, not saying a word. The two women in their late forties are shifting their hands nervously and looking down at the floor, their legs crossed tightly under the bench.

Pepe seems as composed as ever. His alert gaze sometimes roams over the interior of the helicopter and is sometimes directed at the swells beneath. When their eyes meet, he nods at her. Waltraud nods back and looks over his shoulder at Jori, who is monitoring the cockpit displays with his father. He, too, is radiating calm. She wonders what the future holds for young people.

*Does the fast-moving pace of the twenty-first century make it easier for them to deal with the increasing collapse of society, or even of civilization as a whole? Or is that down to the naïveté of youth? And what, on the other hand, can she say about herself?*

She catches herself looking forward despite everything. Because after almost a year, she'll shortly be back in Norway. They have now been in the air for three hours and will soon be refueling on an oil rig, some hundred and fifty kilometers off the Norwegian coast. From there, Immo has confirmed, it's only thirty minutes to her home.

The headphones buzz abruptly, and his voice brings her back to the present. "I can see the platform," he says. "I was stationed there four years ago, before I retrained." Waltraud looks ahead and spots the silhouette of a tower appearing on the horizon like a dark Lego brick. Jens releases her hand and checks his seat belt. She wipes her sweaty hands on her pants.

Immo turns his head toward them. "We'll fly around it two or three times, just to check if anyone else is there. Once we land, Jori will help me refuel. Jens, Waltraud, can you two secure the area? Just in case . . ."

Jens looks over briefly at Waltraud, and they both give a thumbs-up.

"I shut down the engine during refueling, but I don't shut it down completely," Immo adds. "So watch your heads when you get out."

Barely fifteen minutes later, they have landed on the huge production platform. Immo has set down the helicopter expertly on the helipad. They didn't spot a soul as they flew over it. One of the faster rescue boats is missing and the lifeboat is still there. Although they are forty meters above myriads of glitter on the water's surface, sections of the platform still tower above them. There are steel beams and cross braces everywhere, supporting the structure. Countless pipelines made of all kinds of materials wind around them seemingly haphazardly.

Her gun drawn, Waltraud leaps out into the icy morning air. The biting cold generated by the—albeit decelerated—rotor blades takes her breath away. She bends down low and leaves the perimeter of the blades. A staircase leads to the lower level. Jens follows her down. As they leave the fiercest wind behind, she looks back over the edge and watches Immo and Jori insert a nozzle as thick as a fist into the aircraft, locking it into place with a half turn. Then Immo steps over to the control panel, flips a switch, and starts the refueling process.

"Let's take a look around," she calls to him over the noise. Suddenly he looks away from her and opens his eyes wide. Waltraud knows immediately that they're in trouble. She whirls around and finds herself face-to-face with an overweight figure in filthy overalls. Emblazoned on his chest is the logo of the company that had held the drilling rights. His face is hidden under a matted beard. Two restless eyes twitch back and forth. Next to the company logo, a name is embroidered. J. MORRISON, she reads as she slowly backs up the stairs. *Has he been hiding, just waiting for us to land?* she wonders.

The muzzle of the orange flare gun he holds in his dirt-encrusted fingers is pointing straight at her. She has no idea what danger the gun might present to a human, but she feels little desire to test it at this close range.

"Immo," she bellows, not taking her eyes off the newcomer, "we have company."

Morrison pushes her farther back. Then Waltraud hears Immo yell, "Hey, don't shoot. The helicopter's refueling." He pauses and then looks more closely at the man before asking, "Who are you?"

The well-fed creature swings the gun toward him. Waltraud is rooted to the spot in panic.

"I want the helicopter," the individual yells in English.

"Can you even fly this kind of thing? No? Well, I can. I'm a pilot. And we have one seat left," Immo lies. "Just put the gun down, and we'll take you with us."

"That's my helicopter!" he whinnies, waving his gun wildly. "We've been waiting for months to be picked up." *We? Who's we?* The question flashes across Waltraud's mind. She can't see anyone else. "You left us here alone."

The mothers and Pepe watch anxiously through the portholes. Jori and Immo are standing right by the opening to the tank. They raise their hands.

"All right, all right!" Immo placates him. "Let's just disconnect the helicopter, and it's all yours."

"Get your hands off my helicopter!"

"Do you even know where you're going? Do you even know what's going on out there?" the pilot shouts.

"I want to go home." Shrill screeches rise above the noise of the engine. "I WANT TO GO HOME! YOU LEFT US HERE TO DIE!"

"Where's the rest of your crew?" Immo yells back.

"We waited for months—and you left us here to die. No supply ship, no rescue helicopters—nothing!" Threads of spittle fly from his beard with every word.

"Where are the others?" Immo almost shrieks. Waltraud hears anger in it. And only then does she notice the dark brown marks on Morrison's overalls.

Blood. Dried blood.

"WHERE ARE THE OTHERS?" Immo booms even louder.

The platform worker slowly turns his head in her direction and lowers his gaze a few degrees. He smiles conspiratorially at her, revealing a row of darkly stained teeth. Licks his lips. With a crazed expression, he strokes his belly.

Waltraud suppresses the urge to retch. Suddenly, Immo throws himself on him, grabbing the hand with the pistol. Both men crash lengthwise to the floor before she can react. The signal rocket releases from the pistol with a hiss and thunders against the nozzle in the tank. Instinctively, those standing around throw themselves to the ground. The explosion rips the nozzle out of the opening. Fifteen liters of diesel per second shoot out of the writhing hose, soaking everything on the helipad. Waltraud jumps up. The acrid smell of fuel streams into her nose. She runs to push the maniac off the platform. But it is too late. One of the extinguishing sparks of the signal rocket ignites the fuel. Within a heartbeat, tongues of flame are everywhere. Suddenly, everyone is ablaze. A burning Jori rolls away from the helipad and disappears screaming over the edge. Immo holds his grip on Morrison's throat like a living torch. The occupants of the helicopter hammer frantically against the door, its paint blistering in the heat. Waltraud feels the burning creeping up her legs. Everything happens so quickly that she can't quite pin down the pain or what she's feeling—as if she has been decoupled from her own body. And something is tugging at her shoulder. Dumbfounded, she turns around and sees Jens, whose hair is aflame. She opens her mouth to warn him, but the flames suck the remaining oxygen from her lungs as he tugs and pulls at her. The next instant, the blaze reaches the tank—and the helicopter blows up. The brutal shock wave sweeps everything off the platform. Burning debris chases through the rig's gas lines, setting off another chain reaction. Within seconds, everything is exploding. Two minutes later, the thousand-ton structure rears up under the force of a final massive detonation that tears the entire rig to pieces.

All that remains is flaming plastic furniture and scraps of paper from thick safety manuals, which float a while longer on the waves. Gradually, they too disappear into the depths of the ice-cold North Sea while the wind and current disperse the last of the oil slicks.

# CHAPTER 5

# ATLANTIC

## DAY 163 A.I.

I'm enjoying the peace and quiet. I haven't heard anything for days except for the sounds of the elements and Patrick's voice. No discussions that would stress me out. There is no one to distract me or who I need to consider when I plan my day. Just Patrick and me. The hours between sleeping and waking are always the same. Thin coffee and a meager breakfast in the morning and holding our northwest course during the day. In the evening, we have a simple meal of rice, beans, or noodles. Every day we share an orange. We eat the peel as well because we can't afford to waste it.

Four days ago, to the south of Fair Isle, we sighted a flock of gulls that followed us persistently until evening. The birds turned back as soon as they realized that they wouldn't be getting any food from us. The next day the wind dropped. Whether this is usual for our location and time of year, I can't say. In addition, the sun was burning down on us mercilessly and making us drink more. Initially, we had planned two weeks for the eighteen-hundred-kilometer trip and allocated our supplies accordingly. But if we remained in the doldrums, we'd have to figure out a different approach.

The thought of even setting foot on any of the islands we would pass on the way to Reykjavik was repugnant to me. After everything we went through in the Mediterranean, my enthusiasm for islands was limited.

But the mainland repels me even more. Which is the main reason I didn't want to go to Berlin with them.

I know that Iceland is the mainland, too. But my hope is that it will be free of the infected and that I'll be able to be close to my elderly parents. After months of permanent fear, I long for safety and a deep, dreamless sleep. I fantasize about a world where that's possible, to give me enough positive thoughts to get me through the day. But I realize that I'm also trying to distract myself from the pain of loss that has plagued me since we separated. The peace and quiet is great, to be sure. But the longer I'm away from my friends, the more I miss them. I miss the friction between Backup and Patrick, and I miss Franca's commanding voice. I long for Jens's sanity and Waltraud's dreamy madness. The certainty that I'll never see them again tears me up inside. But I don't let any of it surface.

Am I trying to shield Patrick from my worries and problems? It's possible. And yet it's foolish to attempt it because he saw through me long since.

My impulse to write is stirring again. He's watching me furtively as I labor over these scribbles in the old notebook. My sweaty fingers are making the pen slip, but with each sentence, I find it easier to put the next one on paper. Unfortunately, I'll have to limit myself because I only have a few sheets of paper. Since there nothing's happening out here on the open sea anyway, it shouldn't be difficult.

## DAY 165 A.I.

Last night we slept out on deck, using the cushions from the seating area down below as a bed. Shortly before sunrise, we used the last of our coffee. Our water supply is running low.

"We need to ration it more strictly," Patrick said. "I did the math again: If we keep drinking this much, we'll be out of water in seven days. And I don't think we'll make it to Iceland in that time."

"Where are we now, exactly?" I asked.

He disappeared below for a moment and returned with a map, which he smoothed out with one hand on the table.

"If I'm right, we're here." He pointed to a spot between the Shetland and Faroe Islands. "At our current speed, we won't pass the Faroe Islands for another five days." Then he looked me in the eye. He knew exactly how I felt about landing on an island. "We have no choice, Eva. Unless the wind picks up tomorrow at the latest. Or we at least get some rain in the next few days."

"And how do you think it'll pan out? We sail in to the harbor, have a gossip with the locals, and head back out again?"

"Hey, if you've got a better idea, just say the word! I don't want to get the blame when we're dying of thirst halfway there. "

"What if we only drink half a liter a day?"

"I've already factored that in. Seven days, then it's all gone. It's supposed to be possible to distill seawater, but I have no idea how."

I thought for a long while. Every fiber of my being was crying out against it, but I realized we had no other choice.

"All right," I said reluctantly, "we'll stop at the Faroe Islands. Take on water and sail on immediately. "

He nodded. "That's exactly what I had in mind."

Despite the late summer sunshine, I shivered suddenly. I moved closer to him, and he put his arm around my shoulders. "What a load of crap," I heard myself grumble. "Island hopping isn't what I thought it would be."

## DAY 168 A.I.

The worst thing I could have imagined right now has happened. I should have seen the signs days ago. As I was hanging over the railing half asleep and vomiting earlier, I finally had to admit it to myself.

I am pregnant. My period is late. We used up our contraceptives on Mallorca. Since then, we've had to take the utmost care when we've been intimate. I noted when I was bleeding and tried to restrict our activities on the days I was fertile. With little success, as I realized before. The next shock came when I told Patrick at breakfast. He had already suspected it, he said, and he was looking forward to becoming a father.

"Are you out of your mind?" I berated him. "Who on earth would want to bring a child into the world right now?"

"Well, I would," he replied, unmoved. "And you, too, now," he added with a splutter of laughter.

"How can you laugh about it? We barely have drinking water for today; we've no idea what might happen tomorrow, and you want to start a family?"

"What else should we do? Spend every day waiting for evening to come so we can go to bed?"

"No, but having a child now . . ." That was all I could say. Suddenly I jumped up, bent over the railing, and donated my half-digested breakfast to the fish.

"And the way you're throwing up, you're going to need more than a pint of fluid a day. Here, drink this," he said, passing me his ration. I rinsed my mouth and gulped it down, not wanting to waste anything.

I was queasy the rest of the day. At noon I had no appetite, which didn't stop Patrick from eating my portion, too. I wondered what the hell I would do with a child in the times we were living through. The events of the last few months nipped any sensible idea in the bud.

## DAY 170 A.I.

The night before last, we got company. Three fishing boats approached, their engines roaring, and barred our way. We had some diesel in the tank, but their boats would have been faster if it had come to a chase. So we lowered the sails and waited. The boats had armed Faroese on board and stopped about fifty meters away. They had apparently seen our guns. There was a tension in the air that made me uneasy. They weren't there out of curiosity.

I just hoped they weren't going to push their luck and test our will to survive. The drills that Franca had fortunately put us through and our combat experience gave me confidence.

"What now?" Patrick asked, cradling a pump-action shotgun in the crook of his arm. "It's us who want something from them, after all."

"I still think it's a bad idea to head for the islands," I began, and immediately had to raise my voice when he started to disagree, "but I also realize we have no other option." I kept my hand close to the Beretta at my hip.

"Well then, I'll leave it to you to do the negotiating—if you want," he said, moving to stand behind me.

I then raised a hand and waved. It took them a few minutes to communicate with each other and wave back.

I raised my empty palms to them. Patrick put his gun down.

"We don't want any bother," I shouted at the top of my lungs in English. "And we don't want to bother anyone else, either. But we're running out of water. If you could let us have a few liters, that would be very kind."

This time it was less than half a minute before they responded. A bearded Faroese man with a heavy Scandinavian accent boomed across the sea between us: "Water's not a problem. But we don't have much on board. If you come with us to Vágur"—he gestured with his thumb over his shoulder—"we can supply you with food and water."

"What kind of food?" Patrick whispered. "As far as I know, they used to have to import everything apart from fish. And I have no interest in smoked pilot whale meat. But if they could let us have some of their dark little potatoes, I wouldn't say no."

"Stop thinking with your gut all the time," I replied softly. "There's something very wrong here." I thought frantically, then spoke, "Thanks for the offer, but our food supplies will last until Iceland. All we need is water."

"As you wish. But you'll still have to follow us. And since there's no wind at all"—he indicated a tornado motion with his index finger—"we'd be happy to tow you." One of the boats approached slowly. A sailor in yellow dungarees picked up a thick rope from the stern and held it out to us invitingly.

"I have a really bad feeling about this, Patrick. Why can't they just give us the water they have with them? We don't need more than three or four liters."

"How am I supposed to know? Maybe they only have two liters or just one. That's no use to us. And in your condition . . ."

"What do you mean, in my condition?" Anger flared up inside me. "Am I sick or what?"

"No, you're pregnant. I don't want lack of fluids to harm the baby."

"First—it's not a baby yet, it's a fetus. And second—in a world infested with zombies, being short of a little water will be the least of its worries." Somewhere in the recesses of my mind, a voice fretted over what I had just said, undermining my certainty. Out of the corner of my eye, I saw Patrick stiffen, as he did every time we went toe-to-toe.

As I expected, his voice sounded composed and distant. "All right, we'll do it your way. I've told you what I think, so do whatever you like," he said and fell silent. I racked my brain. Only after considering all the available options for the fifth time did I raise my hand again—and wave the tugboat over.

In less than ten minutes, we were on our way to Vágur with an escort. The airstream cooled me, and my anger subsided. I tried to ignore the fact that, between the boats that flanked us, we looked like a prisoner convoy.

Patrick was silent the whole time. Shotgun in his hand, he stood at the main mast, looking in the direction of travel.

Two hours later, we chugged into the long bay of the southernmost Faroe Island. The land was covered in meadows and crisscrossed by countless streams and rivulets of melted snow. Vágur—hardly more than a village, but nonetheless blessed with several churches—stretched across the northern edge of the bay. Red, green, white, and gray houses with dark roofs adorned the green, treeless landscape. They allowed us to moor at the old dock. As I looked back, I shuddered. There were so many fishing boats behind us that I couldn't count them. The closer they came, the louder their engines roared.

"I'm starting to lose interest in this," I said. Patrick had seen them as well. "Let's load the fucking water and vamoose."

"How are we going to vamoose without any wind, Eva?" he hissed.

"Hello, friends." A high voice suddenly echoed from the jetty. We turned and saw a short, roundish man coming toward us. "Where are you coming from?" He sounded friendly and seemed anxious to make a good impression. Behind him came half a dozen women and men.

"Good afternoon," Patrick said, raising both hands into the air. "We've been offered the chance to replenish our water supplies. We won't be staying long."

For a split second, disappointment flared on the little man's face. "But no! Where are you headed—when you haven't even arrived yet? Besides, the wind is much too weak for sailing."

"Our tank is full. We'll head back out to sea and wait there until the wind picks up. Really, we just need some water, and we'll be off straight away. "

"Please forgive me, but I cannot accept that." He stamped his foot gently. His friendly grin made it difficult for us to say no just like that. "Allow me to introduce myself at least: I'm Brandur Guðjónsson, mayor of Vágur. And"—he continued while looking at the tips of his shoes that was presumably meant to signal modesty but belied the pride in his voice— "starting tomorrow, we will begin our festivities to pay homage to the long-forgotten gods who once watched over our islands. I insist that you honor us with your presence and take part in the festivities—as our very special guests." No sooner had he said this than a handful of fishermen were at his side, some of whom had helped drag us here. A few of them held hunting rifles.

This subtle threat frightened me. Now that I was carrying a child, everything was different. Inwardly, my aversion to risks ramped up. Celebrating! That was about the last thing I felt like doing at the moment. But at least it explained the number of boats that had just arrived in the bay. Patrick clenched his fists, the pump-action shotgun resting loosely in his arm. He turned slowly and looked at me. "I guess we have no choice," he said quickly in our native language, to ensure the Faroese couldn't understand.

"Looks like it," I replied. "Then we'll stay here for day or two, right?"

He took a couple of breaths. Then he said to our host, "We are honored by your invitation and would love to accept." I hoped I was the only person who had noticed precisely how sardonic and cynical his tone was.

"Wonderful! Great!" the mayor rejoiced, clapping his hands. He turned and spoke to his escort, who grinned uncertainly. Then they formed a corridor through which it looked like they wanted to escort us. "Please, friends," Brandur continued, "follow my people to your quarters."

"But we need time to pack some things," I replied.

"Of course, of course," he said placatingly. "Take all the time you need. But please remember to leave your weapons on board. We are a peaceful people. You have nothing to fear here."

"Now why did I guess that was exactly what you were going to say," I muttered, heading below. I grabbed our toothbrushes and toothpaste, my writing kit, and put them into a cotton bag along with clean underwear for three days. Patrick handed me the shotgun, which I exchanged for the bag and hid under the mattress in a bunk.

I was under no illusion—if they searched our boat, they would find it. But what else could I do?

While I was downstairs, Patrick had moored the boat and stepped onto the pier. I joined him. The mayor attached himself to us like a good friend and chatted away. "This is wonderful. We haven't had any guests lately, so forgive my curiosity. I'm eager to hear everything you have to tell. Where have you come from? How have you managed to survive? What's going on out there in the world? And do tell me what brought you here." He was like a child tottering between us who wouldn't stop asking questions. "Do you know anything about the origin of the pandemic? How many have survived?"

Patrick answered, mostly in monosyllables, but I remained silent. At some point, I zoned out and just looked around. If we needed to escape, it would be more than easy to find our way back to the harbor, so I memorized the people who came toward us. They were mostly men dressed in fishing gear, their countenances marked by the harsh northern weather. The women, too, had angular features and weather-beaten faces.

Our talkative host took us to a scout hut on the hill in the north of the town. Rakul, the owner, led us inside and showed us our sparsely furnished room. From the window we could look down to the harbor, where I could even pick out our boat. To the right, westward, we saw rugged cliffs and behind them the endless expanse of the sea.

Behind the hut, the hill rose steeply into a wall of rock. On the opposite side of the bay, the rest of the island stretched southward in undulating elevations.

At some point the mayor finally left, though I only half noticed him go. Patrick's agitated voice snapped me back to the present. "Eva, look here!" I found him in the bathroom, where he had already undressed and was about to step into the shower stall. "Hot water at last," he said. "Won't you keep me company?"

A wave of indignation chased across my mind. I wanted to rave, to ask him how he could possibly think of such a thing in this situation. But as soon as I saw the first cloud of steam, the longing for warmth and physical union with the man I loved overpowered me.

So I undressed quickly and threw myself into his arms. What could happen, anyway? I was already pregnant.

Late in the afternoon, we ventured out of the room and found our hostess setting the table in the hostel common room. Rakul was small and wiry, with blond hair woven into a complicated braid, and large gold-framed glasses.

"Oh, there you are," she lilted when she saw us. The discrepancy between her and how the island had appeared to me caught me unawares. "You're the first guests this year," she added. "And I'm so excited. I love having guests."

We smiled back. Patrick tried to make some small talk. "Did a lot of people use to come here?"

"Oh yes, my boarding house is usually busy at the start of fall. But at least you're here now. Come, sit down; you must be hungry." She was absolutely right. My stomach growled loudly at the smell of the food. Rakul had served potatoes, fish, and some meat that I assumed was lamb or mutton. In a large glass bowl, there were vast amounts of seaweed salad. "Enjoy! I have business in town, so I'll leave you until this evening. I'm sure you've heard about the festivities. We are preparing for it right now."

She looked as excited as a young girl before her first prom. "In Vágur, we never lock the doors. So if you go out, you won't need a key."

We thanked her and tucked into the boiled potatoes and salad. Once we had eaten our fill, we headed for the shower again.

We spent the following day exploring the northern part of the island. Rakul had put a blanket and a packed lunch into my hands after breakfast and encouraged us to go for a hike. Since we had no other plans, we gratefully agreed. We followed a narrow paved road that turned into a red clay path farther up. The sun was shining from a cloudless sky. We walked uphill for an hour and discovered two lakes that kept Vágur supplied with drinking water. The barren landscape and firm ground had a calming effect on me. The tension between my shoulder blades slowly eased, and the feeling of perpetual threat subsided a little. More and more often I found myself taking deep, relaxed breaths in and out. We talked about harmless, everyday things. I welcomed the fact that Patrick did not bring up the pregnancy.

So we strode across the dried grass, picnicking and making love among the pools. We made it back to the hut just before sunset. There we showered and ate—this time with Rakul.

"The preparations are finished," she chirped excitedly. "Today we had a test of manhood. It was so exciting to watch our young men showing what they could do. Oh, I'm such a chatterbox." She sipped her tea. "It's so good to have you with us, my dears. What did you do today?"

So we told her how lovely we thought the island was and how at home we felt here, and she was so proud she seemed to grow a few centimeters taller.

Afterward, we sat in the common room, and I continued to write in the light of the bulb. Patrick discovered an American detective novel on the bookcase, probably left here by a traveler, and within a few minutes was immersed in it. Now he's sitting on the bench in the corner with his legs up. For the first time in a long time, I'm imagining our future, how he will soothe our baby in the middle of the night and rock it to sleep. I'm looking forward to the future with an intensity I haven't felt in a long time. My hands are starting to tremble with fear and excitement in equal measure. Now I'm just sitting here, pretending to write, even though the muse has long since deserted me, watching him surreptitiously. I don't dare interrupt this moment of perfect harmony.

## DAY UNKNOWN A.I.

It's taken me four hours to get over it and start writing again. The futility of my writing, indeed of my whole existence, has become clear to me again. It's laughing at me derisively. It's paralyzing me. Robbing me of my breath. Of the will to live.

I feel only fear, sadness, and anger. But then I listen for my demons and am frightened of awakening them.

On the day after the hike, we'd decided to explore the rest of the island. Rakul was already waiting in the common room with a breakfast that was lavish by current standards. We ate together and drank filter coffee. She told us that the Faroese occasionally sailed to Norway to plunder it, as the Vikings had once done. In one of the harbors, they had located a huge warehouse of goods from which, among other things, they took vast quantities of coffee beans.

Remembering her voice makes me even more furious than I already am. She still said Patrick and I should have a look around the south.

It would have been better to ram the blunt butter knife down her throat at that moment than to accept her suggestion. But we laughed when she cheerfully recommended that we leave at once, hike to Sumba, have lunch there, and then return.

"You'll be back by dinner," she said, clapping her hands with satisfaction. "It's a beautiful route; the tourists love it. And you'll sleep well tonight."

We listened to her. We made sandwiches and set off before nine. The weather was mostly sunny. The landscape didn't change much. The path led along the coast and often up long, steep hills. Sheep bells were ringing everywhere. The animals were eating the dry grass and bleating now and again. Most of the streams in the adjacent meadows had dried up. At the Sumba Road Tunnel, we left the road and walked roughly southeast across the pastureland. After passing through a dense bank of fog, we caught sight of Sumba, but lingered outside the village to watch the breakers. After an hour's rest, we turned around and walked back the way we had come.

We reached Vágur two hours later, at the same time as another convoy of local fishing boats. Standing on the hill, we saw them arrive and moor up at the huge red warehouse we had already passed on our outward hike.

The lower we climbed, the more the building obscured our view of what was happening. We were unsuspecting, tired, and hungry, and we had let down our guard.

At the highest point of the warehouse, we made out guards, who instantly stiffened when they saw us. Then the wind carried a familiar stench to us. We stopped as if rooted to the spot. All the hairs on my body suddenly stood on end. Distinctive sounds reached us. The undead were screaming their hearts out. We looked at each other briefly and sprinted back up the street.

But we didn't get far. Three pickup trucks quickly caught up with us. One of them overtook us, blocking our way. We tried in vain to escape over one of the meadows. But within half a minute, the off-road vehicles were surrounding us.

Five men armed with shotguns jumped from the loading beds and came toward us.

"I told you a hundred times that coming here was a bad idea," I growled, furious. "But you always know better."

Patrick said nothing. Wordlessly, he raised his hands and clasped them behind his head.

I addressed the men. "What do you want from us? We don't have any weapons! What's going on here?"

Resignedly, Patrick answered for them. "Leave it. They're armed—we aren't. Don't make things worse by resisting."

"Are you crazy? Are you just going to give up without a fight?"

"They far outnumber us. Remember what Franca taught us about how to behave in this kind of situation?"

"Give up and, if possible, calmly make an escape plan? Create a diversion?" I muttered between clenched teeth.

"Exactly," he answered. Then the men were on us. They tied us up with rough hemp ropes and led us away. The entire time I was struggling not to hyperventilate with anger. One truck drove ahead of us, and the other two followed us back to the depot at the harbor. A four-meter-high gate was pulled open to let us in. We were led to the right, through a vaguely lit corridor. The left wall was made of wooden floorboards that seemed to have been hastily knocked together. Everything smelled of fresh wood shavings—and zombies. I could hear them screaming and wheezing from the opposite side of the warehouse, but in strangely high-pitched tones. The pounding of my heart increased. The instinct to flee kicked in, but I had no way of complying. The bearded man in front of us opened a door. We were pushed into a small windowless room with a sloping roof. The floor was covered with hay. The door slammed and was locked behind us. Suddenly we were standing in darkness. Only a little light entered through narrow cracks.

"So what now, Houdini?" I asked into the gloom. "What would Franca do now?"

"Don't be a pain in the ass, Eva," he replied, turning away.

"I'm about to kick your ass, asshole. See to it that you get us out of here." Ignoring me, he leaned against the wall next to the door and slid down to the floor.

I was foaming at the mouth. I was like the stinkers who were raging just a few meters from us. I kicked around, trying to kick open the door, but it was firmly closed.

"Save your strength, Eva," I heard him say. But that spurred on my fury all the more. I raged for a few more minutes until fatigue and help-lessness overcame me. Soon my wrists were burning beneath the rope.

"What do they want from us? And what are they going to do with the zombies? Can you fucking tell me?"

He was silent. I dropped to the hay, crying.

After a while, I heard footsteps. Someone was tinkering with the lock. Light from half a dozen flashlights shot into our cell. I blinked. A small, roundish figure entered and knelt in front of me.

"Man oh man oh man . . . That was the worst possible time to walk by here," the silhouette said, addressing me. "But this way, you have spared us the unpleasantness of having to bring you here from the hostel. I regret that we meet again under these circumstances, though."

"What are you going to do with us?" I asked the mayor. Patrick had drawn up his knees as if getting ready to jump. But the sight of the armed men in the doorway was probably stopping him.

"Well, you see," the town patron continued, "we Faroese are an ancient people that has uprooted itself over the centuries, culturally and in terms of religion. We are descended from the Vikings," he said pretentiously, gesturing with both hands close to my face. "Once we were proud warriors who sailed the seas, plundering. Powerful and invincible. We were the ones who discovered America, not some runaway Spaniard or Italian. We, the Vikings, accomplished this." He burst out laughing, as if he didn't understand why everyone hadn't known that long ago. "Our gods have been with us, watching over us, since time immemorial. But we became foolish, we turned our backs on them and began to worship a false deity. The Aesir and the Vanir were amused by us at first. And when Odin saw that we were worshipping another resurrected Lord besides him, he laughed for two thousand years. And then he cursed all those who displeased him. They shall never be admitted to Valhalla. None of them shall sully the memories of fallen warriors and brothers in the Eternal Halls. They shall never be permitted to sit and dine at the table with the gods. He condemned them to return as soulless scavengers, to roam the world as stinking husks until their corpses turned to dust—and afterward they shall dwell in Helheim, the realm of the dead."

Here he left a highly-charged pause. "But he also puts us to the test. Those who truly believe in him are immune to the plague of resurrection. Only those with the strongest will, who are totally devoted to him, remain unaffected. In the coming time, they will be permitted to live on, in a world ruled by the strongest children of Odin. The others, however, will be . . . Well, they were once called sacrificial offerings. And that's where you come in! This is your last chance. Discard the false beliefs and turn to Odin—and you may live. Disobedience will be punished. "

Baffled, I looked over at Patrick. I could see amazement on his face. His eyes wide, he looked away from Brandur and toward me.

"Tomorrow your fate will be decided," the mayor continued, unperturbed. "Tomorrow you may demonstrate your faith. Only true children of Odin are capable of enduring in this world." Then he turned away and spoke to someone behind him. Someone pushed past him and placed a bag in the hay. She took a knife out of her pocket and freed us from our bonds without taking any particular care. "Consider this well. Rest yourselves. Tomorrow is a glorious day for all of us." Brandur brought his speech to an end and left. The door slammed shut. We found ourselves in darkness.

"I've heard a lot of bullshit in my life, but this takes the cake," Patrick declared.

"Oh, you mean I might have missed the fact that this guy is nuts?"

"No, that's not what I mean. He could be crazy, but I don't get that impression. It's more likely that he's afraid for his job because of what's happening in the world, and so he's made up this absurd story. It's what outgoing politicians do when they desperately want to stay on in the role. They exploit the insecurity of the population. And what he said about religion isn't entirely true."

"Again, how do you know that for sure?" I scoffed.

"Remember I wrote a review three years ago, about the Viking series that was on TV back then?"

"Oh, yes . . ."

"That's when I read up on Norse mythology. It was far more exciting than the series, I thought. Anyway, not even Odin himself would have the power to cause a plague on this scale. Theoretically, it's conceivable that another being, like Hel or Loki, might have cast the curse. Then the curse would be in the world, but the gods would have no control over it. There is no omnipotent god in Norse mythology. And Ragnarök—the end of the world—comes with ice and fire, not zombies. That would be the worst story in the world. The guy doesn't have a clue and is just taking advantage of the citizens' confusion. Besides, this is a legend that's supposed to have taken place long ago, not something that is yet to come."

"Excellent! Now you just have to convince Brandur of his wrongdoing. I'm sure he'll accept it and let us out of here right away."

Suddenly we heard screams, coming closer. They were not from one of the infected. This person was screaming his head off. After an angry interjection, there was a fleshy thwack and the cries of distress abruptly ceased. I heard a door being pulled open. A heavy weight was thrown through it, and it was closed again.

There was the sound of footsteps moving away, and it was as if the incident had never happened. But it was repeated several times during the evening.

Most of the time, people we couldn't see called out in panic for help, and rarely stopped once the doors were locked.

"They're bringing other prisoners here," Patrick said quietly. We could hear crying and whimpering from the adjacent cells. Some people shouted out, asking if there was anyone else was there. Others responded. We kept quiet. "I'm curious to see what they're going to do with us."

"Oh, I imagine that they want to sacrifice us as well."

Patrick didn't seem to agree. "No, that wouldn't be consistent," he said thoughtfully.

It must have been late in the evening. One of the guards had appeared and brought us a bag of food and water.

"Do you want something to eat?" I asked.

"No thanks; not now. I need to think," Patrick replied. So I left him alone, forced myself to drink something, and relieved myself in the far corner. Then I curled up at his side. He snuggled up to me, and I was almost overcome by a feeling of security.

"I've been thinking the whole time about when the best time to counterattack would be," he whispered, close to my ear. "I've thought through quite a few scenarios. We could jump them at the door the next time they open it. Or in the narrow hallway while they're leading us away."

I didn't really like those options, so I said, "Definitely not when they open the door. They'll be expecting that. And in the hallway, they'll just shoot us in the face. You don't think they'll tie us up when they come for us?"

And they would unquestionably come for us.

"Yes, that's what I thought, too. We'll have to wait until tomorrow. Improvise. Keep an eye out for our chance and then take it. "

"Like Franca would," I whispered dejectedly.

"Exactly! Like Franca would." He tried to sound confident. "Remember what she always told us?"

"Scout, confuse, strike?"

"Yep. Scout, confuse, strike."

"I miss them so much. I miss them all," I wailed.

"And I thought it was just me," he said.

"Franca would empty a whole magazine into Brandur if she only knew what was happening to us right now."

"Oh yeah, and Backup would so make them bleed. Chop them up one by one."

"Jens would bore them to death with his niceness . . ."

"And Waltraud would drive them to suicide with movie quotes."

It would have been nice if these words had brought some comfort. But they only made things worse. My grief expanded until I felt as if my heart would burst in my chest. Tears and snot ran down my face and dripped into the hay.

"Let's try to sleep, Eva. We'll need our strength tomorrow."

"Yeah, I know," I replied with a sniffle, wiping my nose with my sleeve. "It's just that I don't think I'm going to make it. I'm so . . . worked up."

He pulled me tighter to him and gently kissed my earlobe. "Just close your eyes," he said, "and try to forget everything. That's all we can do right now."

I turned my head and kissed him. "I'll try. I promise." Then I closed my eyes. It was so dark, it hardly made any difference. But it was a long time before my exhaustion dropped me into sleep.

We were woken by thunderous stomping. At first I wasn't sure where I was. But when I felt the hay beneath me, I remembered. Some light was filtering into the cell through a crack, so I could see the most important things.

Patrick yawned and stretched. "Good morning," he whispered fondly. "Remember, if they come for us, we'll let them. But as soon as an opportunity presents itself . . ."

"We strike," I added.

"Good girl," he teased, and my anger flared again.

"Now's not the time to be funny, okay?"

"All right," he relented. He stood up and relieved himself in the place I had yesterday. A little later, I did the same. Then we went to work on the bag of food. I had no appetite, but Patrick was right: We had to keep up our strength. Then we divided the water between us.

The commotion in the building had increased. About an hour after we woke up, I heard footsteps directly above us. Dozens, if not hundreds. They seemed to be coming from all corners and going in all directions. The beams and boards above us were bending under an enormous weight.

Dust and sawdust trickled down. The murmur of many voices rose to an ominous murmur.

"I suspect we're under some bleachers they've been putting up the last few days," Patrick opined.

"A grandstand? What for?"

"It's only logical. If you want to create a spectacle, you have to make sure as many people see it as possible. And I assume that people around here like to get caught up in spectacles like this. "

"You think the spectacle is sacrificing us?"

"On these godforsaken islands, anything not to do with sheep farming and fishing is a spectacle. The mayor must have come up with something treacherous. I can literally smell it."

"Well then, let's hope it's not too treacherous, because I've had more than enough of that lately."

"But let's not waste time now; we need to prepare ourselves. Come on, get up and join in!"

Groaning, I rose and began to warm up. We jogged in place while shadowboxing, performed burpees and push-ups. I began to sweat slightly. We went through some close-quarters sequences and stretched. My anger mingled with my newly awakened desire to fight.

A short time later, we heard frightened voices from the neighboring cells: "What's this?" "What are you going to do with me?"

But answers never came.

We were ready. When our door opened, we extended our wrists to the two astonished Faroese who entered with the rope.

They tied us up and ordered us to follow them. At least three armed men escorted us through the narrow corridors. The place was buzzing like a beehive all around us. We turned sharply left, and in a few more steps, we found ourselves in the middle of the building, where the floor had been strewn with sawdust. The huge gates of the warehouse had been pulled completely open on both sides, letting in the daylight. I looked around me. Patrick and I were not alone.

A dozen people with fear written all over their faces were standing with us in the middle of an arena: women and men of all ages. They had indeed built stands around it, where hundreds of locals were sitting side by side. There were a lot of children and young people crowded into the seats at the bottom. They were looking around curiously, as if they didn't know what was going on. Our escort took off our shackles and went back the way we had come. Behind them, the arena gate slammed shut with a thud. A heavy bolt slid into place on the other side.

Around the edge of the ring was a one-and-a-half-meter barrier made of boards. A wire mesh fence nearly twice that height had been set on top of it and secured with barbed wire. The construction was supported by metal posts, which were positioned every two meters. The Faroese sat behind it, staring at us as if we were cattle at the market.

"So, any bright ideas yet on how you're going to get us out of here?"

"Take it easy, Eva," Patrick said. Our comrades in the ring were turning in circles, looking around fearfully while massaging their wrists. The tension emanating from the onlookers made the air vibrate.

"What are you motherfuckers going to do with us," I muttered. At that very moment, the crowd fell silent. It was as if we had suddenly been moved to a soundproof room.

Patrick elbowed me. "Look who's coming!"

The mayor stepped out onto the gallery that had been erected on the east wall. He was dressed in black as usual and wore a glittering chain around his neck. All eyes were fixed on him. The spot had been carefully chosen. Light fell on him from one of the roof windows, picking him out clearly against the background.

He let several moments pass. When the tension seemed unbearable, he spoke loudly and clearly: "My Faroese! Children of Odin! Descendants of the Vikings! Rulers of the world!"

Someone began to drum their feet. A few seconds later, the hall was resounding with applause.

The mayor raised his hands at the perfect moment and the rumbling stopped. "Our people have prepared for this era for many years. For centuries we have waited for the gods to return. And now we have gathered to reaffirm our devotion to Odin and his warrior host. Ragnarök is at hand!"

Before anyone could even think of applauding, Patrick yelled at the top of his lungs, "Don't give me that bullshit, you pompous ass!" The audience's attention shifted to the center of the ring. "Who's the act for here? Are you making yourself out to be the prophet of the north? You don't have any idea—"

The mayor interrupted him loudly, "The infidels who have abused our hospitality will be the first to be sacrificed in order to increase Odin's powers."

But Patrick was unstoppable. "Abused your hospitality? You don't think anyone's going to buy that crap, do you? If you had just given us two bottles of water, we would never have set foot on your shitty island."

"Yes, that's right," the woman to my right shouted, and I jumped in fright. "You kidnapped us from Norway. It would never have occurred to us to come here . . ."

But the mayor was a brilliant actor. I could almost have bought that he was truly enraged. "How dare you dishonor Odin's land with your sacrilegious words? The islands where his children were born?" He raised both arms theatrically, pointing at the onlookers, earning nods of approval and murmurs of agreement. Filled with hatred, he looked toward Patrick. "The sacred ground at our feet will feast on your blood this very day. Those of us who failed the test of manhood yesterday will be given one last chance to be admitted to Valhalla today. You will send the souls of these infidels"—his outstretched forefinger pointed at us—"to Hel in eternal damnation. You will breathe your last . . ."

"Oh, spare us the sermon and get to the point. And make sure something happens to me. Because if I get my hands on you, I'll break every bone in your body, you runt!"

Deadly silence. Patrick was snorting like a bull. The city father attempted to stare him down—and lost. He then turned his head to the north stand and raised a hand. "Open the gate," he commanded masterfully. Seconds later, I heard the scraping of wood and envisaged the bolt on the other side being drawn back. Wondering how many men might have fallen victim to the ridiculous ritual yesterday, I prepared for battle. The door panels swung inward, and I was gripped by sheer horror.

They were children. A mass of little children with dull, milky eyes. Their skin was ashen and networked with black veins. They came running toward us. Their ages were hard to determine, but I estimated them to be between seven and twelve years old. And there were a lot of them. Involuntarily, my hands went to my stomach. When the first person behind me cried out in panic, the crowd cheered. Patrick roared at me, "See that you survive this day, Eva!" He leaned down and kissed me.

Then he turned and sprinted toward the undead children. Out of the corner of my eye, I saw the others dashing off in all directions. I quickly wrapped my jacket around my right fist and ran after my husband. My heart broke when I saw him crush the first child's chest with a mighty kick. I heard ribs cracking. A gush of black blood poured out of the little mouth over his shoe. Then they were upon us. I lashed out with my protected fist, always careful not to get bitten. Sometimes I connected and the child in question landed on the floor. As soon as it was down, I kicked at its throat and crushed its windpipe. Patrick lifted one up in the air and snapped its neck with a jerk. The cheering from the stands made me furious. Once we had dealt with the first wave, we looked around. Behind us, the zombie kids were picking over three injured people and ignoring us. On the opposite side of the arena, we spotted more people who had fought off the attack but were now screaming at their bite wounds. Patrick and I looked at each other briefly and sprinted toward them. At close range, I jumped knee-first against a man's head. He immediately slumped to the floor. The woman who had spoken up earlier screamed in desperate objection, milliseconds before Patrick's fist hit her larynx with full force. Her arm had long since turned gray, and the disease was making its way up her neck. I turned, suspecting an attack from behind—and my life came to an end.

One of the youngest children had broken away from the funeral feast and had come after us. Enraged, it threw itself at Patrick's back, opened its mouth and began to sink its teeth into the right side of his neck. Startled, Patrick tried to get rid of the weight and reached over his shoulder with his left hand. The child grabbed at it, got ahold of it—and bit into it. Patrick pulled the wriggling child forward, his fist still in its mouth.

I stood rooted to the spot with fright. With his free hand, Patrick grabbed the youngster by the neck and pulled his fingers out of its mouth.

He looked in disbelief at the bloody bones, which had been covered with living tissue only a short time ago.

The zombie child chewed on it and choked it down.

The crowd went wild! It had descended to the level of the enclosure and was bellowing murderously. The onlookers' eyes bulged as they screamed, their mouths wide open.

Patrick screamed as well. He grabbed the child by the feet, swung him in a wide arc and smashed his head on the nearest metal post. Blood and brain matter splattered in all directions. It was pure luck that not a drop hit me. But many people on the other side of the fence were less lucky. With the dead child in his hand, Patrick took a few steps back and threw it over the barbed wire. Then he turned around and saw the last three undead coming running. He grabbed the first child, spun him around—knocking over the other two—and sent him sailing over the barrier. Then he grabbed the prone ones by the ankles and sent them after him. There were no more zombies in the arena.

Panic had now broken out in the stands. For a second, the crowd had been quiet, until they realized there were infected people among them. Then they all ran for their lives. Those whose mucous membranes had come into contact with the dead child's secretions spat wildly or wiped their eyes. But I saw the infection spreading. Within seconds, their cheeks turned colorless, then nearly black. The fungal mutation had the shortest possible path to the brains of the new host bodies. So it took barely a minute for the first of them to fall over and come back to life.

I ran to Patrick, who was kneeling on the floor, tying off his exposed arm with a scrap of sweater fabric. Holding one end with his teeth, he pulled the knot tight with his healthy hand. "Shit, shit, shit . . . ," I cursed, crying. My words tumbled over each other, even as I uttered them. "It'll be okay, we'll wash it out with seawater right away. Saltwater kills the disease, right? Sure, it disinfects! Saltwater has a disinfecting effect. It makes you well." I continued to talk nonsense, but I already knew Patrick was lost. His forearm had turned gray. The spread of the infection was slowed somewhat by the bandage, but it could not be stopped forever.

"Listen, listen to me for a minute, Eva," he said, trying to calm me.

But I was on the edge of despair and babbled on in a panic, "Good, you tied it off. Come on, let's find a way out of here and quickly go to the water and wash it off. We'll have to amputate the fingers somehow, but never mind, that's not important now."

He shook me roughly by the shoulder, "EVA! JUST FUCKING LISTEN TO ME!" I fell silent, but my lips moved like a fish gasping for air. "Eva, I can't be saved, and you know it! I have minutes at most before I become one of them. So let's focus on what we planned earlier: getting out of here!"

"Yeah, okay." I took a quick, shallow breath. "Anything you say. How are we going to get out of here? The gate's barricaded from the other side. The most we could do is cut a hole in the fence, but what with?"

"No, Eva, shut up and listen to me! I'm not going to make it. So you— and our baby—have to escape from the arena. Oh, shit." Suddenly he slumped to the ground. Then he screamed in pain. "I can feel it slowly eating into every cell," he said, once the first surge had subsided. "The blood carrying it through my body. My tongue feels furry. My nerve endings are burning. And my vision's getting cloudy." He took a deep breath and stood. Swayed and caught himself again. "Eva! I only have enough strength to try this once. Come here, climb up me. No, don't look like that, this is your last chance, Eva! Our last chance. Now, Eva."

His voice cut out. He gathered his last strength to help me up. I grabbed his hand, climbed onto his knee, my other foot on his hip, then higher again until I was standing with one foot on his shoulder. He was panting and swaying like a drunk. "Let go of my hand, then stand on my palm. We'll count to three. Then you jump and I'll push as hard as I can. That should do it."

Standing bent over with one foot on his shoulder, my head was just a foot above the barbed wire. "One," he said, bending his knees slightly. On two, I mirrored the movement. "THREE!"

I jumped and he pushed. But he was already too weak, so my upper body flew over the fence, but my shins got caught on it. Then I fell. I grabbed the wire mesh as I did so, clawing my fingers into it. My legs slid over the spikes, which bored through my pants into my flesh. The spikes cut into skin and muscle like the claws of a wild animal. I rolled over and over. My legs hit the ground, but I didn't let go. As my heels slammed against the wooden barrier, a pain I thought I would never survive shot through me. My lower legs felt as if they had just been smashed with huge sledgehammers. I screamed. In pain, I let go of the fence and slammed into the bottom step of the bleachers. I almost lost consciousness, but the thought of Patrick prevented that. Crying, I scrambled to my feet, grabbed the fence, and pulled myself to my feet. My legs immediately started to buckle again.

He was lying on the floor barely three meters away from me. He was scarcely breathing. I saw his exposed finger bones twitch. "Patrick? PATRICK!" I yelled.

Very slowly, he turned his head in my direction, looked at me—and smiled. "You did it. You did it," he said, scarcely audible, raising the thumb of his unbroken hand in the air. I sobbed and shook the fence like a madwoman. Then he waved weakly, and I fell silent. "Go now! I don't want . . . you to see me . . . to see me like this . . ."

"NO!" I screeched.

But it was too late. His hand went limp; his head tilted to the side. And he died. "No. Not like this," I whispered.

His last words kept running through my mind: *I don't want you to see me like this.* This was his last wish. I forced myself to avert my gaze and limped off.

There were corpses everywhere. Several times I had to step over mangled bodies, careful not to slip in a pool of blood. In one severed hand I found a pistol. The magazine was full except for one cartridge. Not far from it I discovered the torso, which I identified as belonging to it from the clothes. The facial skin had been mostly gnawed off, the carotid artery bitten through. I rummaged in its jacket, found two full spare magazines inside, and put them in my pants pocket.

I should have hurried. I should have left the warehouse immediately. But the pain in my legs wouldn't allow it. From the ring, I heard him gasp. It was almost liberating that the being didn't sound remotely like Patrick.

I turned around and looked at it. It scrambled to its feet and paid no attention to the bloody fingers that broke away as soon as it leaned on them. It sniffed. It probably couldn't make me out with all the smells in the room if I stood still. Its face was contorted with anger and hunger.

It was not Patrick who arose from the dirt. It was just another poor victim begging for redemption.

I loaded the pistol—and gave it its freedom.

Most of the details of the hour that followed are unclear to me. I only know that I made my way out into the open through a passage between the stands. I limped back into the village—guided only by my instincts—gun in hand. Countless corpses lined the way. My shoes filled with blood. Shortly before reaching the town, I realized that I had been hearing screams in the distance the entire time. In my delirium, I hadn't registered any of it. But as soon as the edge of the bay came into view, I understood what was happening. The undead had cornered the Faroese.

Presumably some of the bystanders had fled the warehouse at the very beginning, with a crowd of zombies close on their heels. They had been caught in the northern part of the bay—and brutally massacred. Some had turned and then attacked the few townspeople whose curiosity had got the better of them and who had come to see what the noise was. And when the rest arrived there, intending to flee to their boats, they were surrounded by undead. The only way out seemed to be by water, but that proved to be wrong. Zombies followed the fugitives into the bay, mad with blood lust. They caught most of them knee-deep in water. They squeezed the eyes from their victims' skulls with their bare hands, and they bit through the windpipes and carotid arteries of those who were now floating face down in the blood-red water. As I walked past, the killing continued unabated. Everything that could move was in the sea.

Some were fighting for their lives, while others, in a frenzy, were trying to take them. An inconceivable surge of death was before me, like an apocalyptic painting by a mad artist from the darkest of the Dark Ages. The screams sounded in my ears like the screeching of seagulls. Though there were no seagulls to be seen.

The fabric of the trouser legs around my wounds had partially stopped the bleeding, even if it could not ease the pain. But this was nothing compared to the agony that raged inside me. It was so overwhelming that I walked through the settlement and toward the hostel as if in a daze. I met no one. I went to our room, packed my diary in my backpack and Patrick's things in his, and left the building with both bags. In the distance I saw our yacht. The way to it was clear. Arriving at the pier, I entered the whitewashed snack bar on the corner. I plundered the drinks and also took a half-empty bottle of whiskey. I placed it all carefully on the floor of the boat, beneath the steering wheel. Somehow, I got the vessel free and started the engine. Only then did I realize that wind had come up. I didn't care which direction it was blowing. I stepped on the gas and chugged away. Suddenly I heard someone calling my name. For a second, hope flared in me that he had somehow made it after all. Until I remembered that his body was rotting on the other side of the bay with a bullet in its head.

It was Rakul who was running after the yacht, calling out to me in panic. Nine or ten zombies were after her. "Wait! Wait for me!" she shouted. I made no effort to slow down and simply watched her jumping through the air. She managed to grab the railing and slammed heavily against the hull.

"Please, help me, Eva! Please," she begged me, her eyes wide. I stood up and approached her. The bone of her nose broke with a crack when I kicked it. Blood gushed out as if from a faucet. Instinctively, she grabbed her face and let go of the railing. A second later, the undead were upon her. I averted my eyes and steered the yacht out to sea while Rakul went down with a murderous gurgle.

I washed out the blood in my shoes with saltwater. I used the whiskey to clean my wounds. On the boat, we had a small first aid kit. However, I had to cut up a sweater so that I could apply fresh bandages every day. My tetanus vaccination still seemed to be working.

I was often tempted to drown my sorrows with alcohol, but I kept on remembering that I was now responsible for two people. So, I buried the grief deep inside me and sailed toward Iceland. I had no appetite, but ate regularly, albeit small portions.

The weather changed and became harsher. But the wind quickly brought me closer to my destination, until the Icelandic crisis response unit intercepted me fifty kilometers from Reykjavik. I don't remember how many days it had taken me to sail there.

On board, I learned that Iceland did not have a single infected person. They kept a low profile and avoided any communication in order to prevent the flow of refugees. They put me in a cabin and quarantined me. In a prison, I was finally allowed to shower, given three meals a day, and received medical and psychological care.

The fetus was doing splendidly. It developed well. My parents were located. They came to visit me every day. I told them we had planned to sail here in the spring. In our old nutshell. And how we had been stranded on Mallorca and had survived there.

I could not hide my sadness from them, and their loving understanding coaxed out all the repressed emotions I had been carrying around for over half a year.

At night, I cried for hours until I fell asleep exhausted. My psychiatrist took this as a good sign, which was all the same to me, given the circumstances.

After three weeks, I was released and went to stay with my parents. We went for long walks every day. Sometimes we drove inland. They hoped the natural beauty would have a positive effect on my spirits.

And they were proved right.

I found some peace of mind at least. But this would be forever troubled by the fact that I had lost half of my soul, of myself. That I would have to spend the rest of my life without Patrick, who still meant everything to me. Acceptance of this was a peace offering to my inner demons, who finally agreed to it after months of tough negotiation and went to sleep somewhere on the periphery of my mind.

But ultimately, I have to admit I do have a brave ally to support me in this. A little co-conspirator who helps me find new sources of strength every day and tap into them.

Cassiopeia.

The greatest and most beautiful gift I could have ever asked for. I feel her growing beneath my heart. And now I can even hear her heartbeat. It beats fast! *Dah-dum, dah-dum, dah-dum.* Strong and powerful, like her father. I can't wait until she finally gets out of there. And until she understands me, so I can tell her all the stories about her daddy.

He would like that. I wish I was already cradling her in my arms.

I often keep an eye out for my sleeping demons. They haven't shown their faces in a long time. It's comforting to think I won't to have to dance with them for the rest of my life. They seem to have fallen into a deep sleep that they don't want to wake up from. How I would love to believe that. But I know better.

# CHAPTER 6

# BERLIN

It was early morning. The leaves of the trees on the banks of the canal were rustling in a cool breeze. Clouds were drifting overhead. Between them, there was a regular flash of blue, and even the sun was showing itself occasionally. Arriving in Havelberg, we moored the sailboat below the lock on the Elbe-Havel Canal. Franca and Verena wrote a rudimentary instruction manual in various languages for other survivors, which we left on the table, weighted down with a wrench. We could not afford to be so generous with the few food items and the rest of drinking water Hanna had collected, so we took it all with us. The bags, made from bed sheets, were not necessarily ergonomic, but at least we had our hands free. I left Franca, who as usual had commandeered the heaviest things, the backpack that had already served me well in Mallorca.

Climbing the mossy rungs on the wall of the lock, we left the waterway. We marched off determinedly but cautiously, at not too rapid a pace, although we longed to reach Berlin at last. First we went south, crossing a wooded area, and according to plan, we came upon a federal highway that led in a southeasterly direction. Instead of the usual roar of traffic, an ominous silence greeted us, one that seemed more oppressive with each step we took into what had once been civilization. Quietly, our senses on the alert, we began the last section of our zombyssey.

A few months ago, the sight of our troop would have led people to believe we were on a leisurely hiking trip. But anyone who saw us up close would have noticed the tension in our faces. At the next major intersection, we looked around for somewhere we could pick up a map. We had one, but it only showed the major European cities and roads. So we needed one that at least accurately depicted northern Germany. Against all expectations, we quickly found what we were looking for. On the outskirts of the village, about two hundred meters off the planned route, we discovered an ELAN gas station with a turning leading to it. Looking around, we headed for it. Except for Marcus, who stationed himself outside with his gun drawn, Franca, Hanna, Verena, and I entered the store, stepping carefully through the frame of the smashed front door. Shards of glass crunched under our shoes. The looters ahead of us had seemingly been less interested in printed materials, because there were a lot of magazines and newspapers lying around. On one shelf, next to the erotic magazines, we saw spiral-bound atlases of Europe, and half a dozen maps. Three of them showed Berlin and its surroundings. We bagged them immediately, together with the atlases. Who knew where our journey would take us in the coming weeks and months?

"These," Verena said, pointing at some maps of Brandenburg and Saxony-Anhalt, "are the ones we need now." She pressed one into Franca's hand and one into mine. One she kept for herself, unfolding it.

"So, how long will it take?" the Italian asked, a hint of impatience in her voice.

"Sheesh, I don't know," the teenager replied. "By car, it's an hour and a half, two hours if you go through the villages. But on foot? Hard to say. I can't get Google Maps at the moment, I'm afraid," she said sarcastically, folding up the unneeded parts of the map until she held only a narrow strip of paper. We stood behind her, looking over her shoulder as she traced an imaginary line with her index finger.

"We are here, and we want to go there," she mumbled. Then she looked around questioningly. "Does anyone have anything to write with?" she asked.

I walked around the counter while the others inspected the shelves. Franca called out, "Here," and handed her a pencil with a black, red, and gold fringe, covered with pixelated city photos that looked like the kind of souvenir you'd only get in rural parts of Germany.

"Thank you," Verena said and began to make notes on the back of the map cover. "We have to go through Jederitz, Kuhlhausen, Strohdehne..." She listed the towns until she reached Berlin. "Hmm, now we just have to get back on the federal highway."

Franca, who was obviously impressed by the young woman's confident demeanor, nodded appreciatively and replied, "Well then, let's go!"

Verena smiled, put an arm around her sister's shoulders, and led her out. We followed.

We passed Havelberg without incident. From a distance, the city on the hill with the medieval cathedral looked as we'd expected it to: an empty, deserted town, though not as ruined as Hamburg. But we did not let that lull us into a sense of security. Our senses were primed and ready to sound the alarm at the slightest sign of danger.

Our fitness, on the other hand, let us down.

We teased each other about how little we had exercised in the past eight weeks, even though we had traveled thousands of kilometers. After three hours, I could hardly walk any farther; I had pain in my knees and ankles. The others felt the same way. Franca kept us going anyway but made sure we took a short drink break every thirty minutes or so. Most of the time Marcus and Verena led the way, and Hanna hardly left our leader's side. I brought up the rear and made sure we weren't ambushed from behind.

The wasteland had a relaxing effect on me and calmed my nerves. Every now and then, we saw deer or horses grazing in the distance; they took to their heels as soon as they scented us. Whenever the opportunity presented itself, we switched from the main road to paths through fields and meadows. The flora had grown considerably, so it offered us at least a little visual protection. We skirted the towns and villages as much as we could. Our food would take us all the way to Berlin, so we could avoid the risk of being discovered while looting. We refilled our water bottles at the Havel River. It was running reasonably clear, but its shallow level was evidence of last summer's low rainfall. After we had been on the road for about five hours, we saw Rhinow in the distance.

"If we want to bypass the town, we have to decide now. Later it could be difficult because we also have to cross a canal," Verena announced. While she consulted the map, we looked at Rhinow. Verena stretched out her left arm and pointed toward the fields to the east. "If we take that path there, we can bypass almost all the villages before Falkensee. From Friesack, we could even follow the railroad. That's the most direct route from there." She looked at us. "I assume we've done enough walking for today. I don't know about you guys, but I'm tired." Hanna gestured in her direction. "So is she," her older sister translated. "Besides, it's getting dark."

Franca answered for the rest of us, "All right. There's no reason to push our luck. We've made good progress. If we can do this every day, we'll be in Berlin in five or six days, won't we?" she asked.

"Yes, more or less. And starting tomorrow, we'll also have the mornings. So it could well be just three days."

We nodded. "Then we should find a place to stay for the night, guys," the Italian woman said, clapping her hands together.

"What about that yard up ahead?" asked Marcus.

I stretched my neck. Five hundred meters away stood an isolated farmstead. "Let's take a look inside," I suggested. After a brief pause for thought, they nodded and we headed toward it.

Only after carefully checking every room and every corner of the house and yard did we allow ourselves to relax a bit. Behind the barn, which housed only a few bales of hay, we were delighted to discover three apple trees, their branches bending low under the weight of the ripe fruit. We filled our pockets and satisfied the worst of our hunger.

We were under no illusion that the people who had once lived here would return. And if they did, there were only two possible scenarios. Either they would be kind enough to take us in for the night, or we would force them to do so. But there was no indication that anyone was living here. The main building was now serving as a residence for chickens, whose droppings covered a large part of the floor. We shooed the birds out and locked the front door. Upstairs, we discovered rooms they had left untouched. We chose the largest one, which had a double bed. Because the two windows, one facing the yard and one facing the street, were locked, the rooms were clean, if a little stuffy.

As usual, we divided up the watch. Verena placed a chair in the corner of the room between the two windows and kept tabs on the surrounding area in the gathering darkness. Marcus and Franca went down to the first floor to search the shelves and cupboards for food. I set about getting more mattresses so we could all spend the night in the one room. Hanna helped me replace the dusty sheets with fresh ones we had found in a drawer under the bed.

At the sound of a loud clatter in the basement, I reached automatically for my spear. Verena pulled out a pistol and instructed her sister to take cover. Seconds later, there were footsteps on the stairs. I held my breath.

Then there was a knock on the door, and I heard Marcus say, "It's us!"

I breathed a sigh of relief. "Come on in," I said. "What was that noise?"

But I could have saved myself the question. In their hands they held two cooking pots, containing potatoes with long sprouts sticking out of them, and plastic bags, presumably containing food.

"Sorry for the noise. We dropped a pot," Marcus said guiltily.

Franca raised a brow. "We?" she asked, pushing the door shut behind her with her heel.

"I dropped a pot," he admitted. "But look what we found. We're having a real German meal tonight."

"What's this?" I asked, picking up one of the bags. "Sauerkraut? And potatoes?"

"Jawohl!" shouted Marcus in German, in a tone that was presumably meant to sound military, before taking the bag from me. "Here," he said, thrusting a vegetable knife and a peeler into my hands. "You do the potatoes while I build a fire." He took off his shoulder bag and pulled out a green plastic bottle, three cans of beer, and two glasses. Then he opened one of the cans and filled the larger drinking glass. "Anyone want some?" he said, proffering the frothy drink. Franca looked disinterestedly out the window. I shook my head and said no, but Verena didn't need to be asked twice.

"Sure. Whoa, can't remember the last time I had a beer," she said, taking a deep swig. Afterward, she wiped the foam from her upper lip with the back of her hand and grinned with satisfaction. At first it looked like she was going to give the glass back to him, but then she extended her arm in Hanna's direction. "Do you want some?" she whispered, making hand signals. Her younger sister declined the offer with both hands.

"Hmm, all the more for me," Verena said and drank again before setting the half-empty glass down on a dresser. She belched suddenly and so loudly that I winced. "Entschuldigung." She excused herself and looked at Marcus, who was in the process of cutting apart the empty beer can with a box cutter and a pair of household scissors.

He detached the bottom and the top from each other, enlarging the opening as far as it would go, and he cut the two pieces to a height of around two centimeters. He threw the superfluous middle section under the bed, and I watched as he nicked the top all around with the knife. He then used the tip to poke a tiny hole in it before carefully sliding the two pieces together. Then he took the green plastic bottle, which was labeled ethyl alcohol, and halfway filled the can construction.

"How far along are the potatoes?" he asked, looking at me.

"Haven't even started yet," I said. "What were you doing there?" I asked, fascinated.

"This is a do-it-yourself camping stove. I'm about to cook us dinner on it. The electric stove in the kitchen doesn't work," he said. Nodding toward the tubers in my hands, he added, "Get going. We're hungry."

About half an hour later, we were sitting on the mattresses spooning warmed sauerkraut and boiled potatoes into our mouths. I could almost feel the vitamins spreading through my veins and reviving me. After just one plate, I was stuffed; my stomach had got used to small portions in recent weeks.

"Whoa, I can't eat any more," Verena moaned, putting her dish on the floor. She stretched her back, stroked the little bulge in her belly, and exclaimed, "Hey, look! Food baby!"

Marcus snorted and Hanna giggled. Franca gave a gracious smile. It took me a while to understand.

"We can pack up the rest and take it with us, right?" asked Marcus.

"If you found Tupperware, then yes," Verena replied, burping again.

He looked into the pot and said resignedly, "There's not much left in there. We'll easily eat that for breakfast."

"How much spirit do we have left?" I inquired.

"Half the bottle. Why?"

"We'll need it. Your improvised stoves are amazing. Tomorrow morning we'll take a closer look to see if there's anything else useful here. More food. Or coffee. We can take the cooking pots with us; they're not that heavy."

"Oh yes, coffee!" wailed Verena. "A latte macchiato for breakfast! That'd be great."

Franca said soberly, "It will be pitch dark in half an hour. So get everything done by then. I don't want anyone stumbling around the house in the middle of the night just because they forgot to go to the bathroom."

"Jawohl, Frau Kommandantin!" replied Marcus in the same military tone as before and finishing the rest of the beer.

Once we had obeyed Franca's order and were lying under our blankets in the darkness, my mind began to race.

Question after question tormented me. *What would we find in Berlin if we ever actually reached it? Was anyone actually still living there? Should we come up with an alternative plan?* I dwelt on my thoughts for a long time. But when I realized how irritating the absence of the rocking ship was, I surrendered to fatigue and drifted away.

Marcus woke me up for the final watch, then lay down on his mattress and started snoring before I had even sat down in the chair. I wiped the sleep from my eyes with my fingertips. Outside, a new day was dawning, but it was nowhere near as spectacular as the sunrises over the Mediterranean or the Atlantic. My attention was caught by something else. In the distance, a shadow was rippling slightly upward. I waited until Franca was awake and showed it to her. "Looks like smoke," I said. "Almost certainly human activity."

"Why do you think that?" she asked.

"According to the map, this area has a lot of marshland. It's unlikely something would spontaneously catch fire here."

She looked at the smoke for a while and nodded. "You may be right. And that's the direction we have to go?"

"We can certainly find a way around it if it looks like trouble," I replied. She squeezed my shoulder gently and clicked her tongue, unconvinced, before turning to wake the youngsters. Below us in the farmyard, the first rooster of the day crowed. I left the room and did my morning business in the adjoining bathroom. The toilet wouldn't flush. Spear in hand, I descended the stairs. Only when I had almost reached the first floor did I wonder if we'd barricaded the front door securely enough. I was relieved to see the massive closet that Franca and Marcus had placed there the night before. Then I walked the rooms, taking care to step on as few chicken droppings as possible.

In the living room, I was greeted by a sofa that was both outdated and in bad taste, worn veneer furniture loaded with all kinds of knickknacks, and an oversize flat-screen TV. It saddened me to see the cobwebbed family pictures on the walls. I quickly averted my eyes. There was nothing usable in this room. So I set about searching the kitchen. Although Franca and Marcus had already been here, it wouldn't hurt to check the cabinets again. In the back corner of a wall cupboard, hidden behind some pots, I found a handful of vegetable bouillon cubes and some leftover sugar, which I took.

My attention was caught by a door to my left. Cautiously, I opened it and found a storage room pitifully lit by a tiny bottom-hung window. Spearhead first, I entered and groped automatically for the light switch. I almost cried out as a daddy longlegs flitted across the back of my hand.

When my eyes had adjusted to the light, I turned my attention to the shelves that Franca and Marcus would probably not have been able to investigate as closely in the dusk yesterday. I discovered two kilograms of rice, several cans of fruit, and even two cans of coconut milk behind a box of rotten apples, and a small packet of coffee.

With that, I went back to the room. We cooked porridge and stirred in the fruit. After breakfast, we divided the loot and went on our way.

"Who on earth would come up with such sick shit?" I snapped as I realized what the dozens of posts along the road to Friesack were. We had bypassed a large number of villages and farmsteads by then. Around noon, we sighted a rural railroad station, surrounded by fields as far as the eye could see and connected to the village by a road. The sun had now driven off the clouds.

This was where we saw the stakes. From a distance, they could have been boundary markers with round signs on top, but a closer look made my stomach turn. Hanna's eyes gazed out from under her turban, frightened. Verena held a hand over her mouth. Marcus looked around, his gun drawn. Franca took the safety catch off her HK and cautiously walked out into the field, probably to examine the impaled heads more closely.

"Were they . . . people?" I asked dumbly.

"Yes—before they became zombies" she replied casually.

"Can you tell how long ago it happened?"

"Hmm, certainly several weeks. And from the looks of it, the heads were cut off long after transformation, they were so gray. Verena, where do we go next?" she asked, without taking her eyes off the desiccated heads. Their skin looked leathery and dark, as if it had been tanned in the sun, and their parched lips had pulled back, revealing gray teeth.

Verena pulled herself together and unfolded the map. I saw her eyes flick back and forth as she searched for the shortest route. She pointed to it with her fingertip and said, "Here we are. From now on, we follow the railroad tracks to Berlin." She pointed southeast. "For the next sixty kilometers." She sighed, and asked, "How's our water supply?"

"About three liters each," Marcus replied.

"Hmm, that's not much," Verena said. "But it's not too bad. It looks like we'll be passing ponds and canals every so often."

"We could filter the water and then boil it," Marcus suggested.

Franca nodded. Since we had left the boat, she had held back on instructions and advice. I hadn't had a chance to talk to her in private. So I could only assume that she was deliberately letting the youngsters take the lead. *So they could learn to survive in this new world? Quite possibly.* But obviously she always kept a close eye on our surroundings and acted as a silent corrective, which also provided life insurance for all of us.

Our mood sank because of the unspoken message conveyed by the barbaric treatment of the undead. Impaling severed heads on sticks belonged, in my opinion, to the Middle Ages. Zombies or not, this was not something civilized people did. It bothered me that we would be entering the territory of individuals who were capable of doing such a thing. But we had to keep going. After a half-hour break and following Verena's instructions, we walked in a different direction. I adjusted the length of my stride to the distance between two railroad ties, which was significantly longer than I was used to. The single span, on the other hand, was too short. I kept floundering, and so I had to compromise.

Soon I felt a twinge in my left hip joint, probably due to the enforced hypermobility. At that moment, I hated walking so much! I wanted nothing more than to be back in a car, driving down a country road, covering the few crappy kilometers to our destination. I used the spear, the ends of which I had wrapped in cloth, as a walking stick. But even that made it only slightly easier.

We made good progress on the tracks, but it was impossible to avoid marching through villages. We hurried through them as quietly as possible, always ready for battle. In each of the towns we saw more impaled heads. The stabbing in my hip had evened out into a constant pain level. I got used to it and concentrated on observing our surroundings instead.

The strange column of smoke had dissipated in the early morning hours. Nevertheless, I kept staring at the place I had last seen it. I no longer regretted our lack of contact with other humans. Rather, I welcomed it—in view of the dangers it seemed such meetings would bring.

We walked steadily, kilometer after kilometer. With every step, we became more confident that we would soon reach Berlin unscathed. And then, just after we had passed a farm, my left hip began to give me trouble.

I groaned loudly and leaned on the spear. My companions turned around in surprise.

"Backie? What's wrong?" Verena asked anxiously. Franca put a gentle hand on my shoulder.

"My hip is suddenly hurting," I said. When I shifted my weight to my right knee, the pain subsided. "It's like someone stuck a red-hot needle in me." Memories of the concussion resulting from the rescue at Hotel 23 came flooding back. I shuddered.

Franca looked around. Then she said, "I see a building, there behind the fields."

I looked in the direction she was pointing and saw the silvery gray roof of a hangar or hall, half a mile away.

"Can you walk?" she asked me. "We need to get off the tracks."

The thought of having to straddle that distance made me uneasy. "I need a second," I replied.

"Let's walk straight across the field," Franca replied after a brief pause, supporting me as we headed down.

"Thanks, I can manage on my own again now," I confirmed as we stepped onto the level surface. So they strode on ahead, trampling a path through the dry, waist-high grass for me. But it still took nearly ten minutes for us to reach the hangar. About a hundred meters away from it, Franca made Verena, Hanna, and me stop. She and Marcus ran over to it. Ten more minutes passed before he returned.

"The hangar is empty," he told us. "The roll-up door is locked, but there's a regular door in it that's open. We can stay there for now. Franca's waiting for us."

In the hall, which was the size of half a soccer field, we immediately blocked all entrances and exits with objects lying around between three single-prop planes. The door could be locked from the inside with a heavy bolt. We also found several empty distilled water canisters, yellowing paper cups, and dozens of spooned-out food cans. Someone must have sought refuge here before us.

The worst of the pain in my hip had now faded. Nevertheless, I stretched out on the cool floor. Out of the corner of my eye, I saw the figure of Franca approaching.

"What's going on there?" she asked, nodding to my hip.

"I was walking in a totally dumb way. I kept taking two ties at a time. And going as slowly as possible, so as not to have to keep overtaking you. I noticed hours ago that something wasn't right, but I didn't think much of it."

"Let me see," she asked.

I lifted the sweater and exposed the area.

"Hmm," she commented skeptically, "there's not much to see. The skin is red. Can you move it?"

I tried to lift my left leg and felt a slight twinge. "It's halfway okay," I said. Then I drew circles in the air with my foot. "Now the pain's getting a bit stronger." Gently, I put the leg down.

"I get nothing but trouble from you," she said reprovingly, winking at me. "I'm no expert, but a forced march like ours takes a toll on the joints after more than two months on boats without any real exercise. My guess is that the tendons or even the hip joint itself have become inflamed. A hernia is also a possibility. With me, it's my knees that have been causing problems for hours."

"And now?" asked Marcus, who had joined us.

"Well, there's not much we can do," she said, looking at him over her shoulder. "Except lie still and cool it—that is, if we only had something to cool it . . ."

"Oh," Marcus exclaimed in surprise, setting down the bag. He took out the spirit bottle and said, "Something like this?"

"Yes, exactly," Franca confirmed. She looked around and walked off down the hall. A little later she returned with a piece of yellowing cloth she had found in a toolbox. "Pour it over, please," she asked the boy, who promptly obeyed. Then she knelt and pushed up my sweater.

A pleasant coolness spread out from the location of the cloth. Only now did I realize how hot my hip had been. I breathed a sigh of relief. "I'm sure it'll be fine tomorrow," I speculated.

Franca laughed. "I don't imagine it will. And I don't want to take unnecessary risks so close to the finish line," she told me. "We'll definitely stay here tomorrow. And then we'll see. We've covered more than thirty kilometers today. We can afford to take a break for a day. Especially since there's no deadline for reaching Berlin." She looked at Verena, who was watching us. "Right?" she confirmed with the young German.

"No, there's no hurry. We're as good as there. One more day doesn't matter now," she said. "I'm noticing how exhausting the march is, too."

Franca nodded. "Now that's settled," she called out, "who's going to cook us something to eat?"

"Marcus and I will get some water," Verena interjected hastily before she could be condemned to the stove. "According to the map, there's a river on the other side of the tracks . . . or a canal . . . or something," she hemmed and hawed. Marcus cleared his throat and rummaged intently in his shoulder bag, not looking at us.

Franca gave the two teenagers a piercing look. "Hmm," she said. "Check your weapons before you go out there. Hanna and I will take care of dinner."

"You got it," Verena chirped. She then conferred with her sister, who merely raised an eyebrow. Pointing to Franca and me, she whispered while making hand signals, "You stay here, okay?" Then she unlocked the door and stepped out, Marcus in tow. They carried two canisters each. Franca went after them and slid the bolt back into place. She and Hanna took out the two makeshift stoves and the aluminum cooking pots. A little later, I smelled basmati rice cooking, which made my stomach growl.

An hour after we had eaten dinner and the sun had set, I felt fit enough to get up and take a few steps. I relieved myself in a plastic bin in the far corner, which I could barely make out in the darkness. Then I inspected the doors. They were all heavily barricaded. Calmer, I limped back to my seat, lay down and covered my hip with the wet rag. That was all I could do for the inflammation at the moment.

It had taken Marcus and Verena half an hour to return with full canisters. Just as we had begun to worry about their whereabouts, there had been a knock at the door. We'd let them in and agreed on a new knocking pattern that was easy to remember but not so common as to be used accidentally by strangers.

After dinner, Verena offered to clean the dishes. Outside, the sun had set. Meanwhile, Marcus filtered the water he had brought with him through a microfiber cloth he had discovered, still in its packaging, in the hangar's kitchenette. Verena brought him the rinsed pots and he set about boiling the water in them. Since our ethyl alcohol had almost run out, he used a few deciliters of kerosene that he had taken from a fuel canister. Though it stank terribly, it burned at a higher temperature than the alcohol.

Within an hour, all the water had been boiled and decanted via a long rail that once fixed power cables to the wall, where it could cool down enough without damaging the thin-walled plastic vessels.

"Now we each have five liters. That should be enough for the next two days, right?" inquired Marcus once the task was complete. The shadows on his face danced to the rhythm of the flames in the can stove.

"Maybe three," Franca replied. "One and a half liters a day is realistic, even if we cover long distances. Luckily, it's already turning autumnal. We'll sweat less, and we won't need to drink as much."

"And if we keep making good progress like this, it won't take us much longer," Verena said, adding a fleeting sideways glance at Marcus. "And if we actually stay here tomorrow, we can easily fetch more."

Franca gave them a knowing look. Then she looked around the hangar and said, "This place reminds me of the last time I flew. Have I told you the story?" she asked the youngsters.

"No, not me," Verena replied. Marcus shook his head.

"Do you want to hear it?"

"Sure—but take it slowly, please. So I can translate it for Hanna."

Franca nodded.

And so I heard her story again. Although I already knew it, the story gripped me. Shortly before the end, before I fell asleep, I felt wistful, as if I had been transported back to the comfort of our refuge on the Mediterranean island.

The night was miserable. On the hard floor, with only a piece of cardboard beneath me, I woke up several times and rolled from side to side, looking for a position that would relieve the pressure points. I only had limited success. So I slept in half-hour segments. Tiring of this, I got up around five o'clock and relieved Franca.

"Are you fit?" she asked me.

"Well, not fit, but awake at least."

"How's the hip?"

"If you hadn't asked, I wouldn't even have thought about it. Seems okay," I said, circling my thigh back and forth at waist level.

"Good, I'm going to hit the hay for a bit."

"Sleep well," I replied. "I'll see you later."

She nodded and left. I heard the soft rustle of her blanket as she wrapped herself in it.

Reddish light gradually filtered through the translucent glass in the upper part of the hangar walls. Over time, it gained in strength but lost its warmth. Diffuse outlines and shadows became sharper. Objects in the hall regained their size and shape. Listlessly, I washed two apples and cut them into small cubes. I steamed them in a pot with a little water, with a view to adding them to porridge. Glancing at my sleeping companions,

I wondered how Patrick and Eva and Waltraud and Jens were doing, and I realized how much I was missing them. My attempt to overcome this feeling by preparing breakfast failed miserably, although the smell of freshly brewed coffee did distract me somewhat from my sadness.

Verena whooped as she stretched with her eyes closed, "Awesome, coffee!" She sat up and handed me her cup as if it was the most natural thing in the world. "Thanks, Backie," she chirped in advance.

I handed back the half-full vessel, "You're welcome, kiddo."

"Oh, don't call me kiddo. I'm nineteen already," she complained, sipping her coffee.

I poured oatmeal into the boiling water. "You got it," I placated her, grinning, and stirred the pot. When the porridge was thick enough, I asked her, "Do you want sugar?"

"Sure thing. And not too little, please," she whispered, rubbing the sleep from her eyes. In no time at all, she emptied her cup. "I'll go get rid of the coffee for a minute," she said, mostly to herself, and disappeared behind me into the hangar. I took the porridge off the heat and put on water to boil for tea. Hanna woke up and looked around in wonder. She looked as if she were having one of those moments when you don't recognize the place you've woken up in. Then she saw me and grinned. I put my palms together, brought them to my right ear and tilted my head in the same direction. Hinting at a question, I raised my thumb in the air. She yawned, nodded, and pointed at me. I grimaced and shook my head in displeasure before showing her a chamomile tea bag. She agreed.

I shared the porridge between the galvanized bowls we had taken from the farm. Marcus woke up and a little later, so did Franca.

"I'm ordering a rest day today," she said between bites, continuing the previous day's conversation. "I need to give my knees a rest." She sighed. "And Backup's hips seem to have benefited from the short break."

"We're not getting any younger," I added resignedly.

"No big deal," Verena said. "It's a bit uncomfortable for sleeping, but at least it's dry. And safe."

"Do we still need water?" interjected Marcus abruptly. "I mean, now we have time . . . to . . . because two of the canisters are already almost empty. Verena and I could . . . maybe get some more," he stuttered awkwardly.

Verena blushed slightly and looked over at Franca as if asking for permission. The latter nodded and advised again, "Check your weapons first and take ammunition with you!"

"Don't you think it's enough to just take the guns?" asked Verena. "We'll be right back."

"No," she said emphatically. "Because if I thought that only the guns would do, that's what I'd tell you."

"That's okay," the younger woman replied, slightly piqued. "We'll just take some ammunition with us." She dug out two packs of fifty cartridges for each of the pistols from her pocket. She tossed one of them to Marcus, who caught it one-handed. They then took out their firearms, which as usual they had put on as soon as they got up. Scraping together the last bit of porridge, I watched as they ejected the magazines, checked them, and slid them back into the pistol grips.

"And remember the knock we agreed on," the ex-Carabinieri cautioned.

"What was that again?" asked Marcus. Verena tapped it out for him. Franca and I nodded.

"We'll be back by ten at the latest," said the young woman. I looked at my wristwatch—it was nine o'clock. She turned to her sister, but Hanna had obviously long since grasped what was going on. Her head slightly bowed, she accompanied them out to the gate and locked it again.

When she looked at me, I said slowly so she could read my lips, "Let's clean up here together until they get back." We had nothing else to do. Now that she had to share her sister's attention with a boy, Hanna could use some distraction. She nodded impassively, and I read a certain sadness in her face that she tried unsuccessfully to hide.

Franca helped us collect and wash the breakfast dishes. Afterward, we cleared the papers and blankets away from our sleeping places and packed the rest of the provisions—just in case we had to leave quickly. Franca inspected the weapons while Hanna and I scouted the planes. But we found nothing of interest. All I managed to do was make a faux pas by handing her the headphones when I went to test one of the built-in radios. She didn't take offense, smiling compassionately at me instead, and shaking her head. Bored, we collected the rest of the empty canisters and placed them under one of the planes. Franca, meanwhile, had finished. I saw that Hanna was daydreaming, and I set about sharpening the spear.

If only I'd honed my hearing just as assiduously over the preceding weeks!

I only became aware of the approaching vehicles when they stopped in front of the gate. I froze. Outside, the combustion engines fell silent.

Car doors opened. A voice used to giving orders rang out. German. Nasal pronunciation. The footsteps of unseen people rustled through the parched grass in front of the hangar. I looked over at Franca, who grabbed her HK and silently stood up. I put my whetstone down and looked around for Hanna. She was right by the door. My throat tightened. Whether she had sensed a change in the mood of the room or something else, I didn't know. But she turned and looked at us innocently. A voice called out. I didn't understand a word. Someone pounded on the hangar door from outside. Franca and I jumped and stared at it. Then I saw that Hanna had seen Franca and me glancing over, she and was also looking at the door. Her smile widened. Without noticing our horrified faces, she skipped lightly toward the entrance. Franca called after her and ran. But she didn't get there in time. Hanna unlocked the door. Rays of sunlight slanted in, and the girl shielded her eyes against the light. We saw a silhouette standing outside. Too late, Hanna realized her mistake. She tried to retreat into the hall. But the figure shot one of its hands forward, grabbed her by the hair and pulled her toward him. A blade flashed in his other hand, and a moment later it was being held against Hanna's throat.

Franca and I froze where we were. We looked into the eyes of the bald man who was smiling as he threatened the girl. He barked something at us in German. Franca responded in English, which enraged him. Two seconds later she slowly put her HK on the floor. I threw the spear angrily behind me. Surrendering, we raised our hands.

Verena gripped his hair tighter, panting with desire. She tried to pull his face forcefully toward hers. But Marcus suddenly resisted. What the hell had got into him? Didn't he want it anymore? Only three seconds before he had been literally lusting after her—at least that was the impression she had got. Now, as he grabbed her roughly by the shoulders and threw her backward into the withered grass, she wondered if he liked it a bit harder. She moaned with pleasure. One of the canisters landed on her forearm. "What the fuck bro, are you crazy?" she complained angrily. She felt Marcus's hand on her mouth as he suddenly dropped down next to her. "Mmm," she resisted, but he squeezed tighter and looked urgently into her eyes.

"Quiet," he whispered. Only now did she hear the thrum of the approaching engines.

*Hanna.* Verena went to leap up, but he put all his weight on her. "Calm down, damn it. We can't let them see us!" he whispered in her ear. "And remember the training!"

Three seconds later, she had calmed down a bit and nodded at him. He removed his hand. The vehicles came closer. Verena wriggled free of him and turned onto her stomach. They drew, unsheathed, and loaded their weapons in one fluid motion. The blood was pounding in her ears, in time with her hammering heart. Through the low bushes and across the grass, she peered toward the hangar, barely fifty yards away. Four cars pulled up in front of the door. Several people got out of each car. Bald, their necks tattooed. Bomber jackets, army fatigues, and combat boots. She couldn't see many firearms, but they had baseball bats, knives, and machetes. The spray-painted graffiti on the car chassis caught her eye. She saw the number eighty-eight and made out runes and what looked like a double lightning bolt symbol, as well as black, red, and white stripes and swastikas. A broad-shouldered skinhead leaned on the roof of his car. Looking around, he called out, "I told you guys it was going to be warm today, huh? You there," he addressed the last car in the line, "go around the back. The three of us will go in. Everyone else, make sure the zombies don't bite our asses off." Without waiting for a response, he ran toward the hangar. A blade flashed in his hand. Verena held her breath. When he thundered his meaty fist against the door, she almost breathed a sigh of relief. It was not the agreed knock. But barely five heartbeats later, the door opened. Hanna appeared. The girl flinched suddenly, and the bald man reacted with lightning speed, grabbing her hair before pulling her into a rough embrace.

Marcus's hand pushed Verena back to the ground. "Stay down, for fuck's sake! There are too many of them," he warned.

She whimpered. Tears of fear ran down her face. Then she heard the bald man shout in the broadest of Berlin dialects, "What kind of little birdie have we here?" His voice dripped with sadistic exhilaration. "No, no English. You're in Germany now, darlin'. One false move, and I'll slit the little girl's throat. Understand?" He turned his head slightly over his shoulder and called out, "Boys, get these two beauties out of here. But be careful, they're armed. Don't let them give you any trouble." Keeping his arms around Hanna, he took a few steps back. Four bald men went past him, stepping over the threshold into the hall. A few moments later, Franca and Backup stumbled out. Verena watched in horror as one of the men took cable ties and tied the hands of all three in front of them.

Meanwhile, the group that had circled the hangar had returned. "Going to have another Zomblympics?" one of them asked when he spotted the prisoners.

"What kind of dumb question is that?" he answered. "Of course we're having another Zomblympics—first thing tomorrow!" They both let out a loud laugh, and the other bald heads joined in. "You pack them up and get going. We'll check out the hangar. We'll be right behind you," he added. They shoved Franca and Backup roughly, stuffing them into a different car trunk. Hanna was installed next to a bald man in the back seat, who grinned at her lecherously.

Verena clenched the pistol grip so tightly that her knuckles went white.

"Then we'll see you in Falkensee in a bit, right?" shouted one of them.

"Yes," confirmed the leader. "But let's be clear: No one touches that bitch!"

"You got it, you horny goat," came the reply and the laughter broke out again. Two engines started up. The vehicles maneuvered onto the hangar forecourt before moving off down the dusty landing strip. A couple of the bald heads stationed themselves by the hangar entrance. The rest set about inspecting it.

*Hanna! Hanna! HANNA!* Verena's head was screaming. They had been so close to the finish line. She had lost her sister after they had sailed around almost the entire continent and crossed half the Republic! Little Hanna, who had been entrusted to her care. And she had failed to protect her. What would her parents say if she came home alone?

Only the steady pressure of Marcus's hand on her shoulder kept her from jumping up and rushing to Hanna's aid. Crying, she watched as the looters brought out their food and weapons and loaded them into the cars before getting in themselves and driving away.

"Do you still have the map?" asked Marcus, removing his hand.

"Yes," Verena said, reaching into her back pocket and handing it to him.

"Is Falkensee anywhere nearby?" he inquired, unfolding the map.

Verena noticed that he'd changed. The sexual tension between them had vanished. He was giving off a different energy that she couldn't immediately place.

Through her tears, she pointed to the map. "That's Falkensee. And we're about here."

"How far is it—twenty, twenty-five kilometers?"

"Yes," she replied. "Why do you ask? What are you up to?"

Marcus looked at her in surprise. "We're saving our people. Getting your sister out of there. What did you think?"

Verena was now sobbing uncontrollably. He took her in his arms and said, "Hey, everything will be all right, but I need your help. Pull yourself together. I can't do it on my own."

She nodded and wiped away her tears. "We were so close to Berlin—"

"All is not yet lost," he cut in. "And we know where they took them. Now let's have a quick look around the hangar to see if those fuckers missed anything. And then we'll be on our way."

"Okay," she said, taking a deep breath. Cautiously, they crept toward the hall; there was no guarantee the Nazis wouldn't return. Verena spotted Hanna's scarf hanging from the door of a plane. She took it and wrapped it around her neck.

"Hmm. The bastards were thorough. Our weapons are all we have left," Marcus noted.

"They weren't quite that thorough," Verena replied, picking up Backup's spear. "They missed this."

Marcus looked into her eyes. At that moment, she realized what had seemed so surprising about him. His determination. His unbending will to save his companions. To save Hanna. To risk his own life in the process. How was it possible that a young man barely two years older than herself suddenly possessed such maturity? Or was it inevitable that in this kind of situation you'd start behaving like this sooner or later?

And who was it that had suddenly put these thoughts in her head? Had she changed, too? Undoubtedly, she realized. But what was she willing to do to survive? Marcus's fearlessness was infectious. Hope flared up in her. She went up to him, pressed a kiss to his lips, and said, "Let's do it!"

At a quarter past ten they were off, the blade of Backup's spear wrapped in scraps of cloth. They walked along the tracks as fast as they could, taking three ties at a time. Three and a half hours later and after a short rest on the western outskirts of Nauen, they were halfway to Falkensee.

They saw more and more impaled zombie heads pointing the way, like a dark reminder. In Brieselang, the next village, three wandering corpses saw them and gave chase. The undead moved ponderously and had difficulty keeping up with them, but it was clear they were unlikely to give up. Besides, it was possible the screeching would attract more of their kind.

Verena finished off two of them with well-aimed shots to the head. Marcus used the spear to eliminate the third. Then they ran on. Around five in the afternoon, they saw the first houses of Falkensee.

"Didn't Backup mention a column of smoke to Franca yesterday?" Verena jerked her chin to the southeast, where a thick gray cloud of smoke had appeared, rising into the sky. She had to keep fighting her fear for Hanna's safety. But being on the move, being constantly on the alert, and not least, being with Marcus, helped her overcome it.

"Do you think it's something to do with the baldies?" asked Marcus.

"It's in the right direction," she replied. "It could well be them because that's where Falkensee is. And my gut's telling me they're the ones behind the impaled heads as well."

"Hmm, yes, it looks like they could be. I suggest we find a place to hide and don't move until it gets dark," Marcus said.

"I really need a drink," she replied.

He nodded. "Let's get off the tracks." They stepped away from the rails, crouched down, and ran through a withered thicket, jumped over a ditch, and arrived in Finkenkrug, a district in the west of Falkensee. Ivy and other creepers had overgrown the paths in many places, and Verena and Marcus had to be careful not to trip over them. The streets, yards, and vehicles were empty and deserted. They went into the first house they found whose front door was open, pulling the door shut behind them.

Weapons at the ready, they checked the rooms, but the building, which had obviously been renovated shortly before the disaster, had long since been looted and abandoned. The empty kitchen cupboards stood wide open. Nothing came out when Verena turned on the faucet. But there was water in the toilet cistern. The ceramic vessel was almost airtight and had remained half full. Greedily, they drank from the toothbrush cup, dipping it in again and again until the container was empty. Seconds later, sweat shot from their pores as their bodies absorbed the water.

Verena sank weakly onto the toilet seat. Marcus sat down opposite her on the edge of the bathtub. "Just like back in Hotel 23," he said, smiling.

"Just don't remind me." She sighed. "At least Hanna was still with us then."

"Shall we rest first?" he suggested.

She nodded. Exhaustion and low spirits made themselves felt as the adrenaline in her body dissipated. "Can you leave me alone for a minute? I need to . . ." she said with a nod toward the toilet bowl.

Marcus blushed, well-mannered as he was. "Um, sure. I'll check the rooms while you wait," he stammered and disappeared from the bathroom. Verena was too exhausted to respond. She lifted the lid, relieved herself, and used some toilet paper from the roll under the window to her left. It could no longer be flushed.

She then stood up, buttoned her pants, and looked through the window—straight into the faces of two children who were watching her from a room in the neighboring house. She froze. The taller of the two boys moved his lips. Barely three seconds later, a skinny female figure with a baby in her arms appeared behind them. Her jaw dropped. Verena swallowed, raised her right hand uncertainly, and waved.

The youngsters grinned and waved back. The emaciated woman put her hand protectively on the shoulder of the middle child and almost looked as if she wanted to turn and flee. But then she thought better of it—and waved, too.

"Quick, come in," said the woman, who was in her forties and had her hands full with her offspring. She closed the door quietly and introduced herself as Kirstin.

"Thank you for letting us in," Verena said, noting how relieved her host seemed as she and Marcus turned their attention to the boys.

The children bombarded them with questions: "What are your names? Where are you from? Where are you going? What are you doing here?"

They were happy to reply, formulating answers that would not traumatize the kids and that would give Kirstin a picture of their journey so far.

"You traveled that far?" asked seven-year-old Finn, visibly amazed.

"Yes," Marcus replied theatrically, gesturing with his hands, "first across the sea, then up a river. And then we walked for days."

"Just the two of you?"

"We were with some friends, but they were . . . captured by bad people."

"Like the people who took away my dad?" the boy said. Verena and Marcus pricked up their ears. Kirstin stiffened, looking at them both questioningly.

"The weird men with no hair?" inquired Verena tensely.

The boys' mother nodded, and Marcus added, "We heard they were going to Falkensee. That's here, isn't it?"

Kirstin stiffened, frowning. "Who said that?" she asked. Marcus told her the story of the morning.

She nodded. "They're probably the same ones who kidnapped Dominic. There's only this one gang here," she continued. "They've been terrorizing the area since before the outbreak."

"Do you know where they're holding the prisoners?" asked Marcus.

"They've cleared an area on the former sports field. Dominic and a handful of others work for them like slaves. Tilling the ground, watering the fields, weeding. Slaughtering animals and cooking for them. They're using the clubhouse as a kind of prison." She fell silent and looked at the wide eyes of her two older boys.

"How long is it since your husband was taken?" asked Marcus.

"A good three months," she replied.

"Do you know how we can get to the sports field? Without being seen?" Verena asked.

Kirstin thought quickly. "It's just under three kilometers to the facility. Just follow the tracks in the direction of Berlin."

"Have they posted guards or put up fences?" asked Verena.

"I assume they have guard posts. But I don't know for sure. The whole sports field always has been surrounded by a high fence. There's just one building on it—that's where the prisoners must be."

The children had obviously become bored with the adults' conversation. They retreated to a corner of the living room to play with their miniature cars.

Meanwhile, Kirstin was now nursing the smallest one, who was gurgling contentedly.

"Hmm," Marcus said, "yesterday we saw what we thought was smoke rising into the sky not far from here. And hundreds of impaled corpse heads. Is there a connection between the two? Do you know anything about it?"

Kirstin nodded and took a deep breath before saying, "They've come up with some sick games. I guess they used to think it was fun to chase the zombies and cut their heads off. Now they have a big party with bonfires when they capture someone. That might have been the column of smoke you saw. They call it the Zomblympics."

"We heard them talking about that, too. What's is it?"

Kirstin snorted. "They make someone run away from the undead on the cinder track and bet on which zombie will get the victim first."

"Holy shit," Verena said in horror.

"Not good," Marcus mused aloud. "How many are there, anyway? We counted twelve this morning."

"There shouldn't be more than twenty or twenty-five. I haven't seen them in a long time because I'm in hiding with the kids."

Verena swallowed. "How did you even survive this long?" she asked.

Kirstin sighed. "Now that it's fall, we're getting more and more fruits and vegetables from the gardens. But in the summer, we had to live on what we could steal from the houses."

"I wouldn't call it stealing," Marcus said. "After all, there's no one left to claim anything."

"Didn't the skinheads raid the town for food?" asked Verena.

"Well, not themselves. That would have been too exhausting for them. They blackmailed and threatened people now and then, to get them to do it for them. But there were vast numbers of undead here to begin with, so they weren't very successful."

"Son of a bitch," Verena said, shaking her head. "And now? Are there any zombies around?"

"Hardly any. That's the only good thing these bozos have managed to achieve," Kirstin reported. "They keep the village clean. And if any do stray here, they torture and kill them for fun. Or even abuse them at the Zomblympics."

Marcus shook his head. "Do you have a little something we could eat?" he finally asked.

"Sure. Can you guys watch the boys for a minute? I'll put something together."

"Um, sure," Verena said in surprise.

Handing her the baby, Kirstin called out to the older children, "Finn, Leonas, stay here in the living room with Marcus and Verena. I'm making us something to eat." The two looked up briefly, nodded, and immediately returned to their game. "I'll be in the kitchen," their mother said and went out.

And out of the blue, they found themselves back in civilization, in normality, where you could leave your children with trustworthy young people, even if you'd only just met them. Verena couldn't help feeling that Kirstin was pleased to be able to be alone for once instead of having to look after the children.

"What do we do now?" asked Marcus.

She reached out and put her free hand on his.

"Like you said this morning: We have to think about training. Scout, confuse, strike!"

Marcus intertwined his fingers with hers and squeezed them tightly. She had the impression that her confidence did him good.

They ate dinner together by the light of a candle. Kirstin had placed two large plates on the table with sliced juicy apples and small, hard pears, and raw zucchini slices. She held back while the boys ate, Verena noted.

She and Marcus also let the youngsters eat their fill before they gorged themselves in turn. After everyone had eaten around two whole fruits, they were halfway full.

"I'm going to put the kids down now," Kirstin said. "It's their bedtime."

Leonas and Finn grumbled, not at all happy about their mother's plan.

"Boys, we'll play with you again in the morning, but only if you go to bed now," Verena replied. Her little trick actually seemed to work because they stopped whining. They headed upstairs with somber expressions. "We're going to bed soon, too," Verena called after them.

"When do you want to leave?" asked Kirstin quietly.

"Around three in the morning," Marcus replied. "That way we'll have enough time to scout the area before sunrise, and maybe we can make a rescue attempt at dawn. If all goes well, we'll be back for breakfast. With guests!"

Kirstin teared up. Verena stood and hugged the trembling woman.

"Don't worry. We learned from the best how to pull off something like this. We were once rescued from a similar situation by them ourselves."

"Absolutely," Marcus agreed. "And we can easily deal with those bald wieners."

"Never underestimate the dark side," Kirstin cautioned.

"Waltraud would have said that, too," Verena replied, suddenly seized by melancholy.

Shortly after three, they stepped out into the night. There was total darkness. The sky was cloudy, and it was drizzling. "Best weather for this kind of thing," Marcus said, rechecking the two small fruit knives tucked into his socks. The sharp, slightly inward-curving blades would be damn effective in close combat. They had put the spare ammunition for their pistols into some children's socks they had found lying around the house. That way they jangled less when they walked. And it meant they always had at hand the exact number of cartridges they needed to quickly fill an empty magazine.

Their pockets also contained a small flashlight and some rusty combination pliers, in case they had to cut their way through any fences.

Verena carried the spear. "Let's get going then, shall we?" she asked.

"We're getting our people out of there right now," he confirmed, hugging her. She felt his lips on hers. They kissed passionately, broke apart, and ran off. The rain became heavier. By the time they were about halfway there, they were soaked to the skin.

But since they weren't out for a walk, they paid it no heed. Even the map was soaked through by now. If everything went smoothly tonight, they wouldn't need it anyway. After following the tracks for close to an hour—they couldn't possibly maintain the previous day's pace in this visibility—they came upon the high grille that had once prevented soccer balls from flying out into the surrounding area. "We're here," Verena said softly, straining to make out anything beyond it.

"Too high to climb," Marcus whispered back.

"And too dangerous, in the rain," Verena agreed, marching on. "Let's follow the fence around to the left." The rain was pelting down and didn't look like it was going to stop anytime soon. The grille soon gave way to a six-foot-high chain-link fence.

"That light up ahead will be the clubhouse," she noted. She spotted a figure in front of the building. "Do you also see the guard?" she asked in a whisper.

"Guard? Where?" said Marcus in amazement.

"To the left of the entrance, under the canopy, half in the shadow, there's one."

"Shit, I wouldn't have seen that one if you hadn't said. Um, what's that on the floor in front of him?"

"Oh, fuck!" cursed Verena as she spotted a large mound of fur at the skinhead's feet. "What do we do now?"

"At least it hasn't scented us yet. It's the rain, I guess," Marcus speculated. "Let me think for a minute," he said. "Hmm," he continued a moment later, "what do you think of this idea?"

After discussing it in detail, they were sure their plan would work. As quietly as possible, they used the pliers to cut a chest-high opening in the fence and bent the wire mesh back. Verena crawled through and took up position thirty yards to the side of it in a ditch, while Marcus moved backward to attract the attention of the guard dog. At first, Verena could hardly hear him. But her hearing wasn't as good as the dog's, she reasoned. When she heard a soft, high-pitched sound, however, the dog also looked over, presumably to the place it thought the sound had come from. Given the noise of the rain, it was likely the skinhead would neither hear it nor identify it. But the dog's curiosity was piqued, which was the most important part of their plan. He rose to his feet. His silhouette revealed him to be a German shepherd. On stiff legs, he peered through the darkness to where Marcus was lurking. *Come on, move it, you lazy bastard*, Verena thought, eyeing the human figure in the bomber jacket.

Secretly, she cursed the weather that kept the man from leaving the shelter. But the dog was now tugging at the leash. Marcus whistled again. Abruptly, the German shepherd lunged forward. At first, she found it strange that he had not even barked. But as soon as the meaning of this became clear to her, the blood froze in her veins. This was no guard dog, whose mere presence was meant to keep uninvited guests away. No, this beast was probably trained to hurt people without warning, really hurt them. *Shit*—it flashed through her mind—*what have we gotten ourselves into here?* But it was too late to warn Marcus. The guard reached into his back pocket and pulled out a flashlight. The beam of light slid over Verena and illuminated the ground just outside the fence. Thousands of raindrops fell in bright lines in the cone of light. But they had chosen the spot behind the compost pile wisely. From the guard's position, the opening would not have been visible even in broad daylight.

The guard shouted angrily at the dog. But with the next whistle, the dog tugged savagely at the leash, throwing the skinhead off balance. The leash slipped from his fingers. The guard dog sprinted into the darkness. The man cursed loudly and stumbled after him, jerking the beam of light ahead of him in all directions. Only now did Verena see the HK Franca had never wanted to part with, dangling from his shoulder. She shuddered, tensed all her muscles, and pressed her face into the mud. The dog approached. She hoped fervently that the rain had washed away enough of her scent. The animal lumbered through the puddles just a few feet away from her. Again, a whistle sounded. The German shepherd ran off. Seconds later, the fence swished as he squeezed through the opening. From now on, Marcus was on his own. Verena let out a tense breath and focused on the task ahead of her.

"Rocky, you idiot!" An enraged voice rang out from somewhere between her and the chain-link fence. "Where are you? Get back here right now! Here, Rocky!"

She could see the guard's outline against the beam of light. Before any doubt could creep in, she reminded herself that this was a member of the group that had kidnapped her sister and intended to do God knows what to her. Her need to protect ignited. Verena would not let anything happen to Hanna. Anger coursed through her. She scrambled to her feet from the slippery ground. Mud dripped from her face. She ran through the pelting rain at the cursing silhouette. She and Marcus had decided it was too dangerous to shoot. That would be bound to alert the rest of the gang. And they wanted to avoid that at all costs. Five steps away, she slid the shaft of the spear past her left hip, the blade slightly raised. Nine steps later, she thrust with all her might without slowing down. But a split second before the spearhead could break through his skin, the skinhead moved. Had he heard her coming, despite the rain? Or had she hesitated at the crucial moment? Verena merely succeeded in cutting a long, harmless slice through his jacket before crashing unchecked against his back, knocking him off his feet. In flight, the guard emitted a sound of surprise. Out of the corner of her eye, Verena saw the HK fly off in a high arc. Then they both crashed headlong to the ground.

The impact drove the air from her lungs. She rolled, as Backup had taught her, and used the momentum to get to her feet immediately. She looked around. The skinhead, who had dropped his flashlight, was nowhere to be seen. Fear flooded through her. Where was he? Did he have any other weapons? She waved the spearhead in a semicircle. A tremendous blow from a fist caught her on the cheekbone, sending her back into the mud. Her hands involuntarily released the shaft. Her shoulder broke her fall, painfully. Verena groaned in a daze, tried to get up, and saw the skinhead straddling her. His hands found her neck and squeezed. Panicking, she thrashed, scratched, and squirmed beneath him, hoping to shake him off. But it was no use. As if through a veil, she saw his outline.

Dimly, she heard him rail, "How did you get in here, you little bitch?" The back of her head hit the earth with full force. The fact that the ground was soaked by the rain kept her from losing consciousness completely. Nevertheless, she saw stars. Something scratched her ankle as she pressed her feet into the ground. *The fruit knife*, she remembered! Verena let go of his wrists, fumbled in panic at the cuff of her socks, and caught ahold of the plastic handle. With a desperate jerk, she plunged the blade into the soft tissue under the man's chin—and tore at it. The pressure around her neck eased abruptly. A second later, her face was doused in a warm, metallic-tasting liquid. Gasping for breath, she choked on the torrent of blood pouring from the skinhead's carotid artery.

The rain made it difficult for Marcus to whistle. He had taken up position on the other side of the ditch separating the sports facility from the estate. Water kept flowing down his upper lip no matter how often he wiped his hand across it. Only when he formed a small canopy below his nose with his right hand did he manage better. At first, he whistled so softly that he could hardly hear it himself—and waited. Nothing happened. He whistled a little louder and listened to the night again. Marcus increased the volume until he saw movement where he thought the guard was. He could only vaguely identify the light coming from the small lamp at the clubhouse. He whistled again, at the same volume. The guard under the canopy moved around more. Soon, he heard shouts—and whistled again. Holding his breath, he listened to the darkness. There was a rustling at the fence. Marcus jumped up and ran through deserted gardens. He had memorized the route before Verena had gone to the other side of the fence. Every few yards, he turned on the pale light of his flashlight so he wouldn't stumble. Behind him, he heard the sound of rapidly approaching paws. The dog was fast as hell. Faster than he would have liked. Still, he reached the front door of the house he had chosen for his plan before the quadruped did. Headlong, he rushed inside. The German shepherd slid on the slippery tiles in the hallway. Marcus, who had barely a four-meter head start, sprinted through the living room and jumped out onto the terrace. At the last moment, he pushed the glass door shut behind him. The guard dog slammed into it at full speed. Marcus started, collected himself, and ran back toward the front door. He hoped the dog was not as intelligent as he feared it was.

When he reached the entrance, he grabbed the doorknob and pulled on it, panic-stricken. He heard the animal's paws racing through the hallway. The door closed a second before the dog could spring at him. Relieved, he dropped to the ground, leaning his head against the wall of the house, panting. The German shepherd scrabbled frantically at the other side of the door. Marcus groped for his pistol and the concealed knives, found everything where it should be, struggled to his feet, and hurried back to the sports field. From a distance, he saw the beam of a flashlight, half-submerged in a puddle, shining into the night. A few meters away, he spotted two scuffling figures and rushed toward the fence. Without pausing, he slid through the opening on his knees. In the process, his right shoulder caught on the cut wire; he lost his balance and slapped the mud. It took what felt like an eternity to free himself. When he finally hurried past the compost heap, he found Verena kneeling over a corpse.

"Are you okay?" Verena heard Marcus's voice close to her ear. Had he whispered? Or was she just hard of hearing? All she knew for sure was that he had turned off the flashlight so they wouldn't attract attention. She was still spitting, afraid she might have swallowed some of the blood. But at least she was breathing again.

"Yeah, I'm fine," she groaned hoarsely, massaging her throat.

"Look what I found," he said, holding the mud-smeared HK under her nose.

"Awesome! Franca will promote you for this. Did you search the guard?" Despite whispering, it hurt like hell to speak.

"Sure. He had a bunch of keys on him. I guess they're the keys to the clubhouse. And there are two car keys. But I couldn't find any trace of the vehicles."

"Good news for once," she said. "I guess I'm not as skilled in hand-to-hand combat as Backup. You'd better take the spear," she suggested.

"You got it," Marcus replied, handing her the HK. "Now let's get our people as fast as we can and get out of here."

Verena felt his hand on her forearm. With a jerk, she got to her feet. The initial dizziness passed quickly. "Okay, go," she whispered.

A few moments later, they were standing at the entrance to the clubhouse. The bunch of keys jingled as Marcus searched for the right key.

On the third try, the door opened. They stepped inside. He turned on the flashlight for a few seconds, shielding the beam with his hand. Two dark corridors branched off to either side. The shadows created by the light indicated where the doors were. Marcus pointed to the right. Verena nodded, took a tighter grip on the HK, and released the safety. Water dripped from the tip of her nose. Her feet squeaked in her soaked shoes as she walked toward the first door.

Ahead of her, Marcus was fiddling with the keyhole. With a click, the lock opened. He turned on the flashlight and shone it into the room. On the floor and on the changing room benches, she saw emaciated figures gazing fearfully into the blinding light. They were all men, dressed in rags. They smelled of body odor and despair.

Gently, Verena put a hand on the light Marcus was holding and directed it to the ground. She saw relief on the prisoners' faces as soon as they realized they weren't part of the skinhead gang.

"Dominic," she called softly. "Is there a Dominic here?" Muffled murmurs came in response. "Dominic?" she asked again, a little louder this time. "Kirstin sent us." Someone stirred in the corner to her right.

A bearded man hesitantly raised his hand. "I . . . am Dominic."

"Are you Kirstin's husband?"

"Yes, I am."

"How many children do you have and what are their names?"

"Three," the potential Dominic replied and gave her the names. Verena couldn't help but grin. "We're here to get you out," she said. Then she looked across the room and added, "We're getting you all out of here. Are there any others being held captive?"

Dominic replied, "Yes, the clubhouse is full of prisoners. Just yesterday they brought in a handful of new ones."

"Do you know where they are?" asked Verena as if electrified.

"Can't say for sure. Probably in one of the other locker rooms," Dominic guessed. Several of his fellow sufferers nodded.

"What do we do now?" Verena turned quietly to Marcus.

He was silent for a moment and then called into the room, "Please stay here until we check the other locker rooms. We'll be right back." He took her by the arm and led her to the nearest door. In each locker room they were greeted by more or less the same sight, but there was no sign of Hanna, Franca, or Backup. With each successive room, Verena's hope of finding her sister unharmed diminished.

Marcus opened the final door. Holding the HK in front of her, Verena stepped inside, close to tears. She had barely taken two steps when the door slammed into her shoulder and the gun was taken from her. For the second time in half an hour, she found herself disarmed and lying on the floor. Dazed, she looked up and spotted Franca's silhouette pointing the muzzle of the automatic weapon at her face.

"What did I teach you about entering an unsecured room?" she hissed furiously.

"Verena! Marcus! Boy, am I glad to see you. We've been here twenty minutes already," said Backup, whose face was contorted into a broad grin.

"Is the spirit of Waltraud walking around here somewhere?" Marcus replied exuberantly. Leaping past him, Hanna threw herself into her sister's arms as soon as she had sat up. "Hey, Backie, catch!" Marcus shouted, tossing the spear to Backup.

"This toothpick will probably follow me to the grave. Thank you!" Backup replied, kissing the shaft.

"Then we're even, I'd say," Marcus speculated.

"That we are, kid." Backup laughed. Franca nodded appreciatively.

"What about the rest of the skinheads?" asked Verena.

"They're probably sleeping it off. One unit came back last night having looted a liquor store," the Italian replied, shaking her head. "Apparently, they hadn't got hammered in a long time. They made up for it in a big way last night. Only two of them had the sense to stay sober. But those two didn't seem to be able to cope on their own. So they brought us straight here while the others went mad at the feast."

"We've taken care of at least one of them," Marcus said.

"And how come you're free? Surely they didn't take your shackles off of their own accord?" Verena wondered.

Backup replied with a smile. "Franca asked me to pull her cable tie as tight as possible. Then she slammed her wrists down on one knee as hard as she could. That broke apart the clasp of the plastic cuff. Hanna and I copied her. Luckily, they were cheap hardware store cable ties," Backup explained, then asked irritably, "You guys heard how they captured us?"

Verena nodded, "We were lying in the grass barely a stone's throw away," she said meekly.

"I see," Backup said meaningfully.

"Good thing you didn't do anything rash," Franca interjected. "And now let's get out of here!"

"We still have to release the others. And take Dominic home," Verena said.

Franca glared at her. "Who the hell is Dominic?"

"Long story," Verena replied. "I'll tell you later. Just come along."

Within a minute, all the occupants were gathered in the vestibule. She heard Marcus ask, "Which one of you knows where the vehicles are?"

"Sometimes they're parked in the front of the clubhouse," someone reported. "But most of the time, they leave them on the street in front of the house where they're living."

"Is that far from here?" asked Marcus.

"No, but if you don't know the area, you'll have a hard time finding it."

"Dominic can help. What about you guys; are you going to be okay?"

"Don't worry about us," someone said in the darkness. "We'll be fine."

"What do you want to do?" inquired Marcus.

"We've got some unfinished business. Some of us haven't seen our families in months and may have lost them forever while they kept us penned up like cattle. They'll have to pay for that."

"I can understand that. But you're all unarmed, and they . . ."

"We gather they were drinking all last night," another voice interrupted him. "From experience, they'll be pretty much unresponsive until tomorrow afternoon."

"Much less prepared for an attack," Dominic said.

"Yes, except for one," Marcus warned.

"We can take care of him," someone in the darkness chimed in. "We know where the shed with the garden tools is. So don't worry about it. By freeing us, you've already achieved much more than we dared hope for in the last few months."

"What's going on, Marcus?" asked Franca impatiently. "What's taking so long?" In three terse sentences, he translated the conversation to her. "Yes, then let them do it that way," she urged, "but we have to get out of here as fast as possible!"

"It's okay," he placated her before turning to the former inmates, "Are you all ready?" Murmurs of agreement rang out. Verena hugged Hanna as tightly as she could. Marcus opened the door. With the elegance of a cat and her HK at the ready, Franca stepped out.

Seconds later, through the patter of the rain, she whispered, "The coast is clear. Come on." As quickly and quietly as they could, they strode out into the twilight.

In the clubhouse parking lot, we found a car, which we drove through an underpass and then back via Finkenstraße to Kirstin and the children. Marcus had started it and given the remaining keys to the former captives planning to get rid of the Nazi gang.

Those who were prepared to stay would go on as before and try their luck at the sports field. Others would go in search of their families—or a whole new life.

Dominic guided us to Falkensee train station. From there it was easy to find the house where his family was hiding.

The reunion was tearful, and even Franca brought herself to leave them alone for a whole hour. Afterward, as we sat together in the living room, Dominic told us that one of the prisoners, who had died a few days before, had been spreading rumors about a functioning enclave in the capital. They would have a hard time surviving out here, he said, and asked us to take him and his family with us. We did not have to deliberate for long about whether to take them, but rather whether it was possible, because we had only one vehicle at our disposal.

So when the sun had barely risen and the rain had stopped, the ten of us squeezed in. Marcus sat at the steering wheel. Franca shared the passenger seat with Hanna. Dominic and Kirstin sat between Verena and me on the back seat, with the kids on our laps. They didn't have much to bring with them. A pillowcase full of toys, a pair of children's shoes that we had put in the trunk, and that was all.

"I hope we don't come across a police checkpoint," Marcus said anxiously. "I don't even have my driver's license with me."

"Do you mean because the car is so full?" interjected Dominic. "Years ago, I visited a childhood friend in the Balkans. It's quite usual to travel like this there."

We chugged off through the clear morning air toward the capital. After a few minutes, we reached a multilane federal highway that ran straight ahead for kilometers.

We were only twenty kilometers from the city center. Moreover, Verena said that if we just followed the road, we would pass very close by the Charité university hospital.

The children soon fell asleep again. I envied them; I would all too gladly have escaped my worry about reaching the end of our journey alive for a while.

At first, we made good progress. There were no barricades and hardly any abandoned vehicles on the road. However, the outbound lane was chaotic. Countless vehicles of all types, many of them burned out, were blocking the lane. We regularly saw corpses in them. Some of them were moving. But even our side of the highway became more impassable the closer we got to the city center. Soon it was taking us minutes to advance just a hundred meters. But leaving the safety of the vehicle and walking was not an option. So Marcus searched tirelessly for ways to get us through. The situation eased slightly once we reached the eerily empty Charlottenburg district, which was indicated by a green sign with yellow lettering.

"We're here," Verena whispered. In front of me I saw Hanna, who looked like she was sitting on hot coals. She was staring around, wide-eyed. The rest of us hardly dared breathe. Imposing Art Nouveau buildings towered left and right, separated by a fifty-meter multilane boulevard. At walking pace, we slid toward the Victory Column, which was a mere line in the distance. We passed the Deutsche Oper, whose glass front was demolished. Two hundred meters past a huge traffic circle, Marcus stopped beneath a railroad bridge and drummed his fingers on the steering wheel.

A park stretched out in front of us. Birds—the first I had seen in weeks—swooped in the air from the trees, which had yellow and red leaves.

"What's wrong?" asked Franca. "Why have you stopped?"

"I can't say. Just a feeling," Marcus replied without taking his eyes off the road. "It's like we're being watched."

"We have been since we arrived in the city," she said. "They can't be the undead. They would have attacked us by now."

"And what's stopping the others?"

"Our national emblems, perhaps?" the Italian said with a touch of gallows humor, pointing to the symbols on the hood.

"Oh shit," Verena snapped. "I totally forgot about those."

Almost panicked, she looked around, pushed open the door, and jumped out.

"What are you doing?" Franca called after her. Verena walked around the vehicle, opened the trunk, and returned a few seconds later with the empty pillowcase.

"Backie, pass me the spear, please," she demanded.

"Backie?" said Franca, looking over her shoulder in my direction. "Is that a thing now?"

I merely shrugged my shoulders and pushed the weapon toward Verena.

She knotted two corners of the pillowcase to the shaft and held it out the window. "What's that supposed to be?" I asked.

"White flag!" she replied.

"What do you want with that?"

"Trust me, you don't want to drive through Berlin in a vehicle covered in swastikas. Apocalypse or no."

But the fabric's a little yellow, I wanted to say, but Marcus was already moving ahead in second gear. At walking speed and keeping the engine as quiet as possible, we approached the Victory Column. The sinister tension in the air increased with every meter. The streets branching off from the traffic circle were all blocked.

Marcus soon switched to the sidewalk. Strangely enough, we found a path there, as if someone had cleared it with a snowplow. Countless cars were piled up to the left and right. Franca and Verena held their firearms in their hands, safeties off. Marcus had his Glock in his lap. "Let's see what it's like when we have to continue on foot," he said worriedly.

Kirstin, Dominic, and I woke the children—in case we had to escape quickly. Five hundred meters ahead of us, I spied the Brandenburg Gate. Then suddenly zombies burst out of the bushes, barely fifteen meters away.

It wasn't that we weren't expecting them. But the coordination and speed of the attack surprised us more than the assault from the bridge in Hamburg. Within three seconds, they were upon us. Gray fists pounded on the bodywork. Colorless heads banged against the windows in blind rage. Marcus stepped on the gas and tried to zigzag the car out of danger. Verena almost lost the spear when the pillowcase was torn off.

But our driver lurched on, undeterred. The children were screaming and crying. A few seconds later, we left the undead several meters behind us. The distance grew steadily, but our escape came to a halt at the Brandenburg Gate. There was no way through for the car. Abandoned vehicles and a muddle of barriers were everywhere.

Franca tore open the door and fired a short volley over the roof. I waited for the next gap, jumped out and hurried around the car. Together with Verena, I helped Kirstin and Dominic get the children out. Marcus joined us from the other side and fired at the undead, who were within thirty meters of us. The familiar stench made me shudder.

"What now?" roared Franca. I could see in Verena's face how the fear was filling her. And then—a flying object buzzed down from the sky and paused ten meters above us and halfway to the Brandenburg Gate. One second, we were staring at it, stunned. But the next, it turned around and whizzed between the pillars.

Verena grabbed the baby, yelled, "Follow me!" and rushed after the drone. Marcus and I grabbed the two older boys. Kirstin and Dominic were so weakened that they would have barely made it another hundred meters with the extra weight. I yelled at them to start running. Startled, they stumbled under the gate. Hanna needed no prompting. She had already followed her sister. Franca fired one last volley, then she too ran.

On the pillars of the monument, I saw hundreds of scraps of paper with photos emblazoned on them. Rushing past, I saw they read *Missing* and *Wanted*. There was no time to decipher more, especially since the rain had made several of the sheets illegible. Verena sprinted across the deserted square, ten steps behind the flying drone. After a hundred and fifty meters, they turned left around a corner. Like a single organism, we followed them, running and panting as the zombie howls grew louder behind us. Then suddenly we heard the bang of countless rapid-fire weapons.

Tracer bullets whizzed past me, close to my head. My first impulse was to take cover. I quickly suppressed it, for fear of the undead. Behind me, I heard Franca's HK rattling every few seconds. The child in my arms grew heavier. We made our way between the haphazardly abandoned buses and cars. I realized that the shots were being fired from the vehicles themselves. Their bodies had been reinforced with grilles and thick wooden boards. Rifle muzzles were poking through narrow slits.

The entrances to the courtyards and adjoining streets were blocked with all kinds of garbage. Over the heads of the others, I saw a bridge that seemed impassable, even from two hundred meters away. Three shipping containers had been placed on it. The drone flew over it and disappeared. With the last of our strength, we broke out of the shadow of the buildings. The roads leading off from the intersection offered no further opportunity for escape. Either we jumped into the shallow current in the next five seconds, breaking our legs, or we let the horde of undead tear us to pieces.

Franca fired with all barrels. Hanna was the first to run across the bridge crossing, and she fearfully awaited our demise. Kirstin joined her. She was crying, close to despair. At her side stood Dominic, looking around like a caged animal. Marcus and Verena placed the two children in their arms and hurried back to Franca. As I was about to set down the boy I had been carrying and join the fray, I heard a metallic squealing, followed by a deep voice yelling at us. We all looked up. The door of a shipping container had been opened from the inside. Inside, I could see pulleys controlled by some invisible mechanism. A helmeted, broad-shouldered man with dark skin and a jet-black beard stood on the container roof, beckoning us over. A bulletproof vest bulged over his muscular chest. The muzzles of half a dozen assault rifles appeared beside his legs. Again, he shouted at us.

Verena translated, "GET IN! NOW!"

The man then pushed down the transparent gun sight of his rapid-fire weapon and raised it to his shoulder. The zombies were only a few steps behind us. We had no choice but to obey. Breathing heavily, we ran inside. Above us, the automatic weapons set up a furious staccato. It lasted a full minute. The door crashed shut behind us, and we found ourselves in total darkness.

Peace.

Just the low hum of the ventilation.

Was I awake or dreaming? My drowsiness passed bit by bit, but I was reluctant to open my eyes, for fear of destroying the illusion. I tried to recall what had happened. But it felt so good lying here that part of me shied away from any unpleasant memories.

The mattress, on which I happily turned from side to side, was far more comfortable than any mattress I could remember. The comforter, however, felt a bit stiff. My head sank deep into the soft pillow.

Shadows danced on my eyelids, making me open them. Cautiously, I looked around. Light. The whitewashed room in which I lay was lit by the sun's autumn rays. They were slanting in through the huge window, which—when I got bolder and raised my head—afforded me an unobstructed view over the rooftops of Berlin.

This was not an illusion. It was real.

I breathed a sigh of relief.

I remembered why there was a needle in the crook of my right arm, providing me with alternating infusions of saline and vitamins. After my whole body had been thoroughly cleansed and I had undergone a medical examination, I was found to be suffering from malnutrition and given an incomparably tasty stew. I was then given a sleeping pill. Finally, they locked me up and left me to sleep on the seventh floor of the Charité university hospital.

The spear, which had been confiscated for safekeeping, and the discreet wristwatch from Saint Elm that ticked quietly on my wrist were my only remaining possessions. Everything else had been burned. Even the toenails and fingernails I had been allowed to clip before heading into the shower had been collected and professionally disposed of in a dangerous-looking bag with TOXIC and BIOHAZARD emblazoned on it in large letters.

I ran my hand over my shaven skull. My long hair had met the same fate as my nails. My forearms had red patches where people in white protective suits had zealously scrubbed me down. I lifted the blanket and saw the hospital gown they had put me in.

My comrades-in-arms had been subjected to the same procedure and were resting in the neighboring rooms. That was all I knew, except that, despite all our fears, we had made it to Berlin.

After a murderous summer, we had sailed thousands of nautical miles over the open sea and through inland waters. We had marched for days through a world where dangers lurked everywhere—and where the undead had sometimes been the least unpleasant instances of them. And yet only half a year had passed since I had had to leave Barcelona in a mad rush. Everything that had happened since then seemed like a dream from the safety of my hospital bed. This was unlikely to be due to the sedatives, whose effects were slowly wearing off. I had clearer memories of the time since they had opened the doors of the container for us.

Panting, we had emerged into the daylight inside half a dozen shipping containers, seconds after the gunfire directed at the undead had petered out. Guns were trained on us from above.

"Lay down your weapons." Marcus translated the thunderous command.

My back against a corrugated wall, I slid to the floor, exhausted. From my seated position, I pushed the spear away. Franca looked up belligerently, but when she saw several assault rifles being loaded, she too complied. She placed her HK on the asphalt and pushed it away with her foot. Verena and Marcus followed suit with their Glocks.

"We are unarmed," Dominic shouted, hugging his family.

"My sister and I are from Berlin! We just want to go home," Verena declared, standing protectively in front of Hanna.

"Ask them if they know Dr. Koller," Franca said. Marcus looked up and did as directed. He received no answer.

However, I heard people on the containers talking on the radio.

"Hello," Marcus called out, louder this time, "Is there a Dr. Koller here? She knows about us." At first, nothing happened. Another ten minutes passed before a figure appeared, wearing a face mask and a white jumpsuit of the kind worn to avoid contaminating crime scenes in detective stories.

It looked down at us for a long time through its transparent safety goggles before saying in a deep masculine voice, "How do you know Dr. Koller?"

Marcus translated for Franca and me.

"Is she here?" Verena's words escaped her throat.

"I'm asking the questions here! Who are you guys anyway? And what do you want?" the man demanded.

"It's a long story. But Dr. Koller can explain everything. Just tell her that her pen pals from Mallorca are here. My parents . . . ," she continued, close to tears. "My parents are also here in Berlin. They got in touch with us months ago through Dr. Koller. Now we are finally home."

His curiosity was piqued. "What's your name?"

Verena told him. The masked man turned around. Again, I heard the sounds of a radio. A minute later he turned back to us. "Listen carefully! This is purely a precautionary measure, and it is for your protection as well as ours," he said firmly. "You will now have to go into quarantine; I can't say for how long. But before that, you will undergo a medical exam-ination. It's a condition of being let in here. If you are cleared by the examination, of course, and if you want to."

"Please tell me if my parents are still alive!" pleaded Verena.

"I can't. I have no idea who your parents are. But"—he dragged out this last word before she burst into tears—"we've initiated inquiries to find them as soon as possible."

Verena wiped her cheeks. "Thank you," she says wanly, letting Hanna put her arm around her.

The rest of us were too exhausted to ask questions. Meanwhile, he continued, "We will now lower food and drink down to you. In return, we expect you to surrender your weapons to us." Given the lack of alternatives, I gave a thumbs-up. The others saw this and followed suit, though Franca hesitated briefly. The figure gave an imperceptible nod and took two steps back.

A contraption with a long chain dangling from it was pushed to the edge of the container. It held a basket, which was lowered to us, rattling. Marcus approached it and peered cautiously inside. He grinned triumphantly at us, lifted out a large pot and some bowls that appeared to be made of dried plant leaves, and asked, "Who's hungry?"

We eagerly slurped the stew, which consisted of potatoes, lentils, and various vegetables, from the bowls. Finn and Leonas refused it at first, but when the smell of the food hit their noses, they quickly gave in and ate. There was even enough for seconds.

"Please finish it all," the figure from above asked. "We hate to throw food away." We didn't need to be told twice. As soon as the pot was empty, we put the dishes back in the basket, including the weapons and ammunition.

I had to put the spear in vertically and fix it in place with a shoelace.

"Tell them to watch the blade. It might be contaminated," I said unnecessarily. "Don't want anyone to cut themselves on it." Marcus translated for me. Above us, they followed this instruction with all due caution.

Then we sat around in a circle in silence while Kirstin nursed the baby. Half an hour later, someone spoke to us again.

"We will now open the inner door and escort you to the clinic by armed guard. A bus is waiting on the other side of the passageway. Please all get on there and sit in the back seats. Needless to say, we will not take any chances in the event of an attack."

Nodding slowly, we stood up. Weariness and resignation were etched on the faces of my companions. At that moment, we just couldn't take in that we had every reason for rejoicing.

It took barely a minute for the gate to open. On the other side, the vehicle was waiting with its door open. We went through one by one and got onto the bus. Four armed men in protective suits sat down in the front, keeping their eyes on us at all times. We set off. The windows were covered with newspaper, so I couldn't see what was going on outside or what streets we were driving down. Kirstin and Dominic held the children close. Hanna had snuggled into Verena's arms and was resting her legs on Marcus's thighs. Franca sat on the bench in front of me and leaned her head against the vibrating windowpane.

"Hey, are you okay?" I asked quietly, without much hope of getting a detailed response.

But she sighed and replied, "The pressure of the past few months has suddenly fallen away. Don't you feel it, too?"

I listened to my body. "Hmm, could be. I hadn't thought about it."

"It'll come soon, believe me. I'm just tired. Kind of happy, too, that we've completed the mission more or less successfully. And on top of that, I have the impression I should feel free now. But I only feel emptiness. I need something meaningful to do, you know?"

I nodded slowly. "It's totally understandable. But right now, I'm way too beat to think about that kind of thing."

She gave me an understanding smile. From the motion of the bus, I deduced that we had made a few turns. A minute later, the vehicle stopped. The door opened.

"End of the line," the escort called. We got out by the entrance to an emergency room. An automatic door, with white, sterile walls behind it. Flickering fluorescent lights. Long corridors that smelled of disinfectant. Five hooded men waiting for us. Who shoved plastic bags, soap, and manicure sets into our hands before separating us into families.

Marcus, Franca, and I were suddenly isolated. Verena's insistence that Marcus join her and Hanna did not bear fruit at first.

"I'm sorry," a female voice said from behind the protective suit, shaking her head, "immediate family only."

"What do you mean, immediate? But if we were married, he could, couldn't he?"

"Yes, he could. Are you married?" asked the hospital worker without beating about the bush.

"Yes, we are," Verena lied, squeezing Marcus's hand.

Her counterpart sighed, giving in. "All right, just this once." She wrote something on her pad.

Verena looked over at Franca and me. Her face suddenly brightened. She let go of Marcus and came over to us.

"Thank you," she whispered through the tears running down her cheeks. "Thank you for everything. I really must introduce you to my parents."

Hanna came over, hugged me, and thanked me in sign language.

I gave her a kiss on the top of her head and said slowly, "Oh, it was a snap!"

She laughed and went over to Franca, who had just let go of Verena. The older sister squeezed me tightly. "I'll see you later, okay?" she said.

"Of course. Just let me get rid of these rags and take a good shower for once. Then you can show me the town, all right?"

"Sure. Party at the Berghain tonight," she said, giving me a wink.

"Don't care where. The main thing is we'll be able to get ourselves outside for some fun and drinks," I replied.

"If you two could wrap it up so we can get a move on . . ." the nurse warned us.

"All right then," I said. We were led away separately. There was always at least one armed person with us.

I was escorted to a room where I undressed down to my underwear. They shaved off my hair and politely instructed me to put my things in the bag.

"I get to shower by myself though, right?" I asked.

"Not if you want to stay here, you don't."

"I assure you I'll do a thorough job."

I was loathe to give up my privacy, and in front of people whose faces I couldn't even see. "I promise!"

"This is not a request show! Either you allow us to decontaminate you, or you'll be back in front of the barricades in half an hour. By the way, you can wash your genitalia yourself. The rest you leave to us. So, what'll it be?"

Without another word, I stepped into the hot water jet and raised my hands. I was thoroughly soaped up and scrubbed down from head to toe. Afterward I was given a hospital gown, ate again, lay down in bed, and swallowed a benzodiazepine. I didn't even notice them inserting the infusion.

Going over the previous day after I woke up was exhausting. Was it the after-effects of the sleeping pill that made me so tired? Or maybe I was just being lazy after all those months constantly keeping one eye open while I slept. Under the nightstand, I discovered a bedpan and used it. A glance at my saline told me the bag was almost empty. I found a cooler spot on the pillow for my cheek and fell back to sleep.

*　*　*

"Hey, Backie!" Someone was shaking my foot. "Hey, sleepyhead, wake up!"

"Mhh," I grumbled, jolted out of a deep sleep. "Leave me alone!"

"Come on; wake up!" I recognized Verena's voice.

"What is it?" I cried. The IV tube tugged at my arm as I moved. "What time is it?"

"Eight-thirty."

"Fuck off. It's the middle of the night."

"You've already slept for almost a day and a half. It's about time you got up."

"Why? What's going on?" I would have loved to sleep for another day.

"Dr. Koller's here."

My desire to sleep evaporated immediately. "Really? Now?" I sat up in bed.

Verena was standing in front of me in a colorful tracksuit, beaming. Carefully, I pulled out the needle.

"Yes. They told her we'd arrived as soon as they could. And now that all our tests are negative, she's finally able to come and see us."

"What about your parents?"

"They were here yesterday, but they didn't let them in. But we'll see them after we've talked to Dr. Koller."

"What about the others?"

"Marcus is having breakfast. Hanna and Franca are playing Ludo or something."

"Franca's playing Ludo? Are you kidding me?"

Verena grinned. "I think she's depressed because they took away her guns."

We both laughed.

"Anyway," she went on, "she told me she feels a bit out of place without anything at all to do."

"That's what she told me, too," I agreed. "And you, how are you?"

"Well, good, I think. I haven't really taken it in that we might actually have made it. It all feels so weird, so . . ."

"Surreal?"

"Yeah, totally. Plus, everything here is so clean and bright. And safe. Don't you think?"

I nodded. "Yes, that's it, exactly! What's it like? Can you take a shower here?"

"No, unfortunately not; the pressure is too low. Drinking water is probably distributed in bottles and canisters. They've built a filtration plant that filters the water from the Spree." Disgusted, she screwed up her face at the thought of the river. "But a lot of houses collect rainwater on their roofs and pipe it to the apartments through garden hoses. Here at the hospital, we were each given two full buckets in the bathroom. One with cold water, the other with hot water. If you've ever backpacked through India, you'll know what to do." She winked at me.

"I'll call you if I can't handle it, kiddo," I returned.

She laughed.

"Now off you go. Meet me in the hallway in ten minutes." I shooed her out.

"Excellent," she said. Light on her feet, she departed.

After washing, I was hugely hungry. In the closet I found underwear, socks, and a patched jogging suit, neatly folded.

Outside in the corridor, I was overcome by the feeling that we were in a prison. When I saw my companions without their hair and in the same clothing, I saw how emaciated we were. A breakfast table with tea, fresh fruit, and vegetables had been set for us in the hallway. There were also small rolls, which I immediately ate two of, washing down each bite with apple spritzer. I filled a cup with herbal tea.

"Who's winning?" I asked the two players at the table next to me.

"Stay out of this, Backup," Franca hissed.

"Hmm, I guess it's not you," I replied mockingly, stroking Hanna's bald skull and walking over to Verena and Marcus, who were looking out the window at the end of the hallway. The sky over Berlin was mercilessly blue.

"Isn't there any coffee?" I said, sipping my tea and drawing attention to myself.

"Probably not here in the hospital, but we're sure to find some outside," Verena replied. "It's hard to believe that the last time we had coffee was just three days ago in the hangar."

"Seems longer to me, too," Marcus said.

"What went on while I was asleep? I don't see Kirstin's family at all," I remarked.

"A nurse told me that they're being housed in another wing where they have bigger rooms and children can be cared for more easily. He was wearing one of those protective suits, like we were infected with Ebola."

"Can't blame them. But at least they know now that we're not contagious. Which makes me wonder, wouldn't they have been able to see that right away? I mean, if we'd been infected, we would have transformed immediately."

"You could have had fungal spores in your clothes fibers or blood residue from infected people under a fingernail, and you might accidentally have brought that into contact with your mucous membranes," said a familiar voice behind us.

Immediately we looked to the other end of the corridor, where a woman with red hair and an armed escort was coming toward us. "Then we'd have zombies in the place we least want them." She smiled kindly at us and said, "Good afternoon. I think we've met: I'm Dr. Koller. To you, Nadine."

She was sad not to be meeting Waltraud in person. "Where is she now?" she asked, disappointed. Nadine looked years older than she had the last time I had seen her over the internet, about four months ago. It was possible that the image quality had suffered in the transmission. But I was sure I hadn't noticed the dark circles under her eyes, which were now etched deep into her face. Her hair was tied up in a makeshift bun. Only the white coat she wore was the same as it had been then. In her hands she held a notepad. We sat around the table where the board game lay. Her companion had posted himself at the door and was awaiting orders.

"Waltraud and Jens are in Holland, Eva and Patrick hopefully in Iceland," Franca replied. I refrained from saying, *If they're still alive*. Instead, we told the virologist about our expedition across northern Germany. She listened patiently but kept looking back and forth between Hanna and Verena, as if she couldn't believe they were really there.

At the end of our tale, she murmured, shaking her head, "After all this time! And against all odds!

"But now I have your results," she continued, glancing at the stack of papers on her lap. "Except for minor deficiencies, you are healthy, if somewhat malnourished. The infusions will replenish your vitamin and mineral deposits in the short term. In the long term, you'll be able to get all the food you need from our gardens." Before we could bombard her with questions, she cried, "You'll get all the answers you want in the coming weeks. I'm afraid I have to get back to work now." To the two sisters she said, "Your parents are waiting downstairs. You can come along right now."

Hanna had read her lips and was beaming.

"Can Marcus come?" asked Verena uncertainly.

Dr. Koller thought for a moment before answering, "I don't see why not." Turning to Franca and me, she said, "I've assigned a staff member to show you around the town." She glanced irritably at her wristwatch. "He's our systems administrator and should have been here by now. Right now, he has a lot of free time because the system isn't too busy—we hardly have any patients. Which, on the other hand, is rather a good thing." She looked at her watch again and snorted. "It's always the same with him. He's probably still asleep." She turned and yelled to her companion. Her angry shouts—at a volume I would never have thought her capable of— seemed all the more terrifying in German.

A visibly startled Marcus translated in a whisper, "Where the hell is Stefan?"

A glance at his skateboard's remote control told him the battery was full: The small battery icon on the display glowed green. Stefan pulled on the strap of his white helmet, which tightened around his head. Satisfied, he looked down at his shoes: they were correctly laced. He didn't want the same thing to happen to him as when the wheel had jammed after a loose lace had got wrapped around the axle.

That time, Stefan had flown meters through the air. The electric device had flipped over, its tip crashing between his legs and forcing him into the fetal position for half an hour.

His stomach muscles tightened even now at the memory of it.

"You ready?" he called with a sideways glance at Adrian, who was moving his own board into position beside him.

"Yeah, let's go," the latter returned, tapping his helmet with the palm of his hand. "Are you giving the signal?"

Stefan nodded, rolling a tennis ball between his fingers. "Attention," he announced, tossing the ball into the air as high as the hospital ceiling would allow.

The ball bounced once. Then once again. And a third time. At that moment, they pushed the control levers all the way forward.

The first few meters were the most critical. If he stood too upright, the accelerating skateboard would throw him backward. If he leaned too far forward, he lost momentum, which Adrian would know how to exploit. Since he rode like a maniac when they held races on the ninth floor of the Charité, this was one of the few chances Stefan would have to gain an advantage for himself.

If he screwed up the start, he had virtually no chance of overtaking Adrian in the narrow corridors. He had often wondered whether his friend consciously accepted that he was likely to get injured. And how it was even humanly possible to harmonize the body's reflexes and tension in such a way as to be able to take almost any curve of their course at over thirty kilometers per hour.

This time Stefan got the perfect start. With around twenty centimeters to spare, he rolled past the first obstacle, forcing Adrian to slow down.

The upper floors were out of bounds, but Stefan was the system administrator and had unrestricted access everywhere. Besides, he laughed in the face of prohibitions. At the moment, all he could think of was that he would have to push himself to the limit in order not to lose the lead. The course was long and meandered throughout the deserted floor. At full speed, he turned right and banked heavily—something he'd picked up from Adrian—slaloming between the beds jutting halfway out of the rooms.

After the slalom section came the section with tables standing in the middle of the route. At the last moment, Stefan took his index finger off the gas, jumped onto the first tabletop with both feet and ran five steps while his skateboard—invisible to him—continued to roll forward underneath the table. This section demanded total concentration. If the board was too fast, he would miss it. He would have to stop it, forcing him to start again. If it was too slow, he would have to wait for it, and Adrian—who he could hear behind him, jumping onto the tables— would pass him. Stefan would be anything but satisfied with that outcome. He went full tilt, pushed down the gas button, and jumped as far as he could. The skateboard shot out from under the table—right under his feet. He swayed slightly, steadied himself again—and accelerated even more. The path led them through deserted open-plan offices, where he had to master one chicane after another between isolated desks. He kept his center of gravity shifting back and forth, defying the centrifugal forces that threatened to take him off the board at every turn.

Out of the offices he went, into the hallway with two narrow thirty-meter tracks that looped between trash cans. Around the corner, the

"Dark Side" was waiting for him. He turned into the unlit hallway, aligned his feet with the direction of travel, and folded his bent knees together. Putting his hands behind his back, he made himself small and streamlined. Now he could maximize the power of the electric motor. Only the indistinct light at the end of the tunnel helped him keep on course and not crash into a wall or a doorframe. The wind took his breath away and rushed in his ears. Stefan didn't dare look at the display for fear of losing precious milliseconds. But even so, he knew that it was showing forty-four kilometers per hour. He drew his shoulders closer together. What was the maximum speed he could take the next turn at? Thirty-three kilometers an hour? Thirty-five? He would be able to analyze it on his smartphone app afterward.

The light was approaching, and he slowed down and leaned into the curve. Too fast; he was still going too fast. He tried frantically to avoid the inevitable, straightening up, taking his finger off the gas, and dragging his belly along the wall as he turned. He lurched two or three times until he had the board back under control—and Adrian shot past him. "Fuck!" he cursed. It was intolerable to lose the lead so close to the finish! Stefan opened the throttle and followed hard on his heels.

There was just one last bend before they headed for the home stretch. But why was Adrian speeding up? That wasn't good, even with his reflexes. If he turned at that speed . . . Shit, had he forgotten they had rebuilt the section yesterday?

They kept modifying the route to make the race more exciting. The final hurdle—a drawer from the chief physician's office—was now on the other side.

Stefan saw Adrian approach the bend at his usual speed and jerk in shock when he realized his mistake. Traveling over thirty-five kilometers an hour, he crashed into the mattress they had secured to this point. They had been foresighted enough to take this safety precaution, at least.

Stefan dodged the somersaulting board, overcoming the obstacle at the same time, and crossed the finish line first. He immediately jumped off and ran back to Adrian, who was lying on the linoleum floor, struggling for breath.

"Easy, easy," Stefan said, taking off his helmet.

Adrian took frantic, sucking breaths. "Kurwa," he cussed between short breaths, "I totally . . . forgot. That place . . . is different now."

"Did you break anything?" asked Stefan.

"I don't think so," Adrian replied. "But certainly . . . bruised a couple of ribs. And my shoulder."

"Do you feel sick at all?" They couldn't afford for him to be concussed. Adrian ran the drone surveillance department. Less than a handful of people were capable of replacing him. Nadine would go nuts if he was out of action.

"No. I don't think . . . I caught my head . . . on anything."

"It was just the same when you were born," Stefan said, helping him to his feet. At that moment, the phone in his pocket rang. Serj, Nadine's burly bodyguard, was calling on the internal line. "What does he want now?" he grumbled, answering the call. "Hello?"

The answer came promptly: "Where are you, asshole? The boss wants to talk to you."

The elevator stopped on the seventh floor. "Leave your stuff. I'll take it," said Adrian. His breathing was halfway normal again.

Nonetheless, Stefan eyed him critically. "You're quite pale. Do you want me to come with you? Koller can easily wait five minutes."

Adrian shook his head decisively. "If you make her wait any longer, she'll have you locked up." He grinned.

"And who'd look after the systems then? Her?"

His friend pushed him out of the elevator. "Go on, get out of here. I got this."

"All right, I'll see you later, okay?" agreed Stefan.

"Sure thing. And don't make the old lady mad, you hear?" Adrian called after him as the door closed.

*Yes, yes*, thought Stefan. Carelessly, he considered which corridor to take. A door opened to his left, and an armed person in protective gear waved him over.

"She wants you!" he heard Serj shout. His tone told Stefan that Dr. Koller was now boiling with rage.

Relaxed, he walked toward him.

"Who do you think you are, anyway? I have better things to do than chase after you," she greeted him as he passed the guard. Looking over her shoulder, he ignored her. Three teenagers and two adults, all sporting buzz cuts and resembling a miserable German rap band in their jogging suits, were studying him curiously.

"Are these the new arrivals from yesterday that Adrian told us about?" he asked. When she nodded, he added, "He had a little accident," finally looking her in the eye. "I was just making sure he could continue working," he defended himself, more or less truthfully.

"You've been racing again, I suppose?" asked Dr. Koller, struggling to compose herself. Stefan refrained from replying and merely nodded. She brought her clenched fist up in front of his face. "I could have you . . . ," she said through gritted teeth.

Stefan waited a few seconds until her initial anger subsided. Jerking his chin at the people behind her, he asked, "So those are the ones I'm supposed to be looking after?"

"Oh, so you haven't forgotten? Just the two adults. The children are coming with me. We also need a place for them to stay. Have you found somewhere suitable?"

"We prepared an apartment for them yesterday. Two rooms, kitchen, bathroom. Third floor."

"Uh-huh, where?"

"Templiner Strasse, corner of Schwedter," he replied. "Should I take them there now?"

"No, we'll keep them here for another week or two so we can bore them to death . . . Of course you should take them there now!" she snapped at him. She turned angrily away and said in English to the German Rap Gang, "Sorry for the delay. Stefan will look after Franca and Backup. You three come with me." They all nodded to her and paused for a moment. Then they all flung their arms around each other.

"Just get yourselves settled in," she said to the adults in English. "I'm going to carve out some time over the next few days, and then we can meet and talk. I still can't believe you actually made it," she added almost reverently, hugging them again. Stefan heard what felt like a hundred thank-yous before she finally motioned for the youths to follow her.

"Oh, yes," one of the adults called after her. "What about my spear?"

"And my HK?" said the other.

Dr. Koller paused for a moment and replied, "Stefan will explain our weapons policy to you." Turning to him, she continued, "When you get a chance, take them to the arsenal so they can see that their things are in good hands."

He nodded and asked the newcomers, "Is there anything you want to take with you?"

The woman who had inquired about the HK shook her head, "No. We're wearing everything we own."

"Looks fancy," Stefan said, giving her a thumbs-up. "Okay, let's go to your new home!"

We shot eastward along Invalidenstrasse. The white Model X hummed quietly. At the speed Stefan was driving on the route that had been cleared, the buildings to the right and left blurred before my eyes. From the back seat, I vaguely registered that the entrances to the apartment block courtyards and the adjoining streets and parks were stacked five or six meters high with vehicles, trash containers, park benches, and other garbage that usually belonged in the bulky waste section.

"What happened here?" I exclaimed. The sight I saw seemed to have transported us back to 1945.

"The barricades?" our driver countered. "They keep the Grays from straying in. In the beginning, it was decided the enclave should be built separately from the Charité—connected by this road, but at a distance so that both sides would have somewhere to retreat to if the going got tough," he said without taking his eyes off the road. "Back then, some of us went through the district with excavators and put up these barriers. It took weeks. Behind them, at fifty-meter intervals, we put up two more ramparts. We threw furniture and electrical appliances out of the windows to build them with because it soon became clear that the stuff standing around on the streets wasn't enough. And we barricaded the doors of the first two floors so that the zombies couldn't gain access through them."

"Brave," Franca said.

"Stupid, actually—but what are you going to do?" Stefan shrugged his shoulders. "We only had two or three armed escorts as backup. Even with them in tow, I mostly shit my pants. The undead could have been anywhere. And they often were. Once we got cornered. Two of us bit it before reinforcements arrived."

"Didn't the whole barrier project attract the undead?" the Italian asked.

"And how!" replied Stefan. "That's why we had to use diversionary maneuvers. That kept them busy for three or four hours. We were able to secure smaller sections of the road, at least. But then new ones came along, attracted by the noise."

"Hmm, I see," she said.

"The barriers are holding up pretty well. Every now and then one of them loses their way and tries to climb up. Usually they get stuck in a crevice among the trash. Then they have to be dealt with quickly and taken away before they bring in more."

"And how do you know when something like that happens? Do you have guards posted everywhere?" Franca asked.

"No, we don't have the human resources for that. We have a surveillance department that uses drones. My boyfriend heads it up. I'd be happy to show you around soon. But look! We're almost there."

We drove three hundred meters along a barricade to our right. We passed a street sign, and I had to turn my head quickly to decipher the name on it: Veteranen Strasse. Stefan eased off the gas. We crossed an intersection that ended at a barricade made of stacked shipping containers.

Like the day before yesterday, when we had been let in over the bridge, I figured there was an entrance here. As I had seen there, I could make out several automatic weapons on the roof.

And I was not mistaken. The gate in the middle opened, and Stefan drove into the twilight. Only then did I notice that two smaller containers had been welded together; the sides without doors had been removed with angle grinders.

A few seconds later, we were back in the daylight. "So, welcome to Berlin," he said in German. We didn't need a translation; this much we could understand.

A small park with a church in the middle was the first we saw of the enclave. And then people. Dozens, maybe even hundreds!

Driving at a moderate pace, Stefan turned right. Raised beds had been erected in the green area to our left. Crowds of people were walking on the sidewalks and riding bicycles on roads. They were walking hand in hand, pushing strollers in front of them, leading dogs on leashes. Carrying shopping and sports bags. Jogging. Many of them had been shaved bald like me, others looked like they had been there a few months, judging by the length of their hair. My jaw dropped. "Can someone please explain this to me?" I asked.

Stefan grinned. "Looks unreal, doesn't it? Even in the apocalypse, you can find ways to live a normal life. That's just Berlin." At the next intersection, he turned right.

"How many people live here?" asked Franca.

"Around two thousand." Stefan continued along a busy road. Quite a few vehicles were coming toward us. Bicycles had the right of way.

"How do you feed such crowds these days?" she whispered.

"We've built an elaborate system for that. You'll see that in the next few days."

I rolled down a window and heard—not in the least what I had feared. No engine noises. No urgent honking or ringing. No loud shouting. Just the sound of the traffic around us rolling past. Bicycle chains rattling. The airstream rushing past. After months of enforced isolation, I suddenly felt I had been transported to paradise.

The air was free of exhaust fumes. Had the near extinction of humanity helped it reach a higher level of evolution? "I guess people here are aware of the danger breathing down their necks," I said, puzzled. "It's amazing how disciplined everyone is."

"That used to be different, too," Stefan disagreed, waiting behind a dozen bikes to turn left. He gradually worked his way forward. "In the beginning, a lot of people saw the pandemic as an attempt by the government—no, a shadow government—to enslave people. Conspiracy theories abounded. However, those crackpots were some of the first to bite the dust."

"That wasn't how it was in Italy, though," Franca said. "Although I don't even know everything that went down there. Two weeks after the outbreak, I was gone."

"You were lucky, I'd say. Because it was only after then that things really took off. Europe-wide. Italy was hit just as hard as Germany. I often wonder if it could have been contained better if people had behaved more sensibly." We fell silent and let him continue, "Back then, we had orders not to leave our houses or apartments unnecessarily. To wear face coverings. To wash our hands. To avoid crowds. Rules everyone should follow in the event of a global disease outbreak. But hundreds or even thousands of these zombidiots took to the streets to protest. Because they saw their personal rights and freedoms as under threat. Well, as soon as the first infected arrived in Berlin, the demos took care of themselves."

Now he turned left onto Templiner Strasse. "Unfortunately, many of them were infected. I'm sure some of them are still walking around out there."

He slowed down and parked. "Well, here we are." To the left and right I saw Art Nouveau houses, which were becoming a familiar sight. It looked like Barcelona but without the Mediterranean charm.

We got out of the car. Stefan fished a bunch of keys out of his pants pocket, fumbled with them, and tossed me two keys. "Please don't lose them. It's difficult to get them cut these days," he said and walked us to the front door. I unlocked it. We stepped into a dark lobby. Immediately I stiffened, looking around for potential dangers. Franca stood with her back to the wall and reached for her hip, where her Glock normally was. Meanwhile, Stefan went to a switch and pressed it. The light came on. He looked surprised when he saw that we had involuntarily assumed fighting positions.

"You're safe here. But you're right, a little caution never does any harm," he said understandingly, leading us to the third floor.

"And this is your apartment," he announced as we reached a door. He told me to unlock it.

We peered into the rooms. Bright, painted white, with impressively high ceilings. Wide floorboards. Towels folded on the beds, like in a hotel. The bathroom was small. I spotted toothbrushes in packages on the rim of the sink, next to a tube of toothpaste. Finally, Stefan led us into the kitchen, where, judging by the smell, people had smoked for a long time.

"I got some groceries yesterday. Fix yourselves something to eat and get yourselves settled first. I'll be back tomorrow at the latest. Then I'll show you around."

"Sounds good," Franca said. "But what about our weapons?"

"Don't worry; we'll deal with them tomorrow. Are you okay so far?" he inquired.

Franca and I looked around again, looked at each other, and nodded with satisfaction.

He grinned and said, "Great. I have to go now," then turned around and clattered down the stairs.

"Well, looks like it's just you and me again," I said, trying to cheer her up.

Franca smiled and nodded. "Could be worse." Then she stepped over to me and gave me a long, tight hug. I returned it. "It's good to have friends you can count on. Thanks for everything, Backie," she whispered.

Swallowing the lump in my throat, I said, "Um, thank you!" Through my tracksuit, I felt a damp patch against my shoulder. It confused me to see the toughest person I had ever come across getting so emotional. Was the tension of the past months slowly crumbling away?

Anyway, the dam broke for me, too. After we had wept and sniffed for a few minutes, I said, "How about it; are you hungry? Shall I make us some soup?"

"Only if it's spicy," she replied through her tears.

"Oh, you can't take it spicy." I scoffed.

She laughed, punched me in the side, and wiped her cheeks. "I'm going to take a shower. I've got to get rid of the hospital stink."

Freshly washed and with bowls full of vegetable soup, we sat on the kitchen table and looked out the window. Slurping hers straight from the bowl and sitting with her heels on the edge of the chair, Franca asked, "What do you want to do next?" Some of her hardness had returned. I got the impression she couldn't be bothered to locate the rest of it.

"I don't know," I replied. "Right now, everything in my life is changing so fast, I can't judge."

"But if you had the choice, and you could decide what your future would be, what would you choose?"

"You mean if I had one wish that would come true?"

She nodded, without looking at me.

"Hmm. I assume I can't wish to change the past," I speculated. She nodded, and I went on, "Then I'd wish that the zombies didn't exist anymore. Or that we at least had a vaccination against the plague."

"No, that's not what I mean. How would you want to live if it was all over? Where? What would make you fulfilled?" I was surprised by her questions. Was she going through an existential crisis?

"That's . . . hard to say," I stammered. "I think, as a first step, I'd want to get far away from people. I'd like to live in a secluded cabin somewhere. Be self-sufficient and all that. I'd have an animal—a dog or a tame wolf— that I could communicate with telepathically," I said with a grin, making her laugh. "What about you?"

"Oh yeah." She sighed, taking another sip of soup. "Lately, I find myself thinking everything's getting too much for me. Much like you, I'd want to keep my distance from civilization, too. But inside, I know it wouldn't last long." She paused and drank. I wasn't sure she expected me to ask a question now, so I kept silent. Bringing the bowl to her lips with both hands, she sipped and then continued, "I've been trapped in a world of fighting, violence, and death for far too long. Sure, I can get by without it for a while. Three, four weeks, a few months, maybe even a year. But then . . . I wouldn't know what to do with myself. I'm too used to chasing after people and enforcing rules. On top of that, lately I've had to fight for survival. My psyche couldn't take it if I suddenly stopped, you know? I mean, I don't know anything else . . ."

I nodded. "I thought you would say something like that."

She smiled almost bashfully, looking at the rest of her soup. "Delicious," she praised it. "But not at all spicy."

"And I really used loads of chili," I defended myself, pointing to the little spice rack on the wall. "The label even says the spice level is five out of five. But you can't even taste it."

"No one here can take anything spicy," she said, shaking her head.

"It was the same with Patrick," I confirmed.


Their parents' current apartment, where Verena and Hanna had now also found refuge, was not nearly as spacious as their old one. The two sisters were sharing a room, which was in no way unpleasant considering they had been sharing bedrooms with other people for months. After all, they had a living room in which they had spent last night talking with their parents until the early hours of the morning. Verena looked out the window. What time might it be? The sky was overcast, so she couldn't tell exactly from the position of the sun. Based on the brightness, it was certainly after ten, she guessed.

Verena was more refreshed and fit than she had been in a long time. She was lolling in bed. The slatted frame creaked. She looked over at Hanna to see if it was bothering her. Then she remembered that it couldn't. Her sister's shaved head lay motionless on the pillow. The blanket was rising and falling imperceptibly with her breathing. Outside, Verena heard the floorboards creak. The light footsteps told her who was walking down the hall. Under the crack of the door, she spotted a shadow that had come to a halt. "Mama?" she called out.

After a moment's hesitation, the door opened gently. Katrin stuck her head around and whispered, "Good morning."

"You don't have to whisper; she can't hear anything anyway." She said it deliberately. Hanna's injury wasn't going to be hushed up, no matter how much it hurt. It was just part of everyday life, whether they wanted it to be or not. And what was better than humor for helping people accept unpleasant things?

Nevertheless, Katrin reprimanded her, "Oh, do you have to say that?"

"Sorry, you're right," Verena replied, kicking off the blanket. She stood up and approached Hanna's bed. Gently, she kissed her temple. Hanna wrinkled her nose without opening her eyes. "She wouldn't mind. Really, she wouldn't!"

"Let her sleep. Do you want to have breakfast with me?"

Instead of answering, Verena asked, "Where's Dad?"

"He's already gone to work. It's almost eleven o'clock. Actually, we could have lunch right now."

"Or brunch," Verena said. "Is there coffee?"

"Yes, I just made some fresh," Katrin said.

"Oh man, that's awesome. Is it hard to get?"

"Not really. But it's best you ask Olek when he and Marcus get back. What about Hanna?"

"Oh, she wants to go back to sleep. Do you still have the scarf Dad brought you from India?"

"The saffron one? Yes, but I have to look for it. Why do you ask?"

"Put it with Hanna's clothes. I'm sure she'd be happy to see it."

"Okay, I'll go get it," Katrin said, puzzled, and left. Meanwhile, Verena made her bed, found a T-shirt and a pair of washed-out jeans in the closet that halfway fit her, and got dressed.

"I found it," said her mother, who reappeared in the doorway. She put the scarf at the foot of Hanna's bed.

"Great." Verena smiled. "But now I want a coffee!" They stepped into the hallway together and went into the kitchen. As well as a kitchenette, it had a table and four chairs. Katrin had prepared—in the circumstances— a sumptuous breakfast.

There were fresh tomatoes and cucumbers and a large can each of pickled peaches and pineapple slices. In addition, there were small rolls like the ones in the hospital. But first and foremost, Verena was interested in the coffee. She took a heaping teaspoonful of sugar but thought better of it and tipped half back. Then she sprinkled the white crystals into the dark potion. Her mother sat down across the table from her and poured herself a cup. Now that the initial excitement had faded, Verena studied her face more closely. The sorrow of the past months was clearly visible on her mother's face. Many gray strands ran through her blond hair. Her cheeks were sunken.

"You need a haircut, Mom," she said, "Your hair is too long."

"Oh, my hair is the least of my worries. Best I wait until yours grows back, then we can all go together," she quipped. "But tell me more about Marcus! You two seem to be getting along well."

Verena couldn't hold back a grin and took a deep breath. "He's not a bad guy. I told you yesterday how we met at the hotel. And we've spent every day and night together since then." Why was she telling her mother so much? They had never been so open with each other. Although they hadn't exactly been best friends in the past, it wasn't even hard for Verena now. They'd had the usual friction, as all families did. Suddenly she realized how much she had changed in the last few months. How mature she had become. Had had to become!

"He's a bit reserved, but he's not shy," she said, before going into more detail about the night in Falkensee.

As she spoke, more and more anecdotes and stories came into her mind.

"You seem to like him a lot," mused Katrin, starting her second cup of coffee.

"Yes, I think I do. We'll see if it turns into something serious. Do you know where he and Olek went?"

Marcus had been staying with Olek, a young man his age who lived in the same building as Verena's parents. Hardly a day went by without Olek bringing his neighbors fresh groceries or informing them about upcoming literary evenings and theater performances. Marcus and Olek had hit it off right away. Yesterday they had spent the evening with Verena's family after her mother had invited them both to dinner.

"They've gone to collect chestnuts and ivy."

"What do they want with those?" asked Verena, intrigued.

"To make detergent, as far as I know."

"Detergent? Is that in short supply?"

"No, we still have plenty. But artificial detergent smells way too good and the Grays can smell it. An ivy and chestnut solution cleans great and doesn't give off such a noticeable odor."

"Okay," Verena said, impressed. "And how do you do that?"

"I think you chop the ingredients, boil them, and let it all sit for two or three days. Then you squeeze the brew and filter it."

"The detergent manufacturers hate that trick!" interjected Verena.

"What?" the mother asked.

"What?" said Verena.

Katrin shook her head. "But you'd better check with Olek before I fill your head with nonsense. If you see him before I do, please tell him I need a new supply. The stuff he brought me three weeks ago is almost gone."

At that moment, there was a knock. "You can tell him yourself," Verena replied and stood up. She had to orient herself in the new apartment for a second before hurrying to the exit. She yanked open the door and found herself face-to-face with Marcus and Olek.

"Moin," she said in the local accent, and then got straight to the point. "What are we doing today?"

Marcus stood grinning in the stairwell. He was wearing a formerly black but now graying Ramones T-shirt under a blue retro-looking tracksuit top. His washed-out jeans were too big for him, but he passed them off easily as stylishly baggy. He had turned up the extra-long pant legs several times, revealing dark Vans underneath. Freshly shaved, he looked scrumptious. She threw her arms around his neck and kissed him.

Olek was two whole heads taller than Marcus. His long hair fell over his shoulders, its red contrasting with his grungy hoodie made of coarse jute fabric. Every thread seemed to have been dyed a different shade of blue. His long cargo pants, whose hem was fraying at the heels, were probably among the few garments with a long enough leg for him. White teeth flashed at Verena from behind his beard.

She held out her hand, which disappeared into his huge paw.

"What are you up for? Shall I show you the gardens?" he asked in a deep baritone. "There's a little performance tonight. But before that, there's all kinds of things we can do."

"I don't care. Just show us what Berlin is like now. I'll get dressed quickly, then we can go. Oh yeah, my mom asked for more laundry detergent."

"Tell her it'll take another three or four days. But I'll remember," Olek promised.

Verena went to the kitchen and conferred with Katrin. "Don't wait up for me; I might be late," she told her.

"Verena, it can be dangerous out there at night," her mother warned in horror.

Verena laughed loudly and kissed her on the forehead. "Oh, Mom, if you only knew . . . Give Dad a smooch from me, will you? And Hanna, as soon as she's awake. Ciao, see you later," she called and rushed out the door.

Olek led them across the enclave. "I'll show you the gardens first," he said once they had left the house. "That's where we get almost all of our food."

"And the rest?" inquired Marcus.

"Through scavenging. Mostly for things we can't produce locally. Flour, sugar, tea . . ."

"Coffee," Verena interjected.

"Coffee." He nodded.

"But where do you get those kinds of things? On the way to Berlin, we scouted out a lot of towns. The stores there were already empty," Marcus said.

"I can well imagine. The smaller stores were the first to be looted," Olek explained. As he walked, he rocked lightly from one foot to the other, gesturing with his large hands. "But in the general panic, the logistics centers, which got regular deliveries before the outbreak, were overlooked. Usually, they divided the goods up there and shipped them on. But because logistics collapsed relatively quickly, most of the goods are still on-site."

"How long will those supplies feed two thousand people for?" asked Verena.

They crossed the street and entered a small park.

"It's hard to say," Olek said. "We're strict about portions, but new people keep arriving. I'm guessing another year, a year and a half. By then, we hope to ramp up production to the point where we can be self-sufficient. And that place up ahead," he said, pointing at a building whose entire facade was bathed in sunlight, "is a kind of greenhouse."

*It doesn't look like one at all*, Verena thought. She squinted and looked through one of the open windows. "Oh," she exclaimed, surprised. "You grow it all in there?"

"That's right," Olek said, leading them inside. The doors of the two mezzanine apartments stood wide open. They were greeted by the smell of damp earth.

Verena spotted a garden hose snaking down through the stairwell and rooms. A separate hose branched off at each room. "That's the irrigation system, I guess," she said, pointing at it.

He nodded. "On the top floor, we collect rainwater in large vats. We use a simple timer mechanism to water the plants once or twice a day." Workers were going in and out. Verena and her companions had to step aside to make room. Baskets of harvested produce were carried out. "We converted the rooms in the apartments that get the most sunlight into cultivation zones."

They entered the first hallway and peered into the room, which was brightly lit by the sun. The floor and walls were covered to waist height with a sheet on which dark soil had been heaped. Perennials were growing close together on thin cords hanging from the ceiling. Between them Verena could see oblong lamps. The beds were divided with wooden beams. Olek stepped onto them and beckoned Verena and Marcus to join him.

"You can come in, but please stay on the boards."

"What's growing here?" asked Marcus.

"Beans," Olek replied. "And those up there," he said, pointing to the lights on the ceiling, "are our backup sun."

"UV light?" mused Verena.

Olek nodded. "At night, we turn them on for six to eight hours. That enables us to triple the harvest, at least according to our projections. This is already the second harvest this year. However, the summer was very sunny. We haven't yet worked out what the influence of the lamps really is. Not many people have the expertise. That's why we're doing all the pioneering work," he said, leading them to the next room, whose floor was free of soil. Instead, Verena saw, there were dozens of open shelves with elongated planters standing on them. Two-meter neon tubes floated vertically between them. She counted twenty-four of them. Olek led her around the room. "Carrots, cauliflower, various types of lettuce," he said. "So far, we have successfully grown quite a few native vegetables. But the biggest problem was that we didn't know what to use as fertilizer at first. We found artificial fertilizer in hardware stores, but it won't last forever. So we have a shredding machine, which shreds domestic organic waste and waste from the harvest. We mix that with feces extracted from public toilets that we've set up especially for this purpose. The earthworms do the rest. Completely in line with the Hundertwasser principle."

"Hundertwasser, the artist?" asked Verena.

"That's the one," Olek confirmed.

"I didn't even know he was interested in this kind of thing."

"Neither did we at first. But one of the residents brought it to our attention and wrote down and sketched some of his self-sufficiency tricks for us."

"That's some great shit," Verena said. "No pun intended," she added quickly.

"Is there anything we could get involved with?" asked Marcus. "I'm uncomfortable with the idea of having others work for me."

"Don't worry about that," Olek placated him. "There's enough for everyone to do here. Dr. Killer doesn't want people to get any stupid ideas because they're bored. That's why she decided everyone should have a job to do, if only for four hours a day. Even the older people get involved."

"Dr. Killer?" asked Verena, puzzled.

"Didn't anyone tell you?" Olek was grinning now. "That's what they call Dr. Koller sometimes. Because of her approach to human trials."

"Whoa," Verena said in horror, changing the subject. "Is she in charge of the city? I thought she was only employed at the Charité."

"Ha-ha, you thought wrong. She controls everything—fortunately. Without her, we wouldn't be half as far along as we are today. But I'd like to introduce you to someone," Olek said, leading them out. "We need to hurry. I don't want to miss him." They walked through a few streets. As they went, he told them Dr. Koller had prescribed that they should not neglect cultural development. "Once or twice a week there are readings, poetry slams, and now and then a play. Before, it was all amateurish and—in keeping with the apocalypse—desperate. Today, it's completely different. There are also sports tournaments where streets compete against each other. Soccer, basketball, and now volleyball, too. And once in a while, a party kicks off in a basement."

"Bread and circuses," Marcus mused.

"Yes, well, Dr. Koller's not stupid," Olek countered.

"You haven't even said what your job is yet," Verena said.

"Oh, this and that. I help out where there's a need. Coordinate cultural meetings, sporting events. Lend a hand with the harvest. All-around stuff."

"Detergent production," Marcus added, and Olek laughed.

"And detergent production," he confirmed.

"What is this place? A kindergarten?" Verena asked as they walked under an arch past armed guards into a courtyard with a huge playground in the center. Happy laughter resounded all around.

Olek nodded. "And the school." Verena followed him across the facility, toward a group of children sitting on the floor, listening spellbound to someone in a white shirt.

"We're in time. The bard's still there," he said.

"Bard?" asked Marcus, intrigued. "That guy on the bench?"

They were a good forty meters away from him when Verena heard the sonorous, far-carrying voice. The storyteller gestured with his right hand. In his left, he held a book from which he was reading. His pitch switched effortlessly from low to high, from threatening to fearful. The children burst out laughing. With one last paragraph, he brought the reading to an end and noisily closed the volume. His young audience laughed again. He stood up, bowed, and took his applause. Verena, Marcus, and Olek waited behind the flock of children. The reader, they now realized, wore round glasses set in thin frames. His Poirot-esque mustache was trim, his goatee tapered to an immaculate point. He picked up the leather bag that lay beside him on the bench and stowed the reading book away. As the children scampered off, he pulled on his coat and put on his hat. Olek strode toward him. Only now did the bard seem to notice his new audience. In a low, serious voice he said, "Olek. Greetings! I'm glad you're here. I meant to contact you long ago, as we are struggling to decide which work to perform next week."

Olek put his right fist over the heart. His arm performed a horizontal arc with his index and middle fingers pointing upward. "Greetings, noble bard," he replied. "First, allow me to introduce you to my friends."

"How inattentive of me. Please forgive me!"

Verena and Marcus looked at each other wordlessly as he bowed to them and told them his name. They awkwardly followed suit, introducing themselves in turn.

"What problem are we talking about?" inquired Olek.

"The director is longing for . . . A crime story."

Olek grimaced in disgust. "No more crime stories, please. We have three of them on the program every week."

The reader nodded. "Correct."

"What alternatives might there be? Or let me put it another way: What would be close to your heart?"

The bard faltered for a moment, as if he had never considered the possibility that he would be asked this question. "Um, me? Well, I would . . . tell a historical story. Or something from the science fiction repertoire."

Olek's curiosity seemed piqued. "Hmm, science fiction. That would be something new. Do you have anything in particular in mind?"

"I do indeed! I was thinking of a vision of a society of the future that experiments with human DNA—with fatal consequences."

"That sounds pretty good," Olek said thoughtfully. "Do you have to sing while you do it? Like you did with the *Deep Impact* story the other day?"

"Sing? No," the latter responded, surprised.

"Very good. Then tell your sci-fi story. Anything is better than hearing a crime story again. I'll sort it out with the director myself."

The bard did not seem entirely satisfied with this answer. "But why did you bring up singing? Didn't you like it?"

Olek tried to placate him with a friendly remark.

But his interlocutor wouldn't let it go. "Tell me! Were you not satisfied with my singing?"

"Yes, it was fine. You sing very well, much better than . . . Dirk Nowitzki, for example." Quietly, he turned to Verena and Marcus, "Come on; let's go!" Walking backward, he said to the bard, "That's settled then! Read the sci-fi story. It's sure to be a doozy! I can hear it now. And don't worry about the director; leave her to me! Sorry, got to go! See you at the reading. I'm looking forward to it."

With these words, he turned and ran away. Verena and Marcus ran after him in amazement. "Why does he express himself so strangely?" she asked once they had fled the courtyard.

"Oh, leave him to it! The bard makes a huge contribution to society. He entertains the children during the day and the adults in the evening. And believe me—without him, our day-to-day life would be pretty bleak."


Franca and I were having breakfast when there was a knock at the door. We started, and I spilled some of the coffee she had prepared on the camping stove.

"That will be Stefan," she said, and went to the door to let him in. I wondered if I would ever be able to relax again and not be terrified by a visit from an acquaintance. "Would you like a coffee?" she offered as he stepped into the kitchen.

"No, thanks. I've already had one today. How about you guys? Get through the night okay?"

"I tossed and turned until well after midnight," I said, yawning. "Didn't fall asleep until about four. I'm okay now, though." I stretched and yawned again.

"I slept through the night, no problem," Franca boasted.

"Well done," Stefan replied.

"Have you thought about what's on the agenda for today?" I asked.

He nodded. "Before Nadine gets any ideas about a pointless job creation scheme, I'll show you around a bit. Agreed?"

We grinned at him.

Fifteen minutes later, we were driving with him through the enclave. After only a few minutes, we arrived at our destination. He parked the vehicle in front of an entrance secured by four armed guards and told Franca and me to follow him. The guard let us through without comment.

"Do you want to see the recording of your escape through Berlin?" he inquired.

"Sure," Franca replied.

And I asked, "Where are we?"

"This is our IT department," Stefan said proudly. "As well as surveillance and security, we also take care of logistical issues such as housing, food, and health. This is where Adrian works."

"Who's that?" I asked.

"My boyfriend. He runs the surveillance team," Stefan explained. He led us past a disused elevator and up a flight of stairs. "We don't have enough power for elevators in this building. We need that for more important things, especially now that it's fall, and the solar power yield is dropping."

The space on the second floor was a combination of a modern loft and open-plan office. Exposed concrete and a large bank of windows around the edge, dozens of desks with monitors in the middle. Thick cable harnesses were fixed to the floor with gray tape in a makeshift manner. Seven or eight people sat in front of the screens. Some were looking at what looked like aerial photographs. Others were interpreting tables and writing lines of code.

"Before you go on, I've had a question on my mind ever since we got here," Franca said.

Stefan looked at her briefly and nodded. "And that would be?"

"Dr. Koller told us a long time ago that you were working on a vaccine. Is that true?"

He looked at her and replied. "You'd best discuss that with her directly."

"And how do I get to her?"

"You have an appointment tomorrow afternoon." Stefan nodded at me. "She thinks a lot of you—she's postponed or canceled everything else in her schedule."

"Oh, okay," Franca said, surprised.

"She's also instructed me and Adrian to be there. In case she can't answer all of your questions herself."

Behind him, a glass door to an office opened and two men came out. One of them, with a receding hairline and deep blue eyes, came over to us immediately. He was wearing jeans and an anthracite business shirt. Stefan and he kissed before he held out his hand to us.

"Hi," he said pleasantly, "I'm Adrian. You must be Backup and Franca if I'm not mistaken."

Grinning, we returned his greeting.

He introduced us to the tall young man he had been talking to in the office, "This is Olek." His paw literally swallowed my hand.

"Nice to finally meet you guys," he said. "Verena and Marcus have told me a lot about your adventures."

"Thank you," I replied. "How are they doing? What about Hanna?"

"Oh, everyone's doing great. I'm on my way to see them right now. Maybe we can have lunch together later?" he suggested.

I looked at Stefan, and he nodded. "One o'clock in the canteen?" I asked.

"Perfect; we'll be there," Olek replied. Turning to Franca and me, he said, "Glad you're here. I'm afraid I have to go again, but I'll see you later, okay?"

Everyone nodded. We watched him leave the same way we had come. Stefan lowered his voice and said conspiratorially, "Nadine's spy."

Adrian smiled artificially, as if the subject made him uncomfortable. He told us to follow him into the office. The door behind us slammed shut.

"What do you mean, spy?" I asked.

"Spy is a bit of an exaggeration. But we have reason to believe he's providing Koller with info," Adrian said, overemphasizing each word and looking at Stefan urgently. "He's the only one who doesn't have a specific job, but he has his fingers in a lot of pies. No one knows more about life in the enclave than he does, about the rumors and the intrigue, but also about the concerns of the Berliners. And he regularly meets with her in secret."

"How do you know that?" asked Franca.

"It's not just us who know that. It's an open secret," Stefan interjected. Adrian pointed to a dresser next to Franca. On it lay a drone the size of a plate.

"And that's why you spy on each other?"

"Don't get me wrong," he said placatingly. "You can trust Olek completely. We all play for the same team."

"Why was he here?" asked Stefan, changing the subject.

"Because of the UV lamps. Some of them have disappeared again."

"What—again?"

"Yes, for the fifth time in two months. And no one will admit to having seen or heard anything. Plus, twelve solar panels are gone." Turning to us, he said, "We need to increase surveillance, but we don't have the hardware."

"By hardware, you mean . . . drones?" interjected Franca.

"Yes. Right now, we have nine in use. But that's scarcely enough to keep a permanent watch on all the barricades. And we lack the human resources to get any more."

My palms were suddenly sweaty. "How would you get more of them?" I asked.

"There's a logistics center about thirty kilometers outside the city where electrical equipment is stored," Adrian replied. "It has everything we need—from refrigerators to e-bikes. Unless it's burned down. Personally, I'm hoping to find drones with infrared cameras. Only then would I be able to sleep peacefully at night. But Koller—"

"Won't let you go out," I finished the sentence for him.

He nodded sorrowfully. "She doesn't want any more losses."

"Hmm, what are the chances of finding something that sophisticated?" I asked.

"There's no doubt models with integrated thermal imaging cameras—it's not standard, but it's not uncommon. The more recent devices even let you differentiate between thermal ranges."

"He means by displaying only a certain temperature spectrum," Stefan explained. It hadn't occurred to me before that zombies might have a different body temperature, so I asked about it.

"Yes, it's about twenty-six degrees Celsius," Adrian said. "We assume that this saves them energy if they have to go for longer periods without food. But the real problem will be registering the equipment before the first flight—back when they were produced, it was essential. Unfortunately, I assume all the services needed for that are down now."

"I might be able to fake something there," Stefan said. We looked at him questioningly. "Well, I could clone the certificates of old models. We're already emulating a server. It should work with that."

"That sounds feasible," Adrian noted.

"Do we know what the undead population is at the logistics center?"

"Relatively low, I'd guess. It's an isolated industrial area off the highway, away from any housing developments."

Out of the corner of my eye, I saw Franca rubbing her thumbs against her fingers nervously. "How do we get our weapons?" I inquired.

"They're in the armory," Adrian said.

"I realize that. I wanted to know how we could get them back."

"Well, you can't move around the enclave with firearms unless you have a special permit. Or unless you're a member of the security forces. Neither of those applies to you."

I sighed. Stefan looked out the window, bored.

"Okay. We'll discuss it with Nadine herself tomorrow afternoon," I said. "Will you please compile a list of things that are urgently needed? Is there anyone who knows their way around the logistics center?"

"What are you going to do?" he asked, avoiding my request.

"Earn my keep," I replied. "How long will it take you to make the list? Can you make it by noon tomorrow?"

"Um, yeah, that should be doable," Adrian said.

"Very good. I need it before we go to see Dr. Koller. Now show us the recording of us," I demanded.

He sat down at the computer and began clicking the mouse. Next to me, I noticed Franca furtively wiping her hands on her pants. Just the thought of the potential mission made our hearts race.

"First of all," Adrian said, "look at the map on the wall!" I turned around. Above the discarded drone was a map of the city, showing two different-size areas—the smaller one to the west and the larger one to the east—connected by a slightly curved blue line. All of this was outlined by three red lines. Between these boundaries were two wide areas shaded in blue.

"In the eastern circle is the Charité," he went on. I stretched out my arm and pointed to the spot. "Exactly," Adrian confirmed. As I moved my finger along the curved shape, he said, "That's the route Stefan took you on,"—I had arrived at the larger outline—"to the enclave. The green dot up there, that's our current position. We've been tracking your path through the city—that's on the far left of the map. Four drones per compass point fly over the city limits every hour at a height of two hundred meters. That's how we spotted you. But see for yourself, uncensored and uncut," he said, gesturing to us to stand behind him. I saw a still image and on it, a hand frozen in motion, either letting go of the drone or trying to grab it.

Adrian clicked on the play icon at the bottom of the screen, and it hastily moved away. The office was filled with the hum of rotors. A few seconds later, the drone rose, and the camera panned down. I caught a glimpse of several flat roofs with photovoltaic units.

"Where did all those solar panels come from?" I asked in amazement. Meanwhile, the drone headed on a southerly course.

"Some from nearby hardware stores, others were already there. We took a lot of them from nearby fields where electricity used to be harvested," Stefan replied. "Which has proven to be a safer alternative than stores. These areas are secured with high fences and are also easy to keep an eye on."

Adrian stopped the recording. The buzzing stopped. The surveillance drone had arrived at the southern edge of the enclave, as was evident from the roadblocks. "No-man's-land begins within a hundred to a hundred and fifty meters of here. This is our protective buffer, designed to offset the smells and sounds of civilization on the outside and keep the Grays away."

The recording continued. I had seen so many ghost towns by now that these images did not strike me as strange at all. The drone climbed higher and flew southward. At a certain point, it stopped. It paused for three seconds and then moved westward, making a large arc northward. Again, Adrian paused the recording.

"That's you, there!" he exclaimed.

"Where?" I asked skeptically.

Adrian enlarged the image. A vehicle with a swastika on the hood appeared in the center of the screen.

"Oh there," I said. "How did you see that at that distance?"

"Software," Franca said, without taking her eyes off the monitor. I saw Stefan and Adrian nod. The buzzing started up again. The drone descended and flew after us. The scene now showed Verena crafting the flag.

"That was very smart of you. Otherwise, we wouldn't have sent out a rescue party."

"How high is the drone flying now?" I asked.

"A hundred meters," Adrian replied. "I'll fast forward a little until it gets interesting." The vehicle drove frantically through the half-clogged streets until it arrived at the zoo. Here, the spotter rose higher again. "Watch out," Adrian said. The camera was now filming the park to the right of the avenue.

"My God." Franca gasped. Beneath the defoliated treetops, it was swarming like an ants' nest. The undead were swarming toward the spot in the picture where our vehicle was. Then the drone turned away and filmed the other side of the road—with the same result. In the meantime, we had arrived where the road had been plowed clear.

"Had you cleared the route?" I asked, shaken to the core.

"Yes," Stefan replied. "Preventative assistance for just such a case as this."

On the screen, the zombies charged out of the park. Breathlessly, I watched our escape to the point where we got out. The drone seemed to drop abruptly from the sky and floated down. From its perspective, I saw myself helping Kirstin and Dominic. The reconnaissance aircraft suddenly veered off, sweeping through the Brandenburg Gate and across the empty square behind it. With a click, Adrian stopped the recording.

"What was that all about?" I ventured to ask.

"Strange, isn't it?" he said.

"How could they coordinate like that?" whispered Franca, looking at the two Berliners. "They can't communicate with each other, can they?" To my ears, her question sounded more like a hopeful prayer.

"I'm afraid they can," Stefan contradicted her.

Before he could say any more, Adrian interrupted him. "We don't know that for sure."

"Bullshit, that's exactly what we do know."

"And if that were the case, we wouldn't be allowed to brag about it in public," Adrian admonished him.

"What do you mean?" Stefan snapped at him. "I'm getting tired of all this secrecy. They'll find out tomorrow anyway."

Adrian fell silent. For a moment, it looked as if he wanted to continue arguing, but he let it drop and just nodded. Franca and I hardly dared breathe. We looked insistently at Stefan, who continued, "I suppose you know how the whole thing came about? With the fungus-infested ant and the rabid dog feces?"

We nodded. "I can't explain it all in detail, but basically this is what happened: Through a chemical reaction . . ."

"Through radioactivity!" Adrian corrected him.

Stefan rolled his eyes. "The mutation caused by radioactivity—or whatever—does not stop at DNA. Just as it amplified the host's sense of smell in the first generation, so it focuses on the sweat glands further down the line." He let us process what we had heard. It meant nothing to me.

"Holy shit," Franca suddenly cursed, then clasped her head in her hands. "Pheromones! Ants communicate via pheromones!"

I looked at her skeptically, "How d'you know that?"

"You learn a lot about insects when you're preparing for a jungle trip in Brazil," she said, as if that were explanation enough.

"Tomorrow, Koller will tell you about it in more detail—if you ask. But ultimately, you're guessing right," Adrian added.

"That also explains their behavior in Hamburg," Franca recalled, recounting the attack at the bridge.

The two nodded. "Yeah, that makes sense."

"How are we going to stop the hell-spawn now?" she asked, running her hand over her millimeter-short stubble.

"That," Stefan said, "is something we don't have the slightest idea about."


"How dare you put a bee in their bonnet like that?" roared Nadine. Stefan translated quietly for us.

"We didn't," Adrian defended himself. "Franca came up with it on her own."

"That's right," I said.

After watching the video yesterday, our general mood was low. At one o'clock, as arranged, we had eaten lunch with Olek, Verena, and Marcus. They were infected by our gloom as soon as they heard about the latest development with the zombies. Not even a discussion about a possible looting trip to the electronics warehouse could lift them. Nonetheless, Verena and Marcus expressed interest in participating, even though he felt her parents would certainly not take a positive view of it.

After lunch, we had wandered listlessly through the city. Stefan showed us various electricity warehouses, piled high with truck and car batteries. At nightfall, I went home with Franca and went to bed early. I tried to read in a novel but couldn't muster enough concentration to stick with it. So I turned out the light and, after tossing and turning for a while, fell asleep.

The next day I stayed in bed until Stefan came to get us. Quickly, I ate one of the rolls, devoured a tomato, and downed some cold leftover coffee.

Adrian was waiting in the car. On the drive to the Charité, we discussed how to get Dr. Killer onside with our plan without her tearing our heads off. Still, it had taken barely five minutes for her to get worked up.

"Do you have any idea of the danger you would be putting yourselves in?" she asked me indignantly.

"Absolutely," I replied confidently.

She became even angrier and looked at Adrian. "What do you expect to get out of this? What else could you possibly need?"

"Some infrared cameras would be very handy. And a few spare drones are an absolutely necessity," he said, presenting her with a sheet of paper covered in writing. "That's the list of the other things that occurred to me. I can't say much more until I get a better picture of the warehouse.

Nadine looked at him in horror, not taking in the list. "If you WHAT? You want to drive out there yourself?"

"Someone has to do it. I'm the only one who can choose the right things."

"And who's going to cover your surveillance duties if something happens to you?"

"Don't worry. I've already briefed four people in the event of an emergency. Operations can be maintained in my absence without any problems."

Dr. Koller massaged the bridge of her nose. "What support do you need?"

"Two armed people at the wheel, two to carry the gear. Franca and me," I answered for him. "Two vehicles. And our weapons."

"Well, if that's all," she said sarcastically. "But you'll have to get volunteers for that. I can't think of anyone who'd be stupid enough to join your suicide squad."

"I would," said the guard behind her, known as Serj to the staff, in a heavy Russian accent.

"Great! That's all I need," wailed Dr. Koller.

"I'll ask Hussein if he wants to come along," Serj suggested. "He's currently guarding the border," he explained to Franca and me. "He's been on a few trips like this before."

"With him, we'd be up to strength," I said, adding, "Verena and Marcus decided yesterday that they wanted to join us."

Adrian grinned cockily.

Nadine looked at us in amazement for a few seconds before admitting defeat. "Whatever. You two have temporary authority to borrow weapons," she said, addressing Franca and me. When we didn't reply, she changed the subject. "I'd like to move on to the last point, if we're done with this," she announced. Everyone nodded with satisfaction. "It's this: Is there anything else you want to know?" she asked.

As if she had just been waiting for this moment, Franca spoke up, "Where are you with the vaccine?"

Dr. Koller sighed. "The vaccine . . . What I am about to tell you must not leave this room! Is that clear? Oh yes, Stefan should feel free to leave, since he can't keep anything to himself." She looked at Serj, who escorted him outside with a serious expression on his face. "What do you want first, the good news or the bad news?"

Franca said, "The good news first."

"The latest tests were successful. We have found a cure that makes humanity immune to the zombie fungus."

"What?" we both said at the same time.

"Wait, I'm not done yet! We've been working hard on this for months and are now having some initial success. The last of the subjects who survived the infection have been under close observation for three weeks. They are doing well. To be on the safe side, we are keeping them in quarantine a while longer. We are not aware of any long-term side effects. But so far, everything is going well."

"That's . . . that's great," I said, dumbfounded. "Now does that mean if you get bitten, you won't transform?"

"Yes, as long as you've been vaccinated."

"So what are you waiting for?" I asked uncomprehendingly.

"This is where the bad news comes in," she said. "The tests we've done so far are specific to the individual subjects' blood groups. With the resources we have, we can't produce the relevant vaccine for each blood group. So we want to produce a universal serum."

"A little more background info would be nice. I have zero idea what you're talking about," I complained.

Dr. Koller took a deep breath and looked me in the eye: "We tested the blood groups one by one. As soon as an antiserum was available, we used it on the next test subject. We have now gone through all the blood groups. Except for blood group B."

"I still don't understand what the problem is," I urged.

"We are short of subjects for group B." Icy silence spread through the room. Since no one spoke, Nadine continued, "If we haven't successfully treated this blood group, we can't talk about a universal vaccine."

"But group B's not that unusual," said Franca, who had turned pale.

Dr. Koller nodded, "Correct. However, no one wants to volunteer."

"Have you had at least rudimentary success with this blood type?"

"Absolutely. And beyond," the virologist boasted. "Not least because of the knowledge we gained from working with the other groups. The next batch of tests will be ready in the next two days. However," she added, "the amount is only enough for a single trial. The subject treated with it will give us the formula for the universal serum. Provided the test is positive, of course."

Franca put her head back and closed her eyes.

I asked, "How many people who live here have type B blood?"

"Thirty-seven," Nadine replied.

"Okay, I'll do it," Franca said abruptly.

"You'll do what?" I asked. And then the scales fell from my eyes: "YOU are type B!" I exclaimed. She nodded. "And which am I?" I suddenly wanted to know. They had taken our blood on the very first day, so they must know.

"Also B," Nadine affirmed emotionlessly.

"Then you'd better take me!" I said hastily. "Franca's a better fighter. A better leader. That's much more important for society." I was convinced my argument made sense.

Ignoring my objections, Franca continued, "Tomorrow we'll get the equipment Adrian needs. And then you'll run the test on me. You'll have the batch ready in three days, right?"

Nadine thought about it for a moment and nodded.

"But why don't we go after the test?" I asked.

"It's not certain the vaccination will work," Franca explained. "That's why we should make the trip in advance. Who knows if there'll be a second chance? Besides, I don't want to have to think about the experiment all day tomorrow."

Suddenly, a few things became clear to me. I glared angrily at Nadine. "You let this meeting go the way it did because you had a specific outcome in mind. Now I see what it was."

She looked uncomprehending, but I saw from her face that I was not mistaken. "Why would two people be granted a half-day audience if nothing was expected of them?"

Franca tried to smooth things over. "It makes no difference now, Backup."

"It does to me, though. It would have been fairer to ask us directly." I rose to my feet in a rage. "And not to manipulate us so as to make it seem as if we were volunteering of our own free will."

Dr. Koller raised a hand and said, "You're absolutely right. It was stupid of me to put on a show like that. I'm very, very sorry."

I faltered. The wind had been taken out of my sails, and I had no choice but to nod and go along with it.

Serj was tracking the group of undead through the scope mounted on his sniper rifle. The overcast sky ensured we had diffuse light and no dark shadows. "I count seven," he said. "They look fresh. Of the fast variety."

Franca lay next to him in the dry grass, looking through binoculars in the same direction.

They had parked the two cars in which they had driven here at the edge of the property that belonged to the warehouse. Then they had moved onto the three-meter embankment bordering the area. In their camouflage gear, they were blended almost seamlessly with their surroundings.

"Correct," Franca confirmed. "What do you think of this plan: You and Hussein cover our backs until we're across the parking lot and at the entrance. Then you guys follow us."

The sniper thought for a moment and nodded. They were two hundred meters from the warehouse. Only a few vehicles in the parking lot provided any cover. "Ready when you are," he rumbled without lifting his head.

Franca patted him on the shoulder and scrambled back. He heard them talking quietly under the protection of the embankment, then she called out to him, "Okay, we're ready."

"Good luck!" The grass rustled as they crept past him. He kept an eye on Franca and Adrian as they darted across the parking lot, closely followed by Verena and Marcus. All were carrying rapid-fire weapons; only Backup ran with a homemade spear. Serj had taken a look at its ragged blade that morning and decided without further ado to replace it with one made of Damascus steel, which could still be found in many Berlin households and restaurants. With his other eye, he watched the wandering corpses through the telescope.

No sooner had the first one lifted its head to sniff the air than Serj burst it open with a high-speed projectile. Its abrupt demise made the remaining six sit up and take notice. Serj let off more shots, their blasts softened by a silencer, until he had wiped out the entire group. He then looked through his sights at Adrian, who was beckoning to him from the entrance. Serj glanced over his shoulder to make sure Hussein was ready to follow him, grabbed his rifle, and took off at a run. By the time they had covered the distance, the lock to the warehouse had also been picked. They positioned themselves in front of the heavy roller door and trained their weapons on it.

Hussein dug thick leather gloves out of his backpack and pulled them on before bending down and trying to reach under the gate. Groaning, he pushed it up. Franca and Marcus threw themselves to the floor and peered into the dark storeroom, weapons at the ready. Stale air reached Serj's nose.

"So far, so good," he heard Franca say softly. She propped up the gate with a knee-high trash can and rolled through the gap, disappearing inside for a full three minutes.

"Okay, come on in. There's no one around for miles," she announced afterward, lying on her back. A small lamp shone from her forehead. Serj and the others standing outside pulled their own headlamps from their pockets and rolled after her. They barricaded the gap with pallets that were lying all around inside the store. Once they were sure no one could gain entry and surprise them, they positioned themselves behind Adrian, who needed a few seconds to get his bearings. Silently, they followed him into the huge warehouse, which was sparsely lit by a few windows. The silence, occasionally disturbed by an indefinable cracking sound, was so oppressive that Serj involuntarily held his breath from time to time. The beams of their headlamps jerked up and down the ten-meter shelves, searching for anything they could use. They moved almost reverently along the silent aisles.

"Got it," Adrian whispered suddenly as they stood in front of a high rack that Serj could barely distinguish from the rest. "Could Marcus and Backup bring the cars around and wait for us at the gate while we get the goods there? There's more here than I was hoping for."

The two looked at each other and nodded. "We need your car keys," Marcus said, turning to Hussein. Backup caught them as he tossed them through the air. "We'll be waiting for you right outside the gate," the teenager added and moved away, Backup in tow.

While Adrian climbed up to the shelf using the support beams, Serj stood four or five meters to the side, which gave him a good overview of the seemingly endless corridors. Their footsteps had left dark tracks on the dust-covered black screed, like the first snowfall of the year. Hearing a squeak, he turned around. Franca was pulling a hand pallet truck behind her. She slid its fork under an empty pallet, pushed the lever a few times, and returned in time to catch the first packages Adrian threw down to her, Hussein, and Verena from a height of three meters. They stacked them on the pallet. Adrian switched to the left and then threw down other boxes that looked smaller but were heavier. It took him four minutes to climb down, satisfied. "Drones, wireless security cameras, and motion detectors. Everything your heart could desire," he enumerated proudly.

"Then let's get out of here," Serj urged. Franca nodded. They moved away with the squeaking pallet truck and followed their own trail back to the gate. Backup and Marcus, meanwhile, were waiting on the other side. They hurriedly loaded the packages that had been shoved through the gap to them into the trunks while Hussein covered their backs.

"I'll roll the door back down," Serj offered. "We might have to come back in at some point. It would be bad if it was full of zombies."

When everyone else had climbed into the cars, he got Franca to help him remove the pallets. The gate rattled down with a loud bang—in contrast to the Model X's gullwing doors, which closed almost silently once they were seated inside. The vehicles moved away, humming, while Serj wondered how long it would take for the dust to cover their tracks.

* * *

Nadine Koller made sure her office door was locked and sat down at her desk. It was the middle of the night. Most people in the enclave were fast asleep. But she wouldn't get any rest until she confided in someone.

With what was on her mind, there was only one person she dared trouble. She opened the computer, entered the password, and opened a browser. The fact that the global internet was dead didn't affect her plans. Using a satellite connection set up months ago, she logged in to the Stockholm clinic's webmail using her account. Professor Eckström's team had been right in their assessment of the scale of the apocalypse and had pulled out all the stops to maintain at least a makeshift level of communication.

For its part, Berlin had taken the appropriate action. In the final days before the collapse, a transmitter had been set up on the roof of the Charité, which connected to their computer via the intranet. No one expected this to be activated from time to time, and Dr. Koller kept it a secret. Now she thought she was safe, she opened a new message, which she had been drafting in her head all day. Tired, she glanced once more at the office door before her fingers scurried across the keyboard:

*Dear Janis,*

*It's been weeks since I last wrote. There has been nothing new to report. But in the past few days, things have taken an unexpected turn: I've recruited a test subject for our next series of tests. One I have been waiting for for a long time. Her blood sample started reacting in the lab test after coming into contact with antibodies. But not in the way we suspected. At first, I thought it was just another failed test. But after twice the normal incubation time, the blood reacted so aggressively that it began to build up a membrane as soon as it came into contact with infected secretions. One that caused it to literally dry out on the surface. We were then able to extract the DNA sequence responsible for this. Can you imagine? After all our failed attempts, might we have made a breakthrough? For the first time in a long time, I have hope again. We still have the clinical test to go, of course. But I am confident it will be successful.*

*However, I may have made a serious mistake. I am not yet sure what the consequences will be, but in desperation I did not know what else to do. I lied. To get the subject to volunteer, I told her a preposterous story about how far along we were with the tests. How successful they would be. However, she saw through me. Afterward, I corrected myself and told her the truth. It is inexplicable to me why I feel this untruth, of all things, to be more momentous than having sacrificed all those people before. Maybe I don't want to lie any longer—always hoping that if my next experiment doesn't fail, I will save the world. As if there were many people left to save. I didn't have the heart for another kidnapping. There are already rumors in the enclave about the missing people, and I can't afford a riot when we're so close to the finish line. Tomorrow I will be able to test the universal vaccine. Everything looks promising. Even in the computer simulations, the modified antibodies have produced the desired effect. There is no reason to doubt that it will work differently in the test subject than in the test trial. At least I would like to believe that.*

*I'm tired, Janis. I can't remember the last time I slept more than four hours at a stretch. When I even rested and relaxed. Tonight, at least, I want to be lighter of heart (whether I will succeed is doubtful). That's why I'm writing all this to you, to unload at least some of my burden.*

*Wish me luck!*
*With love, Nadine*

*P. S.: I will try to provide you with daily updates.*

Dr. Koller saved the message. She waited five seconds for the webpage to reload and for the number one to appear next to the drafts folder. Janis would check the account the following morning and find that she had written to him. Nadine sighed, shut down the computer, and turned off the light.

I was pissed off, nervous, and unreasonable. I had all kinds of fears about Franca's upcoming vaccination. But I realized that it was useless to give way to my anger about her decision. So I tried not to show I was in a bad mood. Franca, on the other hand, seemed calm and relaxed as she sat at the breakfast table waiting for me to finish my coffee. I took my time. At some point it became cold and tasted awful. She wasn't supposed to consume anything before the experiment so as not to mess up her blood work. So, I poured the contents of the cup down the sink, brushed my teeth, and followed her out of the house. We had agreed to drop by

Stefan's house in the course of the morning, and he was going to get us to the clinic by noon at the latest.

Stefan didn't make a sound during the entire trip; our silence was probably too intimidating. Only when we got out did he wish us luck. We nodded, and he drove away. A nurse was waiting for us at the reception desk, and she escorted us down one floor to the basement. Before we entered the last corridor, we passed a heavily guarded door with all kinds of warning signs about danger to life. The security guards told us firmly to keep moving. Dr. Koller was already waiting in a brightly lit room with her entourage—five people in white coats. She raised her head and looked at us. The bags under her eyes betrayed her exhaustion, and I had the feeling that she had hardly slept the previous night. Nevertheless, she radiated a vitality that I had not yet seen in her.

"There you are," she said. "We need about fifteen more minutes here. That'll give you time to change, over there." She pointed to a screen in the corner of the room.

"All right," Franca replied and disappeared behind it. I moved to a less crowed spot and tried not to get in the way. Dr. Koller and her team of assistants looked at each other's tablets and compared values or did whatever they did.

"Franca, we're ready," Nadine called after a while—I couldn't have said whether it had been fifteen minutes or an hour. Franca came out in a hospital gown, her sinewy arms and legs protruding from inside it. I went over in my mind the conversation we had had the previous night, but I had difficulty remembering our exact words. All I knew for sure was that she had resigned herself to dying a cruel death today. Now I read her willingness to sacrifice in her posture and her slightly lowered gaze. She lifted her head just once to follow Nadine's signal to enter the glass booth in the middle of the room. Three white coats followed her in.

Behind a screen, I spied a small bathroom. Next to a bed was an examination table that reminded me of a dentist's chair. Franca sat down on it. Her arms and legs were secured with straps the width of a hand. Sensors to measure her vital signs were attached to her head and neck. An assistant inserted a cannula into the crook of her left arm. The third person checked the connections of the tubes sticking out of various devices. They then went into a huddle, looked through one of the glass panes at Nadine, and nodded. She ordered them out. The door was locked. I saw that Franca was breathing deeply because her chest was clearly rising and falling.

"Can you hear me?" said Dr. Koller into a microphone on the desk where she sat.

"Yes, almost too loudly," came back in response, whereupon the doctor adjusted a control.

"Better?"

Franca nodded. I was so worked up that my heart seemed to be pounding in my ears.

"I'm going to give you the vaccination now."

The Italian closed her eyes. With a motion of her head, she agreed. Nadine looked down at her tablet and tapped it with her fingertip. Suddenly, a low, whirring sound came over the speakers as a colorless liquid flowed through the tube toward Franca's arm. She clenched her hand into a fist and stiffened. The closer the fluid got, the more her blood vessels and muscles stood out. I held my breath. And then the vaccine flowed into her bloodstream. A little later, the whirring stopped. Half a minute passed, during which no one dared to breathe, until Franca exhaled audibly and slowly opened her fist.

"How do you feel?" asked Nadine. Her voice betrayed the tension she was under.

"I don't feel any difference at all yet," Franca replied. "It was just a little cool around the injection site to begin with. Nothing else."

"All according to plan then," Nadine murmured. "We're going to observe you for an hour now before we draw your blood. That will show us how the vaccine and your immune system are interacting. If everything is going smoothly at that point, we'll release you from the straps. However, you'll have to stay in the test room for the entire duration of the experiment."

"Okay."

The next sixty minutes passed uneventfully except for occasional inquiries regarding Franca's well-being, which remained unchanged except for boredom. For comfort, I slid to the floor. Clutching my knees, I got lost in different thoughts until Nadine's voice brought me back to the present.

"We're coming in now." Two assistants then entered the test room with a guard. One of them set about removing the tube from the cannula and drawing Franca's blood via it. The other, a man in his thirties with a chalky white face, checked the sensors.

I heard him say, "I'm going to take the strap off your left wrist now. Once we're outside, you'll remove the rest yourself. Do you understand me?" The tremor in his voice was unmistakable.

"Loud and clear," Franca replied calmly.

With a long, hesitant ripping sound, he released the Velcro. Her arm lay free. Suddenly, it jerked upward, accompanied by a guttural, zombie-like moan from Franca's mouth. Her fingers hung limply in front of the assistant's face for a moment, who gave a loud cry of shock and stumbled backward, bringing down the guard. His weapon clattered to the floor. Outside the test capsule, pandemonium broke out.

"Can you still be saved?" I yelled at Franca over the panic and confusion. But Franca just looked at me, freed her other arm from the restraining belt, and stood up. Hanging onto the drip, she stumbled around the chamber, giving me an inscrutable look. Even the guard was crawling over the ground in fear.

As soon as he was out, Nadine slammed the door shut. "Get out, you idiot! Who put you on guard duty?" she yelled at him. "Get out, I don't want to see you here again!"

"You're crazy. He could have shot you," I screamed at the top of my lungs.

It took us a whole hour to recover from the shock.

I don't know whether further tests were planned for the day or whether Nadine called it a day out of revenge and left the test site together with her escort. Only a new guard and I stayed. At some point, food was brought to us. I poked listlessly at my tray. Franca's appetite seemed to have increased because she polished off her ration in record time.

"Are you eating yours?" she asked me with her mouth full.

"Nah, you can have it," I said, sliding the rest of my portion into the hatch. "How are you feeling?"

"I'm incredibly hungry. But otherwise, same as always. Are you staying here tonight?"

"Of course. You can't be left alone for a minute without getting into mischief."

"Thanks. Then it won't be too tedious."

After the guards had consulted with Dr. Koller, they brought in a mattress complete with pillow and blanket, which I positioned against the glass wall between me and Franca. They had even thought to bring us playing cards, which helped alleviate the boredom for the rest of the day.

"How long do you think this will go on?" I asked after dinner. Franca had put her mattress on the floor, too. Separated only by the pane of glass, we lay next to each other.

"Hopefully not that long," she replied. "I'm not a homebody, as you know. I mean, we've been on the road constantly for months, and now I'm supposed to put up with total quarantine?"

I grinned. "But once you're out and I'm vaccinated, we'll roam the world and fix everything."

"But let's face it, that might be a bit too ambitious." Franca laughed.

"Well, you have to have some goals in life," I said with a shrug.

"So, does it work?" asked Adrian.

"Yes, I think so," Stefan replied. "Try number . . . four!"

Adrian turned on the drone, grabbed a clunky remote, and pushed the buttons.

Suddenly, the aircraft's rotors spun, producing a wild whirring sound. "Yeah," he cheered. "Open the window; I'll take a look around!"

Seconds later, the reconnaissance drone made a nightly circuit of the building in which they were sitting. Once Adrian was convinced it wouldn't give him the slip, he flew the drone out into the city. "What temperature are the undead again?" he asked.

Stefan followed the colorful flashing of the position lights. "Supposedly twenty-six degrees Celsius." He then tinkered with the device's settings. The small screen of the smartphone plugged into the remote control turned black. He continued to tap his way through the options until human-shaped colored patches appeared on the display. "Awesome! There we have it! Now we can even run surveillance at night!" They celebrated their success with a high five.

Over the next five days, little more happened than on the first afternoon. Dr. Koller stopped by briefly each day, ran over the current values, asked Franca a few questions, and since nothing significant had occurred, disappeared again.

I waited to see what would happen, despite my burning curiosity and the soul-destroying boredom, because I didn't want to let Franca down.

On day six, Nadine appeared earlier in the morning than usual. We had scarcely got up and brushed our teeth before she said, "Long story short: We can now continue with the experiment."

"Does this mean my body is tolerating the vaccine well?"

"Exactly. Even better than expected."

"And what are the prospects . . . ?"

"Well, no one can say. And I don't want to lull you into a false sense of security by making assumptions. But rest assured, if I wasn't absolutely convinced that we had a realistic chance of success, I wouldn't be taking any chances."

Franca nodded composedly. "So what happens next?"

"We're going to infect you." Icy silence spread through the room. I closed my eyes. Meanwhile, Nadine continued, "And observe how your immune system reacts. For this, we have brought a diseased tissue sample, which we will use to contaminate a scalpel blade. We're going to use that to break your skin. If the vaccine works, the tissue will not change."

"And if it doesn't?"

"For this very reason, we'll start with your little finger. Which we can amputate if necessary."

Franca nodded hesitantly. "Use my left hand. I'm right-handed. And let's get right to it. Before I change my mind."

"Hey, isn't this moving a little too fast? Isn't there another way to test it? In a Petri dish, under a microscope, or something else?" I objected.

"Unfortunately, we don't see any other option, Backup," Nadine replied. "Believe me, if we had an alternative, we would use it."

"Leave it," Franca said to me affectionately. So I stayed by the window and watched skeptically to see what would happen next.

"Good, then; let's start," Nadine said firmly. Whereupon Franca was strapped to the table again. "Just to be sure," Dr. Koller said, smiling apologetically at her. Then she turned and asked for the tissue sample. An assistant approached, carrying a stainless steel box wrapped in plastic and covered with danger signs. Dr. Koller pulled on thick black rubber gloves and took the sample, tearing the packaging and carefully opening the shiny silver box, which she set on the table. From my vantage point, I could see it contained a scalpel and a Petri dish.

Nadine picked up the glass ring, which contained a dark gray mass. She removed the lid and reached for the knife. It almost looked as if she hesitated. Then she guided the blade almost reverently over the zombie tissue.

"We're going to tie off your little finger below the first joint so that the poison can't spread as quickly if the vaccination hasn't worked," she explained. Meanwhile, an assistant did what she described. Slowly, Nadine lowered the knife toward Franca's trembling fist. The virologist briefly placed her free hand on it. "It will be all right," she affirmed in a whisper. My throat tightened. I stepped as close as I dared. Nadine positioned her hand with the scalpel, pausing hesitantly barely five millimeters above the surface of the skin. And then she cut a small wound into it.

When the tissue around it began to turn grayish almost instantly, my heart almost stopped. I had observed such scenes countless times and knew what the outcome was. Franca took a sharp breath. The assistant jumped in to perform the amputation, but Nadine held her back. Just as I was about to protest, I emitted a sound of surprise. The discoloration had suddenly stopped. Like everyone else in the room, my eyes widened. Three seconds passed. Not only had the change of color stopped—it was actually receding.

"Take the bandage off her. Now! I want fresh blood to get to it," Nadine ordered. Seconds later, the grayish color had almost completely disappeared. A whitish secretion oozed from the wound. As dark, red blood flowed out behind it, Dr. Koller shouted in amazement, "It works! It WORKS!" Speechless, we looked at the cut in Franca's finger, which was no different from a normal injury. As relief spread through me, the strength seemed to drain from my legs. I slid down the wall and sat on the floor.

"How do you feel?" Nadine asked Franca, her eyes still fixed on the wound.

"Fantastic. It's burning a little, but otherwise I'm fine." Only now did I notice that her face was chalky white. I probably didn't look much better myself.

"May I do the test again?" asked Nadine.

Franca pursed her lips and shrugged. "Sure. Why not?"

"We'll now try the ring finger next to it," the virologist said, repeating the process with the scalpel. Franca's immune system again fought off the attack. Now some of the people in the room dared to cheer quietly.

"Middle finger?" asked Nadine breathlessly. Franca nodded and, over the course of the next five minutes, collected various cuts in her hand, always with the same end result. Now I too cheered loudly whenever her blood flushed out the secretion.

Then Franca said, "Enough, I need a break," and lay down. "My circulation is shutting down from excitement."

"We'll give you a dose of saline. That should help in the short term."

Franca raised a thumb in the air—and dozed off.

She slept for twelve hours straight. During that time, I watched the tablets that displayed her vital signs almost continuously. Everyone around me looked content, almost euphoric.

But this mood made me suspicious—everything was going much too smoothly for my taste. Nadine appeared almost hourly, kept saying, "Mm-hmm, good," and "Splendid." Then she would leave. When I asked what would happen next, she replied, "We'll keep Franca in quarantine for another week. If nothing changes, we will release her. But she will then have to come in twice daily for follow-up."

"And when can other people be vaccinated?"

"Once we produce the antidote in larger quantities."

"Can you be a little more specific?"

"No. How are we going to do that? We have to extract Franca's serum first, to know what's needed," she answered irritably and disappeared.

As soon as Franca was awake, she asked for food. She again ate a double portion and drank a huge amount. I watched her as she stuffed her mouth. "That's a side effect, I guess. My appetite is enormous." After visiting the bathroom, she began doing push-ups. At twenty, she stopped. "Hmm, my strength hasn't increased," she said, disappointed. "I'm still going to have to increase the effort to convert the nutrients into muscle."

"It wouldn't do either of us any harm to put on a little more weight," I replied.

"Are we playing another round of cards?" she asked.

"You deal," I replied.

For the next five days, our daily routine hardly varied. At one point, Hanna, Verena, and Marcus, with Olek in tow, even spent an entire afternoon with us. Franca continued to eat big portions. I watched her muscle mass slowly grow.

Late one evening, Dr. Koller unexpectedly came in when we were about to go to bed. "You're coming on splendidly," she said to Franca. "I've been meaning to tell you that," she added. Looking more tired and worn out than ever, she kicked off her shoes and joined me on the floor, where she took the cordless phone out of the pocket of her coat and turned it off. "If it were up to me, I'd let you out first thing tomorrow.

But . . . for safety's sake, we're keeping you here until the day after tomorrow." Suddenly we were all grinning.

"Well then. If I have the prospect of being released, I'll easily survive one day," Franca replied.

"You'll finally be sleeping at home again," I added.

Nadine nodded and said, "After quarantine, we'll draw your blood to produce the vaccine. But from what I've seen so far . . ." She raised a thumb in the air.

"This is great news," Franca exulted.

"And when will it be ready?" I urged.

"Oh, in a few weeks, I don't know," Dr. Koller groaned wearily. "I don't want to think about that now. Let's play cards instead."

"There's a lot of commotion down there," Adrian said. The screen in front of him was dark with a few bright spots. In the upper right corner, the temperature to be detected was displayed: 20–30°C.

"Where did so many of them come from so suddenly?" muttered Stefan.

"Wait! Do you hear that?" Adrian went to the window and yanked it open.

"Sounds like a big drone," Stefan replied.

"Like a perversely large drone," he agreed, turning to look at the screen before picking up the remote. The image went dark as the spotter changed position. "Highlight the temperature discrimination, please!"

Stefan touched the keys. The digits on the screen changed accordingly. Nothing else happened. Adrian carefully swiveled the drone clockwise.

"Strange. What's that?" he asked in surprise, flying toward a brightly glowing object two hundred meters above the ground, its contours becoming clearer on the display. "Oh, shit!" he exclaimed as dozens of white lines moved ultrafast toward the camera. The image flashed briefly. Then everything went black.

"Did we just get shot down?" asked Stefan, looking at Adrian, who had gone white as a sheet.

"Rewind!" The view switched to the most recent shot, about ten seconds before the camera cut out. "Stop!" said Adrian. Together, they looked at the blurry image, where they could just make out what they were seeing. "We've been . . . shot down. By a . . . fucking Apache helicopter!"

* * *

Suddenly, we heard shots being fired. First one salvo, then a second, until there seemed to be a battle raging in the stairwell within a short time.

"What is it . . . ?" I asked. But before I could finish the sentence, Franca had run to her couch. She pulled a submachine gun from under the blanket.

"Where . . . Where did you get that?" stammered Dr. Koller at the sight of the weapon.

"Come on, let me out of here!" Franca ordered. I obeyed immediately and unlocked the door. We hugged briefly before she ran to the entrance. Now the gunshots were closer. She peered cautiously out of the room and beckoned us to her.

"Who's shooting?" she asked.

"How should I know?" Nadine replied. In the hallway ahead, I heard quick, heavy footsteps. Franca put her index finger to her lips and motioned to us to stay where we were. She scurried out toward the arrival, or arrivals. I peered after her. At the end of the corridor lay the bodies of the guards who had defended the door marked with security signs. Franca had pressed herself against the wall and was waiting, as tense as a drawn bow. Much too late, I spotted the figure in army fatigues with a digital camouflage pattern, stepping into the corridor and taking aim at me. From her hiding place, Franca rammed her gun into the pit of the gunman's stomach.

But the shot had been fired before I could pull my head back. A bullet drilled into the wall a few centimeters away from me. The attacker toppled over like a sack as Franca smashed her elbow into his neck. In one fluid motion, she raised the submachine gun in the direction he had come from. Without looking, she fired a long volley around the corner. Several sounds of pain followed the clatter. A lifeless body fell stumbling into the passageway.

Franca poked her head around the corner like a snake, moving it back and forth. She then bent down and frisked the unconscious man at her feet. She looked at his uniform before tossing me his rifle. "Come on, follow me," she shouted and jumped over him. I had to drag Nadine by the hand behind me to get her to break free of her stupor.

"Is this the only way out?" asked Franca, pointing to the staircase. The doctor nodded. One floor up, we again heard booted footsteps. Franca glanced past the stair railing and immediately ducked her head. Shots rang out. Concrete shards exploded at her feet. Enraged, she yelled something in Italian and ran to the door marked with warning signs. She pushed down the long, chrome door handle and pulled it wide open. Inside, all was darkness.

"No!" screamed Nadine, "Don't go in there!" But it was too late. Behind us came the crash of countless weapons. Crouching down, we crawled into the unlit room. Projectiles whizzed over our heads, shattering glass in the darkness. Franca closed the door. Bullets pelted against it from the other side. Over Nadine's panicked shrieks, I heard them denting the thick metal. Her screams were deafening. Blindly, I groped for a light switch, picking up scratches and wounds from the shattered window glass. I flicked the switch as soon as my fingertips found it. A second later, cold neon lights flickered overhead. I smelled a familiar stench. Mere centimeters from my hand, I saw a grotesque face that had ventured through the cracked window. It snapped open its mouth and sank its rotting teeth into my forearm.

Franca screamed.

Nadine screamed.

And I screamed more loudly than both. Franca fired a bullet into the zombie's skull. The emaciated monster slumped in the corner of the room where it was held captive with a handful of others. They charged, but the Italian made short work of them before they got close. Then she put the gun aside, stepped to me, and immediately began to tie off my upper arm with a drainage tube, of which there were quite a few lying around in this secret laboratory.

"Oh shit, Backie," she cursed. The skin discoloration around the bite set in.

"I told you not to come in here!" rumbled Nadine.

"How were we supposed to know you were breeding zombies in the basement?" Franca snapped. "What's wrong with you?"

"Where do you think we got the tissue samples from? Do you think we'd be this far along with the vaccine if we hadn't?"

"Can you guys please shut up? I'm about to kick the bucket here."

They both turned to me. "Do we have another shot of vaccine anywhere?" I wailed.

"I don't even know if that would do any good in your condition. A vaccine is supposed to be given before infection, not in the middle of it."

"Speaking of vaccines; what are the Americans doing here?" asked Franca.

"Americans? What Americans?"

"The ones out there—out there!" the Italian commented. "I've been around military circles long enough to recognize troops even when they don't have insignia on their equipment. Besides, one had the Marines emblem tattooed on his forearm. Could they have gotten wind of the tests?"

Nadine thought for a moment. Then she blanched.

"What?" exclaimed Franca.

"They can't have. The email traffic is encrypted," Dr. Koller stammered.

"What do you mean, email traffic? With whom?" Franca was boiling with rage.

"With my old professor in Sweden. He supported me with what I was doing."

"How the hell can you have mail contact with someone in Sweden? The internet is dead!"

"Well," Nadine pressed around, her eyes fixed on my spreading infection. "We have a connection via the Euro-Sat . . ."

"You were sending confidential messages via a satellite, and now you're wondering how they were hijacked?" Franca's world seemed to be coming apart at the seams. "How stupid are you people?"

"Um, hello," I begged. By now I was no longer afraid. I wasn't even close to panic; I was miles beyond it. "Can we see if I can be saved first?" The skin around the bite was burning like fire. And I couldn't feel the assimilated tissue at all anymore.

"I'm immune," Franca said. "Can we do something with my blood?"

"If we had five or six weeks, yeah, sure! But at speed, like this, no."

"I CAN'T LOSE BACKUP, TOO! YOU CAN DO SOMETHING, CAN'T YOU? WHAT WAS THE POINT OF ALL THAT STUDYING?"

"What do you expect me to do: conjure up a vaccine? It doesn't work that way."

"I don't care about that at all! Do anything that will help!"

"You just don't get it, do you? I can't do anything about it . . . or . . . maybe I can . . . ? Wait a minute." Dr. Koller ran to one of the worktables, where she tore open drawer after drawer. As soon as she found what she was looking for, she hurried back. "Give me your arm. No, the one with the cannula," she urged Franca, who promptly obeyed. Nadine took two full vials of blood from her. "There, now it's your turn," she said, looking at me.

"What do you want me to do?" I asked.

"Give me your arm," she ordered brusquely. "We're running out of time." I held it out to her. It had now turned gray all the way to the elbow. My fingertips were losing their healthy color. Dr. Koller looked at the limb, weighing up where to place the needle she had positioned on one of the ampoules. "Ah, screw it," she said, and began stabbing my bicep above the tube again and again, pumping Franca's blood into me. "You both have type B blood. That's definitely an advantage." When she got to the inside of my upper arm, she inserted the needle into the artery and injected the remainder into me.

Suddenly, I felt a chill spreading around the puncture sites and flowing through my arm toward the infection. "What the fuck? It's like ice water running through my veins."

The icy feeling reached the affected area. Tensely I watched what would happen next.

"No way!" Franca exclaimed. The black veins abruptly stopped advancing.

"The burning is starting to subside," I reported in amazement.

"Interesting," Nadine said. "I didn't think that would work."

After a few minutes of silence, I added, "And the feeling's coming back, too."

"What do you mean by that?" asked Nadine.

"It's my arm again. The numbness is gone," I explained and set about removing the tube.

"No!" shouted Franca. "We need to get you to the quarantine room right away. Right now, you're a danger to all of us."

"But how do we get out of here?" I asked.

She then rose and listened at the door. "I can't hear anything," she whispered. "Is there a phone here? So we can call for backup?"

"Unfortunately, not. And I dropped mine earlier," Dr. Koller replied.

Franca stood up—and froze. Her gaze remained fixed on the door. Nadine and I held our breath. Abruptly, she turned and yelled, "TAKE COVER!"

Dazzling light blinded me. The blast hurled us against the wall. The sound of the explosion, which ripped the door out of its frame, nearly deprived me of hearing. I landed on my stomach amid the shards. Dazed, I tried to lift my head, but I couldn't breathe. My eyes burned with the dust and smoke. Beams of light from three or four flashlights made their way through the haze. There was a high-pitched screaming in my ears. I saw helmeted silhouettes stepping over the threshold. They illuminated Nadine's and Franca's lifeless bodies before becoming aware of me.

Apparently I wasn't interesting enough for the intruders, because they left me lying there. The last thing I remember of that evening is two of them grabbing Franca by the arms and dragging her out.

I came around the next day. I had been put down in the quarantine room, filthy as I was, and given water and something to eat. My appetite seemed insatiable. I ate and drank whatever I could get my hands on, and yet was soon hungry again. Later that same day, I was given new clothes: a hospital gown. This is how it went week after week. Almost a month after the attack, I was still in isolation, although Dr. Koller performed daily tests on me.

"I'd love to let you out, Backup," she said at one point, "but I don't know what would become of you."

"But I'm healthy. And I feel good—given the circumstances," I affirmed. "What's wrong?"

"It's not about what's wrong—your test results are excellent."

"Then please explain to me what's wrong. Why is my arm still discolored even though I have it completely under control and am not a zombie?"

"Franca's blood has altered yours so that each of the affected cells is encased in a kind of protective membrane that is preventing the outbreak of the disease. As long as it stays that way, everything will be fine."

"And when can I get out?"

She sighed. "It's not that simple. Let me vaccinate the entire enclave, and we'll see, okay?"

I nodded. "I guess I have no choice, do I?"

"Unfortunately, no."

"And how long will it take you?"

"I'm guessing another three, four weeks, maybe five. But I wonder how the population would react to you and your arm moving around in their midst. That could be a serious problem. We'll have to keep it quiet, I'm afraid."

This time it was my turn to sigh. "Do we at least know what happened to Franca?"

"We suspect she's been kidnapped." Before I could make any sarcastic remark, she went on, "A helicopter dropped a half dozen gunmen outside the main entrance. If Franca's suspicions were correct—and also judging by the hardware we spotted on our drone and security camera footage—they were indeed Americans. But why they had to kidnap her, I have no idea."

"Her blood is now more valuable than oil," I said smugly.

Dr. Koller nodded. "I still don't understand it. They killed nine of our people to get something that we would have let them have if they had just asked."

Nine people. Nine people from a community that numbered barely two thousand—that was a bitter blow. But being deprived of the person I was closest to had unleashed a rage in me that took all my effort to keep in check.

So I lowered my eyes and clenched my teeth until my jaw muscles ached. "I'm sorry about that," I hissed between breaths.

Nadine couldn't say anything; she merely nodded.


One morning, a voice I hadn't heard in a long time woke me up. "Hey, Backie! Hey, sleepyhead, wake up!"

"Oh, not you again! What are you doing here?"

"Nadine sent us so you wouldn't get bored." Verena stood on the other side of the glass wall with Hanna, Marcus, and Olek behind her. "Let me see your arm," she demanded.

I stood up and pushed the sleeve of the gown I was wearing up over my shoulder. Their eyes widened.

"Whoa—awesome," Verena exclaimed. "You're a true nombie!" she said, almost in awe.

"A what?"

"A nombie. A zombie that's not a zombie. No-mbie!"

"Do you ever stop with the nicknames?" I groaned.

"Hmm, I don't think so," Verena replied seriously.

"Oh, never mind," I growled. "You guys want to play a game of cards with me while you're here?"

"Sure," she said as they sat down on the floor. "You deal!"


Crouched in ankle-deep snow, I study the footprints disappearing south along the A100 not far from Babelsberg. If I take the weather conditions into account, they must be between three and five days old. The sun is shining in a cloudless sky, so I take off my knitted cap. Winter is coming to an end, but sturdy hiking boots and thermal underwear are still essential outdoors. I look over my shoulder and say, "About four days. Three hundred zombies heading south."

Olek looks toward the horizon, where the myriad tracks disappear. In his holsters are a Beretta and a machete. Marcus and Verena are also carrying their Glocks at their hips. They carefully secure our flanks.

"We're letting them go, right?" she asks. "I don't feel like starting a fight with three hundred of them. Vaccinated or not."

Each of us is carrying a backpack with two thousand tins containing the antidote, along with food rations that require only boiling water to prepare.

"Of course. We have a different task," I say, tapping the base of my backpack where the vaccines are.

As the young people stand confidently in the wintry sun of our postapocalyptic world, I realize they are no longer merely my charges. They have grown up quickly. Now they are on the verge of bringing the vaccine that holds the potential to save humanity to survivors. They have long since earned my respect. And my friendship even more so.

And yet I feel an emptiness inside me, which has grown deeper and deeper since last fall. It almost plunged me into depression after Franca's abduction. Even though I'm feeling a little better now, I'm regularly seized by great sadness. And then I try, as best I can, to conceal my state of mind until I get the opportunity to give in to the pain in solitude. I have now mastered this art perfectly. Because I'm concealing something else, too.

My gaze wanders to my left fist, holding the spear shaft. A glove covers the gray skin underneath. It's less about protection from the frost because my left arm is impervious to the cold. But it does feel like a part of me and obeys me as it always has. In the same way, the blood flows through it supplying the cells with nutrients. So my bones remain stable.

The medical team at the Charité has examined everything in detail and is well informed about what is going on inside. But they know nothing about the voices that speak to me from it. No one but me knows.

In the end, it's not mere sounds that have been taking shape in my head since the bite. No. It is so much more.

Hitherto unknown primal needs that cause my pulse to skyrocket whenever I smell humans.

The ability to see the outlines of objects around me even in the dark. The colorless glow of warm, living bodies at night.

The strength inherent on the infected arm that I am always reminded of when I touch the spot on the spear where my handprint left its mark during a silent rage.

I adamantly refuse to answer their call. The call of a faction that would welcome me into their ranks. That would accept me as one of their own and integrate me without prejudice. The only price would be giving up my humanity.

Leaning on the spear shaft, I rise and look to the south. A glance at the sun reveals that we have about six hours of daylight left. Behind me, I hear my companions preparing to march on. I stow my cap in my jacket pocket and tighten the shoulder straps of my backpack.

It's time to hit the road.

# CHAPTER 7

# STAVANGER

Professor Janis Ekström strode toward the park bench. All around him was greenery, and the sun was shining above the budding treetops. In his right hand he held his old lunch box, dented from years of use, and in his left a small bottle of diluted orange juice. Just before taking his seat, he looked around for Professor Agnar Sørensen, with whom he had an appointment here in the park at Stavanger University Hospital. Janis had visited him at home last night for the first time in months and had been delighted to see that Sørensen had regained his strength after a long illness. They had had little contact during that time. It was important to avoid the risk of infection. Medication was scarce, and the men were disadvantaged by their advanced age.

At the moment, however, Agnar was nowhere to be seen. Janis sat down, placed his lunch box and juice bottle beside him, and smoothed out his gray suit pants. Now, he didn't mind that they weren't pressed or that his formerly white shirts had a grayish sheen. All the same, he was glad he had taken three suits with him when he fled Stockholm. Then he pulled out a sandwich and bit into it. His upper denture rubbed uncomfortably on the right, so he chewed mainly on the left. He wondered if there were any competent dental professionals left who could fix them for him. Out of the corner of his eye, he caught sight of a silhouette and recognized Agnar's figure. His old colleague was leaning on a cane.

Ekström swallowed his mouthful and exclaimed, "Since when does a youngster like you need a walking stick?"

Sørensen grinned. "Since he survived a combined five knee and hip surgeries, an apocalyptic winter, and three wives. I think a stick is justified."

He sat down with Janis, hung his cane on the back of the seat, and fished a sandwich out of the box. "Gee, I missed this," he said, nibbling carefully at the soft part of his sandwich. "My stomach's still not quite up to it," he explained apologetically.

"It's only here in the park that I notice how much weight you've lost," Janis said. "Take it slow!"

"Well, I was flat on my back for three months, too," the other said defensively. "Damn gastrointestinal infection almost took me out, with the drugs being so scarce. But we're still alive, Janis."

"Which, unfortunately, is more than we can say for the rest of the world."

Janis watched as Agnar chewed thoughtfully on a sunflower seed.

"Quite amazing," said the convalescent, "that we two old farts were involved in saving what was left of it. But Doctor Koller did an exceptionally good job, my friend."

"I completely agree. She had to pull out some stops to achieve the goal. But ultimately, in hindsight, that justifies the means, doesn't it? Oh yes, before I forget. The vaccine will be shipped tomorrow."

"And you're just telling me this now?"

"Hey, I'm an old man too, and I only found out this morning. Besides, my brain doesn't work as well as Nadine's anymore."

"It never has, Janis, it never has. Neither yours nor mine has," Agnar said, looking back at the sandwich in his hand.

Janis's voice snapped him out of his ruminations. "Ah, look, here comes Göran. You absolutely have to meet him." The convalescent looked in the direction Eckström was pointing. Three people were approaching. One young man, who looked like a nurse, was pushing a wheelchair. In it sat a person whose legs and large parts of whose face were bandaged. The third person was limping, and their head and right arm were also hidden under several layers of gauze so that little more than their eyes could be seen. Otherwise, they were dressed in the customary hospital nightgowns.

"Göran is the one pushing the wheelchair," he added.

"And who are the others?" asked Agnar.

"These must be the friends he told me about. I'm meeting them for the first time today, too."

When they were within shouting distance, Janis waved at them and said in English, "Good afternoon, Göran. I finally get to meet you all. How are you today?"

The young nurse grinned amiably and replied, "Good day, Professor. We are doing splendidly." The man in the wheelchair nodded and the woman next to him also inclined her head slightly. "The skin grafts were successful and are healing as expected. Now we're enjoying the day. The fresh air should help with the healing process," he added.

As they came to a halt directly in front of them, Janis heard Agnar inhale sharply. "This is my colleague Professor Sørensen," he explained. Before he could get a word in edgewise, he introduced him to Göran, whose bandages on his arms and legs could only be seen up close.

"I'm glad you're feeling better," he said, turning to Agnar. "Professor Ekström told us a lot about you while you were sick."

"Thank you very much, young man. It was not a pleasant time; I can tell you that." Sørensen sighed.

"So much the better that you're fit again. We are also in the process of recovering. But you two will have a lot to talk about. Please don't be offended if we move right along."

"Not at all, Göran," Janis said. "I'll keep my fingers crossed that you're all feeling fit again soon."

"Thank you very much, Professor. And take good care of yourself."

"I will."

They said good-bye. Slowly the three went on their way. As soon as they were out of earshot, Agnar blurted out, "What on earth happened to them? Their faces are horribly burned."

Janis sighed, drank a big gulp of juice, and said as he replaced the cap on the bottle, "My dear colleague, that's a painful story. A few months ago, it must have been the last week of December, a local man is walking his dog along the beach at Brusand. At the southern end of the bay— right by the local campground—the animal starts barking furiously. It runs away from him. The man runs after it and discovers it yapping at the wreckage of a rescue boat among the stones. The kind they use on cruise ships."

"Like a lifeboat?" asked Agnar.

"Yes, that's right, a lifeboat. The man is about to drag the dog away when he hears faint cries for help. He approaches the boat and peers in through one of the portholes, where he spots those three. More locals turn up, drawn by the barking. There's even an armed patrol. They quickly determine that they are not infected and work to get Göran out. He is barely conscious, and the other two are on the brink of the afterlife. Joining forces, the people then carry out the man and woman, whose skin is already peeling off due to their severe burns and into which their clothing and life jackets have been partially burned. As they strip Göran of the remnants of his faux leather jacket, they also peel off large chunks of skin from his back."

"Good God," Agnar whispers.

"You said it. But it goes on. They are lucky, in that it's winter. In the cold, the pain is probably halfway bearable," Ekström says. "So, the burns are exposed as much as possible and cleaned with drinking water. The owner of a nearby campground organizes clean towels and sheets and drives up in a motor home. Afterward, she decides to bring the stranded people to the hospital here."

Janis pointed his finger at the entrance at the far end of the park. "Half an hour later, they're standing by the emergency entrance, where they're immediately admitted and looked after. The medical team fights for their lives for days. Göran is out of danger after a week, but the other two . . . The attending physician who told me the story said their vital signs were getting worse and better in parallel. Like they were egging each other on to survive—almost like they were connected on a higher level." When Agnar tried to object, Janis quickly raised his hand and beat him to it, "I know there's no rational explanation for it. The doctor just said it was extraordinary. Anyway, the burns were beyond bad. She can't explain how anyone could have survived them for so long. And then, as soon as their condition was halfway stabilized, they started doing skin grafts. Apparently, that went well, too. You saw them."

"Dear me," Agnar stammered. "How did those poor people get into that state in the first place?"

"Tragic, very tragic. They had escaped from the mainland and had to stop over on an oil rig by helicopter. They were going to refuel. They were attacked by the last remaining worker, who was obviously out of his mind."

Janis took another small sip. "As a result, the aircraft was destroyed. The explosion doused them with burning fuel. Göran's parents and a family friend were killed. He himself managed to roll away from the landing platform and hit the ground hard a few feet below. When he came to, the rig was already falling apart. Göran spotted the lifeboat, rushed into it at the last moment and detached it. At the foot of the rig, he spotted two yellow life jackets being rocked back and forth by the waves—with the other two inside them. The detonation of the helicopter had simply swept the pair off the platform. They had plunged nearly twenty meters into the water, which fortunately extinguished the flames and lessened the pain of the burns. He got them into the boat, in which they had been traveling for close to thirty hours. Someone had stored some spare cans of diesel in it.

But three kilometers offshore, they ran out of that, too. It was pure luck that they washed up at Brusand."

"And that someone was nearby who happened to overhear them," Agnar added. "But there's probably always someone strolling on the beach there."

Janis nodded. "Here they come, back again," he said. "Don't let on we were talking about them," he asked.

"I can try," replied Sørensen unconvincingly.

"Hej, Göran," Janis greeted him for the second time. "That was a short walk, though."

"You're right, Professor. My friends are still weakened and unfortunately tire quickly. I'd better take them back to their room."

"You are a good boy, Göran. Your friends are lucky to have you."

The latter beamed, "Thank you, Professor. And I wish you both a pleasant day," he said, inclining his head slightly toward them.

"We wish you the same, Göran," Janis Ekström replied.

The boy was about to walk away, but he thought better of it, turned around, and tilted his head to the right. In a friendly tone, he said, "Professor, my name's not actually Göran. I know by now that it sounds very similar in Swedish, but my real name," he said, smiling now and tilting his head to the left, "is Jori."

# ACKNOWLEDGMENTS

Had it not been for the COVID-19 pandemic, I don't know if the second book in the Anno Initium series would have been written so quickly. I used the time when society was locked down, and we were forced to stay at home to write *The Lost*. Moreover, the release and success of the audio version of Volume 1 gave me so much motivation that now, just one year later, the second part is ready to roll off the production line.

As with *The Stranded*, I would like to thank all those without whose support *The Lost* would not have been written in this form: Mille grazie to Ramon for the Italian translations; Punkrock Miri and Megges Wolf for ghost-reading, criticism, and input—you have been instrumental in guiding *The Lost* on its quest; Stefan Lindecke and Stefan Schulz-Lauterbach for the technical insights into servers, networks, and the like; Adrian (@sikorakete) for his ideas on how private drones might be useful in an apocalypse; Immo Heeling for sharing his insider knowledge on rigs, the Netherlands, and helicopters; Björn Schulz and Daphne Laut for your tireless editing—I realize what I've asked of you; Marcus Dorau for the endless design adjustments; the RONIN HÖRVERLAG audio publishing team: Stanley Schäfer, Katharina Adler-Marquard, Selina Vollrath, Neele Thäsler, Anton Artes, Luis Fensel, David Opoku-Pare, Mamady Sissoko, Nadine Preis, and Anna-Lena Kühner—thank you for welcoming me into the RONIN family; Jill-Patrice (@letterheart), Marcel (@booksurfer), Le(i)a (@liberiarium), Andrada (@andalorian), Lisa-Marie (@weltenentzueckt), Bianka (@bibibuecherverliebt), Josia (@josiajourdan), and Olaf Raack (@olaf_raack_autor) for their support on social media; Tommi Schneefuß and Dennis Schmidkunz (@soundofsnow. com); and of course especially to Vera Teltz and Uve Teschner—thank you for breathing life into the Anno Initium characters!

Dinko Skopljak
Würzburg
February 16, 2021

# ABOUT THE AUTHOR

Dinko Skopljak is the Yugoslavia-born author of the Anno Initium trilogy, which launched with his debut novel, *The Stranded*. Prior to becoming a writer, Skopljak worked variously as a dental technician, a photographer, and a web designer. A lover of science fiction and fantasy, cinema, and nature, he lives in Würzburg, Germany, with his two daughters.

# DISCOVER
# *STORIES UNBOUND*

PodiumAudio.com